The Adventures of

Spud Dempsey and Eddie Stump

There's Money on the Edge

Boone Mortensen

All rights reserved. No part of this publication may be reproduced, stored in a retrieval system, or transmitted by any means – electronic, mechanical, photographic (photocopying), recording, or otherwise – without prior permission in writing from the author.

This is a work of fiction. As such, any names, characters, places, incidents, and dialog are either the products of the author's imagination or used in a fictitious manner. Any resemblance to actual places, events, or persons (living or dead) is purely coincidental.

Copyright © 2020 by Boone Mortensen

All rights reserved.

ISBN: 979-8625678070

Baseball is a hard sport to play,
and then there is pitching.

Prologue

Dodger slugger Hank Keller, an old pro with a square jaw and a golf-ball-size cheek full of chewing tobacco, paused to watch the baseball sail over the outfield fence. Satisfied, he tossed his bat down and trotted to first base. With a mouthful of tobacco-stained teeth, he smiled at the young Giant pitcher. Rubbing salt into the wound of the Dodger rivals, Keller took his time rounding the bases. As he touched home plate, he looked to the heavens to give thanks to the baseball gods for starting another rookie pitcher. Greeted with a loud chorus of boos, Keller tipped his hat as he strolled toward the Dodger dugout.

A disgusted Giant fan, with a protruding white blob sagging below his bright orange T-shirt, threw down his beer cup. He burped, patted his beer belly, and stomped on the cup with his heavy black biker boot. He belched again, wiped the foam off his upper lip, cupped his hands, and yelled, "Hey Stanton, if I wanted to watch Home Run Derby, I'd go to the All-Star Game. Where'd you idiots get this one?"

A woman, momentarily distracted by beer belly's obnoxious behavior, stopped reading her book. Irritated and chilled to the bone, she wrapped an orange scarf tightly around her head to keep the cold breeze out.

Bored, she went back to reading her book. It was summertime in San Francisco and nature was playing its nightly trick. A warm, pleasant day quickly turned cold and blustery as a thick fog bank rolled in from the coast. Swirling gusts howled through cavernous Candlestick Park, turning entry and exit aisles into icy wind tunnels.

A spectator wearing black-rimmed glasses and a Giants' baseball hat, emboldened by beer belly, screamed, "We told you not to trade Parnell. You trade the good players and give us these kids right out of little league. Great. Just great. Send him back to the minors where he belongs."

Turning his back to the field, beer belly pleaded his case to the owner's box on the stadium's second deck. "How you gonna beat the Dodgers with guys like this?"

Giants' manager, Billy Stanton, jerked the hat from his head and slapped it on his wool baseball pants. Wiping the top of his bald head and adjusting his uniform, he mumbled, "Look at what they send me. A bunch of kids wet behind the ears who don't know how to pitch. Hell, I could've hit that one out. How am I supposed to win with this guy?"

Giants' pitcher, Charlie Pierce, lifted his head enough to watch as Keller touched home plate. Keller's reputation as a jerk was well deserved. Charlie arched his back and stretched his workman-like six-foot-two-inch frame. He wiped the sweat from his forehead thinking it was odd to perspire on such a cold night. As he strained to see into the Giants' dugout, a wind gust whipped dust into his fair blue eyes. Stepping off the mound, with the sleeve of his undershirt, he wiped his eyes. Straightening his broad shoulders and stretching his neck, he tried to read Billy Stanton's body language. He didn't have to; Stanton would be angry. He didn't like pitchers, especially rookies. Giving up a home run to the Dodgers, let alone Keller, would not sit well. Charlie waved for the catcher, Lance Perdue, to throw him another baseball. Circling the mound, he expected a quick hook.

Stanton leaned against the dugout wall searching for his pitching coach, Derek Sheets. "What's the matter with him?" he asked, kicking the tip of his shoes against the concrete steps to knock the dirt off his spikes.

Sheets dug his hands into his jacket pockets. "The kid's a bit nervous. He just came up. Rookie nerves, that's all," replied Sheets trying to protect the young pitcher.

Stanton pointed toward the pitcher's mound and then snapped, "Don't sit there; go talk to him. He's got one more hitter."

As Sheets climbed out of the dugout, he heard Stanton moan, "Who said this kid was ready? His fastball isn't fast, his curveball doesn't break, and his location is so bad I don't think he could pitch batting practice."

Sheets looked over his shoulder and started to reply. But then thinking better of it, he held his tongue. He had learned long ago that there was little value in responding to Stanton, especially since he wouldn't listen anyway. Sheets was old school, and like a good soldier, had learned to keep his mouth shut.

Sheets pulled his baseball jacket tight around his stomach, lamenting the need to lose weight. The last thing he needed was a few more pounds to tack onto an already beefy frame. He stepped over the first base line to talk to the young pitcher. This was not the time for criticism, but, rather, encouragement. As an ex-pitcher, he remembered how nervous he was on his first call-up. No matter how much you prepared, the first outing was often difficult. If he didn't calm the kid, he knew Stanton would pull him.

Sheets knew Stanton well. He was an ex-teammate. They had played together with the New York Yankees. Stanton was a star while he was just one of the team, considered a "solid ballplayer." A reliever who was given the occasional start, he was best remembered for the home run he had given up in the ninth inning of a playoff game with the hated Boston Red Sox. It was a hit the New York press would never let him forget; he had almost cost the Yankees the pennant. Fortunately, the Yankees came back to win the game and then went on to win the World Series. Even though he had pitched well in the series, after the season, he was traded. He became a journeyman. First, it was Cleveland, then Kansas City, then Cincinnati, and then, finally, the St. Louis Cardinals. He was always solid, but unlike Stanton, he was never a star. Then it was over. He was headed to work in a steel plant until he caught a break. The Cardinals, an organization with a history of recognizing talent, saw he had a natural rapport with pitchers and offered him a job as a pitching coach. He started at the bottom, but he was still in baseball. After kicking around the minors for several years, he finally got his chance to coach in the majors with the Giants. The reason? The Giants had hired Billy Stanton. Someone in the front office remembered they were once teammates and management was looking for someone to balance the volatile ex-star.

Stanton had the marquee name, but he, Sheets, had what management called the demeanor and baseball acumen to offset his intense and often difficult ex-teammate. That was two long years ago. He was still here, but frankly, he didn't know how much longer he could stomach Stanton's ego.

Stanton's was a classic case. As often happened, being a great player didn't mean you were going to be a good manager. No coach or player could ever measure up to his expectations. To Stanton, players should never strikeout or make an error, even though he had made many. Stanton was especially tough on pitchers. All pitchers were expected to throw perfect games, or at least, never have a bad outing. His attitude toward everyday players was almost as bad. As Stanton's playing days became a distant memory, his ability as a player grew to mythical proportions. He was the best at every aspect of the game and let his players know it. Rather than passing along his vast experience to the next generation, as any good professional would, he guarded his baseball knowledge as if sharing it might diminish his career. Rather than becoming a teacher, Stanton turned into a bully. He instilled fear. Young players, in awe, were afraid of him. Veteran players tried their best to please him. He was unapproachable when access was a must. Using fear as the motivator created many negative side-effects. Giant pitchers, afraid to make mistakes, made way too many. The soft hands every infielder needed to make plays became like rocks, their leather gloves like boards. There was no such thing as a routine play. Outfielders trying to impress Stanton with their arms threw home rather than holding runners from advancing into scoring position. Playing sound fundamental baseball was all but forgotten. Newspaper beat writers lamented that players often made mistakes twelve-year-old kids didn't make.

As the team sank into a losing streak, Stanton retreated. He managed by directive sent from his office. He often sulked at the end of the dugout as far away from his players as possible. He had become Captain Queeg, paranoid and alone. He didn't want to be part of a team that tarnished his image. Players were on pins and needles. Sheets thought about quitting but was bound by his contract, and, he rationalized, baseball jobs were hard to get. It was also hard to quit something you loved. Baseball was his life. The game had rewards, but it also came with a great deal of heartbreak.

Sheets approached the mound, "You okay, kid?" he asked.

"Take me out. I suck," replied Charlie.

Sheets covered his mouth to keep lip readers from eavesdropping on the conversation. "Look, don't worry about it. Just pitch. You think you're the only pitcher to give up a few hits? Focus on making good pitches. You've got guys to back you up. Don't try to be perfect; just pitch," said Sheets as he patted Charlie on the arm.

Sheets recognized that Pierce was frustrated but also knew he had vast potential. As young pitchers often do, he was too hard on himself. Getting *lit-up*, baseball lingo for giving up a bunch of hits and runs, was hard on a pitcher's confidence. Besides ability, successful major league pitchers had to believe in themselves. If they didn't, nobody else would either. There was no getting around a bad outing; they happened to every pitcher. You just had to bear down and pitch through them. Sheets also knew that pitchers who lost their confidence often never recovered. Many careers ended because of the mental rather than the physical aspects of pitching.

Sheets turned to Perdue, the rookie catcher with rounded shoulders, a bull neck, and a chest thick enough to render the chest protector almost unnecessary.

"Set up on the outside. It will help Charlie focus. Now let's go...let's get out of this," he said clapping his hands.

The young catcher shook his head in agreement. "Yes, sir. Set up on the edges."

Sheets turned back to Charlie, "If he beats you, make him beat you with your best stuff. Now go after him. Be aggressive. Com'on now, let's go."

Charlie glanced toward the dugout. "Is Stanton going to pull me?"

"You let me worry about Stanton," said Sheets. "You just pitch. Focus on the hitter. Now make some pitches and let's get this inning over. Go get this guy."

Charlie took his glove off. Reaching down, he picked up some dirt. He roughed up the baseball because he thought new ones were too slick. It also helped him to get his mind straight. Slipping his glove back on, he toed the rubber. Allowing another hit or home run was a sure ticket back to the minor leagues. After three years in the minors, this was his chance, and he was blowing it. He was pitching like crap. He had no control of his pitches, never a good thing for a "control" pitcher. He had a vicious change-up, a curve with a sharp north to south drop, and an above-average fastball that reached into the nineties. He could be tricky, and if his command was good, he could keep the ball in the tight windows necessary to get outs. Problem was, none of it was working. It was his fault. He had read too many articles about his *golden* arm. Caught up in the headlines, he had believed them. Well, his arm didn't feel so *golden* right now. His left arm felt like a piece of dead meat. He shook it to make sure it was still attached to his shoulder.

Positioning his left foot next to his right, he stood on the rubber and peered at the next hitter. Stan Gert, one of the best hitters in the National League, was short, stocky, and had a quick powerful stroke. There could be no mistakes with Gert.

"Concentrate," he said aloud. "Hit the edges."

A minor league pitching coach told him *there's money on the edges.* Successful pitchers won by hitting the edges and mixing up pitches to keep hitters off-balance. Good hitters could always catch up to a fastball down the middle.

Beer belly cupped his hands together around his mouth, "Hey kid, are you going to throw the ball or what? Some of us have to work for a living and I'd like to get home before midnight."

"That fan has a point," said Stanton. "That kid throws the ball in the next five seconds or I'm pulling him."

"He'll be fine. He's just focusing on what needs to get done."

"He gets three pitches. That's it. I'm tired of this crap. I'm going to give the front office hell for sending me these kids that can't pitch and then expect me to win."

Sheets stepped up on the top step. He hung both arms over the protective chain-link fencing. With his index finger, he scooped a large wad of chewing tobacco from his cheek and flung it on the ground. Nasty stuff, he thought. A "chaw" helped with his nerves, but it couldn't be good for his long-term health. Pierce was in trouble and there was little he could do to protect him. He was already on Stanton's bad list. Once you were on it, you were on it. Pierce was the kind of kid Stanton could ruin.

Charlie took the sign from Perdue. The catcher went down to one knee and lowered his glove, an indication that he wanted Charlie to keep the ball down and away. Stan Gert swung the bat back and forth over the plate. Ready to hit, he lifted the bat just above his right shoulder and set his feet.

Charlie raised his mitt to mid-chest level. Holding the ball inside his mitt to keep it hidden, he gripped it with his index and middle fingers across the seams. Using as little effort as possible, he started his windup, hiding the ball as long as he could. At the top of his motion, with maximum leverage, he strode toward the plate with his right leg. He let loose with his best fastball of the night. It screamed toward Perdue's mitt. Everything worked perfectly and then; whether it was a wind gust, the spin of the baseball, or a combination of factors, the ball drifted toward the center of the plate. In that instant, Charlie's stomach sank.

Gert's eyes widened. He took a short step to start his momentum and then swung the bat. The swing, quick and powerful. The contact pure. Gert crushed the ball. The ball left the bat with such velocity that the left fielder didn't have time to make a move. The players, fans, and Stanton watched as the ball, like a small missile shot out of a cannon, streaked over the left field fence for a home run.

"That's it," yelled Stanton as he stomped toward the mound before Gert had finished rounding the bases.

Charlie met Stanton as he crossed the first base line. As he walked by, he handed him the baseball. Walking to the dugout, he softly tossed his mitt on the bench and headed for the showers. Without saying anything to Sheets or the other players, he went to the locker room and tossed his uniform into a pile and changed clothes. Grabbing a few belongings, he quickly left the stadium. He ran to his Chevrolet pickup truck and drove north. The baseball career of Charlie Pierce had come to an abrupt end.

Chapter 1

There was nothing physically special about the place. The area was mostly made up of farms and country dwellings. It was neither rich nor poor. Forgettable, maybe, except for the people who lived there and called it home. The center of the burg was at the intersection of two country roads, South Lone Elder Road and the main Canby-Marquam Highway. If it wasn't for the dilapidated community center, baseball field, and country store, few travelers would have noticed it. Lone Elder was like many small communities that dotted the Willamette Valley between the capital city, Salem, to the south and the thriving port city of Portland to the north. Lone Elder was one of those places with a name, but few remembered, or cared, where the name came from. One old-timer said Lone Elder was named after a Boxelder tree, but nobody remembered seeing a Boxelder tree close by. Another member of an area church, of which there were many, said the name came from an original settler who happened to be an elder at a nearby church. A farmer, always hoping for a bumper crop, claimed Lone Elder came from an Elder tree his grandfather brought from England and planted for good luck. Although those were good for local yarn, accepted history said Lone Elder was named after an Elderberry tree. The lone Elderberry stood close to the current intersection. Centrally located, the Elderberry provided a spot where local farmers could congregate. It was the place for conversation on hot summer days and to break the monotony of cold winter afternoons. The Elderberry gave locals a small respite from back-breaking work, a chance to discuss the price of corn, or have a nip of whiskey with friends. For a hard-working community, one could easily visualize a local farmer telling his wife that he was going to the lone elder. The Elderberry tree was gone, probably a victim of progress or time, but the name Lone Elder stuck.

Across the main road from where the Elderberry tree once stood, residents built a one-room schoolhouse that eventually became a community center when area school districts were consolidated. The community center served as a place to hold meetings, weddings, or other social gatherings. On the south side of the road, situated at the corner of South Lone Elder and Canby-Marquam roads, was the other notable landmark, the Lone Elder store. Built in the front part of a rustic farmhouse, the store became what was once the living and dining rooms. The store was small but functional. The original owners, tired of farming, started the store to provide a few basic items. There were four shelves attached to the back wall for dry goods. In the center of the room were two free-standing gondolas for food and household items. Near the front entrance was a cooler for milk jugs, beer, and soda. A hand-operated cash register sat on the sales counter. The counter was located off to the side of the front door and was stocked with candy bars, real venison jerky, and cigarettes. The entry door was two inches thick and made of solid oak. An electric heater warmed the room and allowed the front door to be left open, except on the coldest days. A wood screen door with a bell attached announced the comings and goings of customers. There were two steps leading down from the main store to a small deck. On the deck was an old freezer. The top had been removed and the freezer converted to an ice chest. In the summer months, the chest was packed with ice, beer, and different varieties of soda. The honor system prevailed. If you wanted a beverage, you left money in the large mason jar sitting on the round end table. The owners emptied the jar once or twice a week depending on how full the jar was. You could also pay for your beverage at the counter inside if you wanted to buy other items. Charge accounts, payable monthly, were provided to regular, well-known customers.

After the original owners retired, the store, now in need of repair, was bought by Gene and Nell Flynn. Nell, a beauty with auburn hair as bright as her smile, was as pretty as she was tough. Her husband, Gene, *The Fly*, Flynn, was an ex-professional boxer. Flynn was known for a mean uppercut and the ability to spend money as fast as he made it. An Irish immigrant, Flynn was good enough to win the Northwest and West Coast Middleweight Boxing Championships. *The Fly* fought officially in the ring. To earn extra cash, he also took on neighborhood toughs in bare-knuckle back alley fights that were little more than street brawls. He made a small fortune and invested in a nightclub. The nightclub went broke as did Flynn. Back in the ring, he wasn't the fighter of old, but he was still good enough to regain some of his wealth. It was during his comeback that he met Nell. They quickly fell in love and married, luckily for Nell, before Flynn spent all his money on yet another wild venture. It was Nell who coaxed, some say demanded, that Flynn buy the Lone Elder store from the original owners who also happened to be Nell's aunt and uncle. The store was rundown and in need of a major renovation, but it was also the start of a new life. After one final fight, Flynn paid off his remaining debts and moved to Lone Elder. Gene and Nell upgraded the store with a fresh coat of white paint and quickly became part of the community.

After the store regained its past glory, the Flynns expanded. They added two gas pumps and a covered bay. Next to the pumps, they added a small storage room stocked with automobile oil, an air compressor to fill tires, a few wrenches, and other mechanic tools to make minor vehicle repairs. They hired attendants to pump gas, check the engine oil, and wash the windshield. In a stroke of genius, the Flynns hired two longtime farmers, Odell and Benny, as attendants. They wore bib overalls and knew every farmer from Lone Elder to Woodburn. They brought in a steady stream of customers to buy gas, shop the store, and have a bit of friendly conversation. There were few complaints about the service, except when Odell or Benny occasionally missed a spot when cleaning a vehicle windshield. The combination store and gas station were unusual but turned out to be a huge financial success. The store and service station were open from six a.m. to six p.m. six days a week; Sundays in Lone Elder were reserved for family and church.

Progress, as it often does, presented new challenges. Better cars and the modernization of country roads made it easier for locals to travel to the nearby towns of Canby, Molalla, or Woodburn. Needing an additional revenue stream, the Flynn's adjusted to the changing times by adding a tavern. The new tavern, an extension built off the store, was noteworthy for the winning combination of having a family atmosphere, good conversation, and ice-cold beer. The rectangle shaped establishment consisted of a bar lined with ten stools fixed on four-inch metal pipes. A jukebox, full of country western and rock-n-roll records, greeted patrons near the entrance. A shuffleboard table with low hanging lights sat against the back wall. Adjacent to the bar were five red leather-covered booths. Around four o'clock, the tavern, serving a variety of beer along with free peanuts and hard pretzels, came to life. Once again, Lone Elder was the hub for farmers, ranchers, loggers, and the occasional bored housewife. It was a friendly crowd unless the bored housewife became a point of contention between two equally bored, or over-served, male patrons.

The Flynns were on a roll and doing well. Then, unexpectantly, Gene died. While telling the story about his championship fight to his beer-drinking customers, who also served as his audience, he suddenly felt ill. Dizzy, he went to bed and died during the night. Doctors said his death was caused by a brain aneurism likely brought on by too many blows to the head. Nell was left to raise their young daughter, Rebecca. Nell, an excellent businesswoman, took the small life insurance money Flynn left her and invested it. She bought the property across the street, that included an old community center and baseball field. Initially, she planned to rent the building for meetings, family reunions, and other important functions, but age finally caught up with the structure and she closed it because of safety concerns. Nell planned to tear it down but other priorities left the building to the mercy of age, the weather, and hungry critters.

Recognizing the growing demand for eggs and chickens, she invested in a chicken hatchery. She sold processed chickens to restaurants and fresh eggs to area grocery stores. She contracted with *Fred Myers* to sell them eggs. To meet the growing demand, she built an egg processing plant and became wealthy selling eggs to stores throughout the Portland metropolitan area. Now with plenty of money, her friends encouraged her to sell the store and tavern, but she refused. Nell said it was a link to her husband, and besides, she said, the store and tavern kept her close to the community. The association also provided many new business opportunities. The other reason Nell stayed was Rebecca. Lone Elder was a healthy place to raise a child, so she built a new house a mile closer to Canby and stayed. Nell's life revolved around her daughter and her businesses. There was little time for anything else.

Possessing her mother's auburn hair, Rebecca Flynn was as fiery as her fair skin with probing eyes that made it hard to look away. Rebecca became a major attraction for young men from miles around. A quick wit, sharp tongue, and her father's temper caused most men to consider Rebecca with a bit of caution. None were quite sure how to handle such a prize. Rebecca was like her mother. She was highly intelligent, strong-willed, and independent. Although she hid it well, those who knew her also said she was loving and compassionate. An excellent student, she breezed through high school as she did the University of Oregon. Tempting offers from Stanford University and the University of California law schools were pulls she couldn't ignore for too long. She decided to weigh her options over the summer months while helping Nell with her businesses. Like her mother, Rebecca considered running the store fun. It allowed her to interface with locals, most of whom she had known since she was a small child. Nell, although very proud of her daughter, disliked the thought of her moving to far away California. It was a decision both avoided discussing. For now, they were content with enjoying each other's company.

Chapter 2

The April morning air was thick with the smell of hot oil, diesel smoke, and the woodsy freshness of recently cut timber. Steam rolled down the mountain as the bright Oregon sun sucked moisture from the previous night's rain. In the distance, the crest of Goat Mountain peeked above the low-hanging clouds. Over the rumbling drone of a diesel motor and the pop, pop, pop of chain saw engines, a black-tail doe and her young fawn bounded from the dense underbrush and disappeared into the thick, dark, menacing woods.

Charlie Pierce inhaled a deep breath of crisp mountain air. Adjusting his blue suspenders, he brushed the sawdust off his logger jeans. With a stick, he scraped mud from the soles of his cork boots. Called *corks* by his crew, Charlie thought the name was a bit misleading for boots made with thick soles and infused with steel spikes for traction. Taking off his skull bucket hard hat, Charlie leaned against a newly cut log and wiped the sweat from his forehead with a red handkerchief. He relaxed but kept alert. He was constantly reminded that loggers were often injured or killed because they let their guard down. A dead limb falling from a tree or a large piece of loose bark, among many hazards, had appropriately earned the nickname *widow makers*, and for good reason.

Although he was still new to the job, Charlie made up for his inexperience by working harder than anyone else on his crew. His job was to attach choker cables to newly cut trees so they could be hoisted up and stored on a roadside log deck. On occasion, when the logs were too long or too large for the skyline cables to winch up the steep grade, his job was to cut them into appropriate lengths to make them manageable. If the tree fallers missed an occasional limb, a rare occurrence, he trimmed the log clean before hooking up the choker cables.

The work was hard and sometimes dangerous, but in a short amount of time, he had learned to like the job. He had failed at baseball; maybe, he thought, he could achieve a certain amount of success as a logger. He also liked the camaraderie of being part of a logging team, and loggers were a team. They had to work together for safety and to make the operation run smoothly. There was also an individual element to logging. Every man had to do his job. Besides the chance for injury and the loss of income, being careless could cost lives. There was no place for a laggard or screw-up. He trusted his co-workers because they were professionals and took their occupation seriously. Charlie figured that working with the best didn't eliminate the risks but minimized them.

His attention was suddenly drawn to a high-pitched scrape. He looked up at the skyline carriage. The carriage, used to hoist logs up the steep grade, had locked up.

"That damned carriage is stuck again," said Charlie's boss, Pete Long. The operation's yarder, Long was also part owner of the Goat Mountain

Logging Company. "It looks like the pulley is locked up."

Long, called Poop by his friends, had been a logger in between deployments in World War II and Korea. An ex-Army Ranger, Long was medium height, had a rough beard, bald head, rock-solid body, and ready smile. He had earned the nickname, Poop, during the WWII operation, Market Garden. Long was part of the 82nd Airborne and attached to the British Army commanded by Field Marshal Bernard Montgomery. The objective of Market Garden was to establish a bridgehead in German territory and pave the way for the Allied advance across the Rhine River. The brainchild of Montgomery, the operation was considered, by many, a military failure.

It was the objective of Long's unit to capture one of the many bridges spanning the Rhine. As they approached the target bridge, they were attacked by German troops. When the Germans attacked, Long was sitting across a log doing his business. Hidden in a nearby woods, Long emerged with his guns blazing and his pants still partially down. He surprised the Germans from behind and quickly ended the engagement. His unit secure, Long calmly went back and finished his business. Long's Army buddies surmised his being regular was far more important than fighting Germans. They nicknamed him Poop, and the name stuck.

Uncomfortable calling the older more experienced man Poop, Charlie just used his real name, Pete.

"Pete, what do we do?" asked Charlie.

"Not much we can do. Bob will try to free it. Generally, that works. If it doesn't, he'll have to release the cable and set the carriage down. Then we'll have to undo the chokers and he'll pull the carriage up the hill. The wire rope has probably frayed and jammed the pulleys, or the gears are frozen. We might be able to fix it. If not, we'll go help the fallers de-limb and buck trees."

Pete signaled to Bob, the yarder engineer, a short man with a thick, black beard, that they were clear with three blasts from the horn. "I hope he can free it. I don't like the idea of setting those logs down again. The wire rope and those chokers can get tangled. Stay clear. We'll have to be on the lookout when he tries to move it," said Long as he adjusted his hard hat.

"It's not moving," observed Charlie.

"It's really jammed up. I can hear those gears grinding and see pieces of wire hanging out of the carriage. He's going to have to release the wire rope and set it down. We'll wait until the carriage is on the ground, then we'll go see what we've got. Now, don't do anything stupid. We wouldn't want you to hurt that *golden* arm."

"I no longer use *golden* and my arm in the same sentence," replied Charlie.

"Hell, you never know; you might get tired of logging and give baseball another try."

"I doubt the outcome would be any different. Besides, why would they give me another shot? I walked away from my contract. They don't like it when a player does that. I think I like it better in the woods. Trees don't yell or judge you."

"I guess not," replied Long.

Long took a drink from the canvas water bag and watched while the crane operator set down the skyline carriage along with the logs.

"Before I went to Europe, I used to pitch a bit. Won a few games in high school but I don't think I had the talent to make it to the pros. It didn't matter because the War had started. I guess I always wondered if I was good enough; you always do if you never give it a try. I'd take a bit of yelling and a few jeers if I had the ability. I'm not complaining; I made it through two wars, have a wife who puts up with me, and have three great kids."

"You're lucky," said Charlie.

"The thing of it is, if you have the opportunity, you should give it another try. You're young and you can always come back to the woods. Logging will be good for a few more years. Lots of houses to build and we'll need lumber. Then I don't know; it depends on the economy," Long said with a sigh. "Oh, well, let's go release those chokers."

Charlie followed Long as he traversed the steep hill. They skirted around stumps and climbed over logs. Out of habit, always aware of the hazards from above, they stopped every few feet to study the slope.

"Pete, you guys be careful down there," yelled Bob from the log deck.

Long waved his arm, "Always am. Just make sure there's slack in the wire rope so we can release the chokers."

"I'll take all the tension out. Watch those logs. They can shift without warning. Be ready to jump out of the way. Find your escape route," Bob warned.

Charlie heard Bob but didn't answer. He was too focused on the job at hand. He'd been in the woods long enough to know this was a dangerous situation. On a steep grade, if a log broke free and started to roll, it could careen in any direction, smashing everything or anyone in its path. The logs were free of limbs, which could make it easier for them to roll. Working their way up the hill, he and Long fought their way through thick brush and downed tree limbs. Looking for a faster route, Charlie climbed up on a downed log lying parallel to the slope. Digging the steel spikes of his boots into the raw log, he started to scale it. A slow walk turned into a sprint. When he reached the end of the log, he paused before jumping off. Picking a target spot, he landed squarely on the logs bound together by the choker cable. He climbed to the location where he had set the choker. The bell and knob were still locked together, but as Bob had told them, the wire rope was loose.

The side with the bell was slack but the other side was tight. The rope was bound up underneath. One log lay on the stump while the other log rested on the lower log. Both logs were of considerable size and appeared stable. There was a gap of a few feet between the bottom of the logs and the ground. There was enough space to crawl under. The area was thick with brush. Charlie slid off the log and dropped onto a stump. Ducking under the log, he inspected the choker cable. He saw where the cable was bound. Fortunately, he was able to free the wire rope from the brush. Climbing back on top of the logs, he disconnected the bell and knob.

"All clear," Charlie yelled as he jumped off the logs. As he moved a safe distance away from the wire rope, he yelled, "All clear!" Then he yelled again, "All clear!"

Odd, he thought, Long didn't respond. He waited, expecting to hear three toots of the horn to signal that everything was clear. Bob would not attempt to free the carriage until he heard the all clear signal.

Suddenly, Long screamed. "We've got a flyer! Run!"

Flyer, on this crew, meant a log had broken loose from above. Immediately, Charlie reacted. He glanced toward the log deck in time to see a snag the size of a small car hurtling down the hill. Where it came from, he didn't know. As he ran for safety, he heard the snap of tree limbs and the dull thud of logs slamming against other logs. The snag hit a stump and quickly changed course. It flipped end over end, directly at him. His position was suddenly dire. What he did in the next few seconds could mean life or death.

Instinctively, he dove under the logs where he had just released the choker cable. He huddled close to the stump just as the snag slammed into the logs just above his head. He glanced up as the snag split in two. One piece flipped high into the air and tumbled end over end, plummeting down the hill before crashing against the base of a towering fir. When the rotted tree hit, the core exploded, splintering into small pieces. A few seconds later, the second section crashed against a large boulder, showering the canyon with debris.

His senses on a razor's edge, Charlie's momentary relief turned into instant alarm when the logs above started to shift. The movement was slow, gradual, and relentless. Reacting, he lunged out from under the logs landing on his shoulder. Unable to stop his momentum, he rolled down the steep hillside until he came to a jarring, abrupt stop after he hit a sturdy huckleberry bush. The sudden impact knocked the wind out of him. He gasped for air as he fought to catch his breath. Aware that he was still in grave danger, he struggled to his feet. He fought to regain his breath. He heard the unmistakable hollow sound of bark scraping against bark. For an instant, he was frozen. The logs, free because he had disconnected the choker cable, started a slow, methodical slide. As gravity took hold, the logs started an unstoppable roll down the hill. The logs turned like a slow-moving train. They lined up like two soldiers perpendicular to the hill. Charlie was directly in their path.

The bottom log got tangled in the wire rope still attached to the skyline carriage. As they rolled, the combined weight of the logs and carriage caused tremendous tension on the tower cable. It was too much. The tower tilted and then snapped back as the overhead cable frayed and came apart. A high-pitched twang reverberated through the valley. Whipping like a wild snake, the wire rope sent the men on the log deck scurrying for cover. Adding to the chaos, the skyline carriage broke free and plunged down the hill. As it tumbled, a section of wire rope snapped like a cut air hose under full pressure.

Charlie knew that when the logs started to roll there would be no stopping them. If he didn't move, he would be crushed. Freeing himself from the brush, he crawled, jumped, and then dove sideways across the slope in a futile attempt at escape.

"Move! Get out of there!" screamed Long. "Get over here! She's gonna break loose!"

Long had seen it happen before; when logs started to move, they only safe course was to move as quickly and as far away as possible. The cutting area on the hill slope was free of logs but the slash remained. Whether Charlie could make it to safety was questionable. He had to fight his way through the brush, and the logs were picking up speed. There were a few stumps to hide behind, but they presented a different hazard. When a log hit a stump, it could fly up and pitch in any direction. When a log careened, anything could happen. In a matter of seconds it could be chaos.

Keeping his eyes on Charlie, Long ran across the hill. Charlie made it to another stump and scrambled behind the base. One of the spinning logs slammed into the stump and launched skyward. For an instant, he thought he would be crushed. He jumped clear and prayed. The log missed him by inches.

Long had preached, '*In the woods, what you don't see can often kill you.*' Charlie heard it before he saw it. One of the logs hit a large branch and snapped it into two pieces. One section, the size of a small tree, came at him like a missile. He jumped to get clear, but he was too late. He felt a sharp pain in his left arm, but there was no time to worry about the injury. If he could move, he had to. The logs and carriage were on a relentless pursuit. They were on him. Small pieces of branch and bark hit him from every direction. Suddenly, he was surrounded by a terrifying confusion of logs, flying limbs, and tumbling equipment.

As he tried desperately to find a clear path, a branch hit him, flipping him into the air. Now, everything seemed to happen in slow motion. Along with the logs and carriage, he plummeted downward. Now flying, he spun like an out-of-control kite. He landed hard, luckily, into a thick bed of fir branches. His arm stung. He was sure he had broken it. From above, he heard a chorus of screams and yells. Completely spent, in one final, desperate attempt, he jumped behind a rotted snag. Then he did the only thing he could; Charlie waited for the inevitable.

Chapter 3

Other than the store, tavern, and community center, Lone Elder was notable for Sunday baseball games held on what could best be described as a country baseball diamond. Opposing players often called it a cow pasture. On the occasion one of the local farmers had the time, they would drag the field with a sled that included three truck tires followed by a square timber. Attached to the timber was a screen to smooth the field and collect rocks. The field could be remarkably smooth unless it wasn't. The dirt infield was generally smooth enough to field ground balls, but there was never any certainty of that. A hard-hit ball could careen off a clump of grass or hit a rock. The resulting bad hops often caused a broken nose, knocked out front teeth, or threatened future generations with what amounted to a punch below the belt. Fielders brave enough to risk it quickly became very adept at fielding balls primarily because there was no other option. Smart players took great care to manicure the infield. In between innings, they often pulled the stray weed or tossed small rocks off the field to prevent bad hops. All of it was worth it to play the popular Sunday afternoon pickup games. With hard farm work consuming the rest of their week, it was the only time most of the men had to recapture a bit of their youth. For a few hours every Sunday, they had fun while they relived the dream of playing professional baseball. For a small moment anyway, it was a chance to emulate greats like Micky Mantle, Willie Mays, or Joe DiMaggio.

The Lone Elder field consisted of a backstop made of poles like those used to support electric or telephone lines. Chicken wire extended thirty to forty feet up the poles to protect the grandstand behind home plate. The grandstand was made of wood with twelve-inch planks for seats. The dimensions of the dirt infield were large; too large. The infield extended well beyond the bases before the outfield commenced with a rough grass edge. The outfield was a mixture of grass, alfalfa, and a combination of weeds. When mowed, the grass became a prickly, gnarly mix better suited for grazing than baseball. Along the first base line between the field and the highway was a massive big-leaf maple tree. On warm summer days, the maple provided shade for spectators and a place to throw out a blanket for a picnic.

Sometimes the women played, but most preferred to spend time socializing. Some women, like their husbands, had jobs at one of the nearby paper or lumber mills, but most were stay-at-home moms. For them, the Sunday games offered a small respite after a week caring for children, managing the household, and helping run the farm.

The games were generally quiet affairs but could turn into heated contests. A bad call was sometimes settled behind the community center or more often over a few beers at the tavern. The games became a regular affair until things changed. The reasons were varied but the generation of men who came of age in the forties and fifties were now older. With advancing age came added responsibilities. Soon, the weekly games became every other week and then monthly until, due to lack of time and interest, the games slowly died out.

As the community thrived, the field fell into disrepair. The infield, never free of weeds, was taken over by them. One of the farmers, recognizing an opportunity, cut the outfield grass and baled it for hay. Over time, the nails attaching the chicken wire to the backstop poles rusted out. There were large holes in the chicken wire. A strong wind tore a large section of the wire backstop from the poles, leaving it in a twisted heap. The poles, now stripped of wire, stood as if they were biblical reminders of the crucifixion. After a particularly long night, a patron of Nell's tavern wisely thought it was safer to sleep in the back of his pickup truck rather than driving home. Waking up before daylight, he swore he saw the image of Jesus on the tallest pole. The message was life changing and it caused him to stop drinking. A changed man, he started to go to church on Sunday. His wife, who had for years tried to get him to stop drinking, thought it was a miracle. There was talk of taking the poles out and cutting down the large Big Leaf Maple, but nobody seemed to have the time.

Then a new cycle started. The kids of the ex-players were now old enough to play. The Lone Elder field had a rebirth. Busy parents had little time to travel to nearby towns to take their sons to play baseball. Adding to the problem, there were too many boys in the post-World War II generation. Boys who wanted to play were often boxed out from playing on crowed town teams. Besides a numbers problem, a rural farm boy had little chance to play on a town team even if he was a better player. In the "real" world of youth sports, money and connection were great equalizers to talent. Over a few beers, the Lone Elder Baseball Association was formed. Lone Elder field was transformed. New, modern backstop wire was attached. The infield was groomed. Bleacher boards were replaced, a new home plate was installed, and new benches were added to the home's and visitor's field-level dugouts. Lone Elder baseball was functional again; it was time to play ball.

Chapter 4

"Dog-gone-it!" yelled Long. "That's the darnedest thing I've ever seen, and I've been in these woods for over twenty years. That dad-burn log barely missed you Charlie. Are you sure you're okay?"

"Well, I'm alive. I think my arm might be busted."

"No. Dog-gone-it. What hit you?"

"It wasn't the log but a flying limb. The butt of a limb caught my arm."

Long crawled over a nearby log, then jumped down the hill to where Charlie sat still a bit dazed, but thankful to be alive. "Which arm?" he asked fearfully.

"The left one."

"Dog-gone-it. That's your pitching arm."

"Well, it was," said Charlie calmly as he held his left arm close to his chest with his right hand.

"How bad is it?"

"I see some bone pressing against my skin. I guess it could be pretty bad."

Long grabbed the "jerk" line and hit the whistle four times to signal that a man was injured. Bob descended the hill in jumps and bounds, the downhill momentum carrying him like a deer leaping over a fence.

"What's going on down here!" he yelled.

"We've got to get you to the hospital," Long said to Charlie. He turned to find Bob. "Bob, we've got an injured man down here. He's hurt pretty bad."

"Can he be moved?"

"Do you have any other injuries?" asked Long.

"Nope. I think it's just my arm. I was lucky. I still don't know how those logs broke free and missed me."

"You're lucky to be alive," Long sighed, relieved. "Can you make it up the hill?"

"If we go slowly, I can make it," replied Charlie.

Long yelled up to Bob who was halfway to them, "He can make it up the hill. Get the truck." He turned back to Charlie and knelt beside him. "Dog-gone-it," he said again. He pulled a red handkerchief from his pocket and looped it under Charlie's arm and around his neck. He tied it off. "There; that should help hold your arm up."

"Thanks," said Charlie. "The slightest movement hurts."

"I know it hurts, but it could have been a lot worse. Come on, we've got to get you up the hill. I'll help you."

Charlie motioned for Long to go ahead, "It's my arm, not my leg. I can walk."

"I'm sure you can, but if you fall and land on that arm, you'll be sorry you didn't ask for help."

With a helping hand from Long, Charlie stood. There was an eerie silence as the logging crew shut down the equipment. The high-pitched buzz of chain saws could still be heard in the distance. Then, they were shut down too as word quickly spread that there was an injured man. Within a few minutes, the whole crew was on the log deck to see what had happened and to offer assistance.

Without the use of his arm, Charlie traversed the hill in a wide zigzag.

He looked down at his broken arm, "I guess my pitching days are really over."

"Don't talk like that. Doctors fix broken arms all the time. You'll be as good as new in a few months."

"What am I going to do to make money? Not much you can do in the woods with one arm."

"Don't worry about that now. We've got insurance that will pay part of your wages for a few months. These things happen. We'll take care of you."

"I'll stay at the logging camp."

"Nonsense. You can't stay way up here by yourself. What if something happens? You can stay at my place. I've got a small shed in the back that I use for an office. It has running water, a bathroom, and a place to put a bed. You can stay there."

"Nah, I wouldn't think of it. You've got a family to feed. You don't need another mouth. I'll find something," said Charlie.

"You can stay with me until you decide what to do. Besides, who's going to cook for you? That's going to be kind of hard with one arm."

Charlie thought for a few seconds and then said, "I guess you're right, but I'll pay for my room and board."

"Okay, if it makes you feel better, you can pay rent."

Charlie grew quiet as he thought of his uncertain future. He wasn't a doctor but knew his arm was badly broken. Doctors could repair broken arms, but sometimes they were never the same. Suddenly, his ability to pitch, a talent he had always taken for granted, may be gone. The thought frightened him, but why should it? He had walked away and vowed never to return. Now that decision seemed impulsive, almost childish. He had quit and now had to accept charity from Long. He knew Long didn't mind, but it felt like he had hit rock bottom. Charlie painfully understood that he had taken an important part of his life for granted. He didn't want to jump to conclusions, but it was like losing a friend. Sometimes you never knew how much they meant to you until they were gone. If that was the lesson, he just hoped he was up to the challenge of making it back. That could be a long difficult road.

Chapter 5

Spud rubbed the windowpane clean with his hand. He turned his baseball hat with the big LE, for Lone Elder, around so that the bill faced backward. He put his face against the windowpane and peeked in.

"This place looks haunted," said Spud.

Eddie probed. "How would you know if a place is haunted?"

"I don't know, but the place looks like it should be. There are cobwebs all over the place and there's a rope hanging from one of the rafters."

"Maybe they hung somebody in there," said Kermit.

"Are you guys chicken?" Eddie queried.

Spud ignored the challenge, "We came here to play baseball and get ready for the season, not to check out this old place and look for ghosts."

As Eddie held the wood ladder for his best friend, Spud Dempsey, he noted a row of cedar shingles laying on the ground directly below the roof edge. Stepping away from the building, he saw the roof was a checkerboard of missing squares.

"There are so many wood shingles missing; I bet this place leaks when it rains," Eddie observed.

"Nobody uses this place anymore," said Kermit. "They probably don't see the need to repair it."

"Crawl in and check it out," Eddie suggested with a wiry smile.

He liked to hang with Spud and that generally came with a good deal of give and take. With Spud, he got as good as he gave. He knew how far he could push him without a serious backlash. If he went too far, he could expect a wrestling match. Spud loved to wrestle but he didn't. Wrestling with Spud was no easy task. Most of the time, they wrestled until they were both worn out. Eddie preferred to negotiate rather than fight, unless he was pushed into it. If he had to fight, he chose boxing.

Spud and Eddie were alike in many ways, but their physical appearance was as different as two boys could be. Eddie was long with lean muscles. Depending on the sunlight or his mood, his eyes became unpredictable shades of blue. He wore his ash-blond hair short. His bronze skin looked like he spent most of his time on a California beach. His smile was easy, and he laughed often. Eddie was full of fun with a good dose of mischief mixed in. One of his favorite pastimes was playing tricks on his friends, but he also had a serious side. Spud thought when he was serious, he was too much like an adult. With his youthful good looks, Eddie attracted the girls, who he mostly ignored. When the need arose, he could be smooth-talking. He was comfortable talking to adults, primarily because he dealt with so many of them while working at his parents' hardware store, Stump's Hardware. A local institution, it was well known in the community that if you couldn't find it anyplace else, the third-generation hardware store had it. When he wasn't going to school, playing sports, or on an expedition with Spud, he spent most of his time helping his parents. Even at his young age, Eddie was a highly sought-after athlete. He was a natural. He could play any sport, and he could play it well.

In sharp contrast, Spud was solid and stocky. He had the look of a rough and tumble farm boy. He was as comfortable working as he was rolling in the dirt. His rough skin had a perpetual tan, understandably so since he spent most of his time outdoors. A ban of distinctive freckles matching his inquisitive brown eyes covered his nose and filtered down his cheeks. His body was hard, almost gnarly, from spending long hours working in the fields. He picked berries, lugged baskets of beans, and hauled hay. He was tough, and although he rarely offered a challenge, he occasionally accepted one. Spud was adventurous, and like Eddie, could be mischievous. His determination was often thought of as being stubborn. Spud was slow to anger but could be fearless if the situation called for it. Like Eddie, he was an excellent athlete. Where Eddie preferred basketball, Spud liked to wrestle. They both loved baseball and committed to playing on the same teams no matter what the adults might want. They were a bit too young for football, but coaches were already marveling at how far Eddie threw a tight spiral and how much Spud loved to make a hard tackle. As much as they liked sports, Spud and Eddie loved to camp, fish, and explore. It was the exploring that often got them into tight spots they mostly thought of as adventures.

Spud pushed up on the bottom rail, but the window was stuck. He took his fist and hit the stile on each side. Still, the window wouldn't budge. Using his pocketknife, he ran the blade between the rail and casing. He repeated the steps between the rail and stool. He tapped the window again with his fist, careful not to break out the loose pane. Once again, he pushed up on the rail and this time, it moved. He curled his fingers under the rail and lifted the bottom section high enough to crawl through.

"I got it. It's open," Spud exclaimed.

"Climb in if you ain't afraid. Watch out for ghosts," Eddie teased.

"I think it's haunted," said Kermit as he helped Eddie hold the wobbly old ladder they had found behind the meeting hall.

Kermit Sharp was a good friend of Spud and Eddie. Sometimes he tagged along on their expeditions. Spud called Kermit "The Book" because he was a wealth of knowledge and smarter than most kids. His appearance was bookish. He was tall for his age, wore dark glasses that matched his hair, and rarely looked up because his nose was always pointed toward a book. When Spud or Eddie had a question they always went to Kermit. He wasn't an athlete, but if you needed to know about history or mountains or rivers or what made things work, he was the guy. If he didn't know the answer to your question, he had a researcher's determination to find it. Kermit was knowledgeable about most things, except girls. Girls scared him. Where Spud and Eddie *tried* to ignore them, Kermit avoided them at all costs. One time, Christy Vance, a girl who sat in the desk in front of him at school, told Kermit that Sally Hanks had a crush on him. Sally, with a reputation of being a little too aggressive, gave Kermit a sudden case of the hives. Pleading sickness, Kermit didn't come to school the next day. Secretly, he hoped the pretty Ms. Hanks' crush was a moment of misplaced passion and that she would quickly forget about him. His hopes were dashed the following day when he returned to school. The crush had lingered. When Sally wanted to talk to him at recess, Kermit developed an immediate case of stomach cramps and ran to the bathroom. The teacher, recognizing the symptoms of his ailment, told Kermit he had to skip recess and stay at his desk. Now safe, he busied himself with reading a history book about Abraham Lincoln. To his relief, as crushes usually do, especially Sally's, they quickly fade away. Kermit was relieved when Sally moved on to the next boy.

Besides Kermit's passion for knowledge, he loved baseball; everything about it. He kept all the statistics on Lone Elder players just like big-league teams did. He knew his friends' batting averages, RBIs (runs batted in), and OBP (on-base percentage). He calculated the pitchers' ERA (earned run average), and just about every other important measurement. Kermit had a passion for numbers and baseball was a game with abundant statistics. He loved the game, but he just didn't play it very well. He played to please his dad who hoped his son would one day play in the major leagues. Kermit, long before his father did, knew there was less than a remote possibility of that ever happening. His thick glasses perched on a thin nose made it hard to see the ball. His legs were as uncoordinated as they were long. It was hard to run, impossible to stop, and an adventure every time he tried to catch a fly ball. If the flyball was hit too high, he circled under it like a fawn taking its first steps. He, along with everybody on the field and in the stands, held their breath. Most of the time, he let it drop because it was safer. He would then pick up the ball, and in a well-practiced move, throw it to the cut-off man.

When hitting, his strategy was one of hope. Kermit figured that if he swung the bat hard, occasionally, he might hit the ball. Sometimes he left his fate to the pitcher and umpire; a walk was a major victory. His goal was a batting average of one hundred, figuring a hit in every ten tries was acceptable. It didn't matter that the other boys were better hitters; if he got that one hit, he was helping the team. He realized that a low batting average didn't leave room for a slump, but in youth baseball nobody seemed to care about slumps. His first hit, the year before, was more like a bunt. The baseball dribbled to the third baseman who didn't field it cleanly. Kermit and his teammates took the opportunity to classify it as a hit. Kermit beamed when he earned the game ball. He quickly wrapped the ball in plastic as a memento. If it wasn't a league rule that every player must play in the field and have at least one at-bat per game, Kermit would have been content to sit and watch. When he did play, generally the last two or three innings, he played right field. He had the awareness, backed up by statistics, that most players were right-handed and hit the ball to the left side of the diamond. Although the chances of batters hitting the ball to left field depended on the pitcher, he liked the odds. Besides, if balls were hit to the right side, they were generally caught by the infielders. He knew that all changed as players grew older, but by that time he could safely move on to other pursuits. Kermit played ball at Lone Elder because his friends did, and they encouraged him to play. He loved Lone Elder baseball.

"How do you know it's haunted?" quizzed Eddie.

"Odell, the old guy at the store, told me it was," said Kermit.

Eddie interrupted him, "Odell? Who's he?"

"He pumps gas with Benny. They work for Mrs. Flynn."

"How does he know about the ghost? I think he's just pulling your leg," said Eddie.

"Odell and Benny know everything about Lone Elder. My dad calls them old-timers."

"Why do they think it's haunted?" asked Spud from the ladder.

"Odell told me and my dad the story. He said a long time ago, right after World War II, there was a wedding. On the day of the wedding, the bride disappeared. They never found a trace of her and the case was never solved. Nobody was arrested. The only evidence was that somebody saw a suspicious black car pull out of her parents' driveway. That's when the ghost sightings started. Odell said the ghost is a woman wearing a bride's dress. She floats above the stage. He said that sometimes she sits in the balcony. The man she was going to marry was heartbroken. He was killed in a car wreck. Odell said he ran head-on into a semi-truck. He said, Carl..."

"Carl? That was his name?" quizzed Spud.

"That's what Odell said."

"Odd name for a ghost," said Spud.

"Who said anything about ghosts?" asked Eddie.

"Nobody, I was just thinkin' he could be," replied Spud.

"He might be," said Kermit. "Carl was a star baseball player. Odell says that sometimes late at night people have seen a man dressed in a baseball uniform sitting in the stands. When the wind starts to blow, you can hear a whistle. The whistle is a sign that he's around watching the game. Odell said it means a bad thing is going to happen."

"A whistle? You mean, like somebody dies?" asked Spud.

"No, I don't think so. From what Odell said, it's kind of a curse on the ballplayers. They make errors or strike out; kinda like a bad jinx."

"We played last year. We never heard a whistle, but we made errors and struck out. I think it was because we played bad, not because of a curse," said Eddie.

"The curse only happens during an important part of the game; when the game is on the line," said Kermit.

"When's the curse supposed to go away?" asked Spud.

"Nobody knows. The curse could last forever."

"Com'on Kermit, a meeting hall ghost and a baseball curse?" challenged Spud.

"This is our second season and I ain't seen no ghosts," said Eddie.

"I ain't afraid of no ghosts," added Spud.

"My dad said that since we started playing baseball again at Lone Elder the man is happy. He said the curse only applies to adults," said Kermit.

"What if he's just saying that so you ain't scared?" asked Spud.

Kermit kicked the ground with his tennis shoe, "He could be. I don't know, but that's what Odell and my dad said."

"What about the woman ghost? What's going to make her go away?" asked Eddie.

"Odell said when they solve the mystery. Maybe find her body. He said she won't go away until then. He said she might go away if there is another wedding at the hall. There haven't been any weddings here since the woman disappeared. People thought the place had a bad omen. Now Mrs. Flynn is going to tear this place down and build a building to store eggs."

"What's the ghost's name?" asked Spud.

"I don't know. Odell didn't mention it."

"No meeting hall, no ghosts. This is stupid. Nobody believes in ghosts," said Eddie.

"Well, there haven't been any weddings. Brides think the hall is haunted. If the ghost shows up, they think it will bring bad luck to their marriage," added Kermit.

"That's dumb," said Spud as he scanned the inside of the meeting hall. He didn't believe in ghosts but decided he didn't want to take a chance on seeing one. He closed the window and jumped down off the ladder.

"What are you doing?" asked Eddie.

"There's nothing in there. It's empty."

"I thought we were going to sleep on the floor," replied Eddie.

Spud knew that if he showed any hesitation, Eddie would tease him relentlessly. "Who wants to sleep on the floor? We brought our gear. Let's go back and sleep at Kermit's house."

"What are we going to tell Adams?" asked Eddie.

Their friend, Tub Adams, had dared them to sleep in the community hall. Tub was Lone Elder's third baseman and sometimes played first base when Eddie was pitching. Tub had a barrel for a body, liked to talk almost as much as he liked to eat, and, in general, caused trouble.

"Tell him we got chased off by adults," replied Spud.

"He won't believe us," said Kermit.

"Let's go play baseball. We can come back later after dark. We can roll out our sleeping bags on the floor and see if there's a ghost," said Eddie.

Hesitant at first, Spud replied, "I'm in."

"What if we get caught?" worried Kermit.

"Nobody uses this place anymore. Like you said, they're going to tear it down; it's a fire hazard," said Eddie.

Kermit was cautious, "Okay, but what if there's a ghost?"

"There ain't no ghosts," said Spud.

Chapter 6

Owen Nance leaned against the base of the Big Leaf Maple and tipped a pint of Jack Daniels whiskey. He held the bottle up high above his mouth to make sure he had completely emptied every drop. Then he tossed the pint into the roadside ditch and slumped back against the massive tree trunk. It was late. The Lone Elder tavern had closed for the night and there was no sign of Ronnie Samuels. He had tracked Samuels until he had finally found him. The question was: what to do now? Through the dim light, he could see a man in the shadows. He strained to see but it was too far across the road to the tavern parking lot to see a face. He stayed in the dark close to the tree trunk in case someone looked toward the baseball field. He watched and waited. When the last car pulled from the parking lot, he staggered to his feet. Dressed in stain-covered baggy pants, a wrinkled, long blue sleeve work shirt, and well-worn, ankle-high PT style boots, he was the model of a drunk. He thought, because of what he'd been through, he might have become the man in the disguise. A knotted beard covered a sunbaked and worn face. A stained Portland Beavers baseball hat protected the crown of his head and pushed the rim of his greasy long hair over his ears. He dressed like a farm laborer because he considered it part of his cover. He wanted to blend with other farm laborers as much as possible. The other reason? He needed the money.

His journey had been long and stressful. He hadn't eaten, and he was half drunk. What used to happen on occasion now had become routine. Drinking was an escape and was now almost a necessity. He was being punished for a wrong he didn't commit. He took a step and tripped on a tree root. Falling hard, he crashed his right knee against the hard ground. Rocking to his side, he cussed as he squeezed his knee with hands as hard as the liquor he had just consumed. A flash of anger made his head explode. The veins in his eyes bulged a deep, dark red. He felt sick to his stomach and fought back the urge to puke. Rolling to his back, he forced his leg straight. Letting his arms flop straight from his shoulders, he lay there as if he were on a cross. Dizzy, he looked to the stars. Whether from the alcohol or the pain, he passed into a dreamless, deep sleep.

Nance woke with a start. He didn't know how long he had been out. Luckily, it was still dark, except for the dim light that came from the Lone Elder store. His head pounded from the combination of whiskey and wine. He needed a drink. Water more than alcohol. Throwing his arm and leg to his left side, he rolled to his stomach. Through the haze of his drunken stupor, he willed his body up to his knees. A sharp pain reminded him that he had badly injured his knee. He fell back on his side and pinched at the pain trying to erase it. He coughed up a mixture of dirt and bile. He spat and sat up. Drawing his shirt sleeve across his mouth, he wiped dirt from his face. He longed for a shave. He took the soiled Portland Beavers baseball hat from his head and slapped the dirt from his pants. With a flat hand, he skimmed the top of a head that still held a few strands of gray hair. He fought to stand straight. Unsteady, he took a step toward the baseball field. Lightheaded, he staggered backward, caught himself, and regained his balance. Carefully, he took a step forward and almost tripped when he caught the toe of his boot on an exposed rock. In a slow, snake-like slither, he made it to the baseball diamond. He stepped into the batter's box and pretended to raise his bat. Through cloudy eyes, he imagined the pitcher winding up and, with all the unnatural forces of a pitching motion, let loose with a fastball that reached speeds of ninety-plus miles per hour. In slow motion, he imagined that in less than a half a second, the ball was at the plate. Now steady, he cocked the bat, made a small stride, and took a powerful swing. He imagined the bat barrel smashing against the baseball, connecting at the *sweet spot*. There was a loud crack. Then the familiar momentary hush as the crowd heard the sound and collectively searched for the ball. Then, as they saw the ball rocket into the stands at a greater speed than the pitcher threw it, the crowd roared its approval. He raised his arms and dropped the imaginary bat. He stole a final glance at the ball and danced to first base. As he reached first base, not ninety feet, the regular distance of professional baseball, but the shorter youth distance, he slowed. His lungs burned and he coughed again. The cough was deep and painful. His body started to shake. His head spun and his stomach churned. Violently, he bent over and retched up the yellow mixture of the beer he had for lunch and the wine and whiskey he had for dinner. Exhausted and sick, Nance fell to his knees and collapsed onto his stomach. Just as the moon dropped behind an ominous dark cloud, he passed out. Another day, and night, had passed and he was no closer to bringing a murderer to justice.

Chapter 7

"Push me up," instructed Spud.

Eddie lowered his shoulder and pushed up on Spud's butt. Spud shimmied through the window opening and fell to the floor. Eddie tossed up their sleeping bags and a pack with a flashlight, peanut butter and jam sandwiches, beef jerky, and a can of cola each. Spud helped Eddie and then they pulled Kermit into the meeting hall. Just in case they needed a quick exit, they left the window open.

"This place smells," said Spud.

The boys walked the floor in different directions. The meeting hall was one large room. There were four sash windows along the east and west walls to allow, if they were all opened, cross ventilation. It was hard to breathe. The heat from the afternoon sun lingered. From the one open window, a cool evening breeze flowed through, replacing hot, stale air trapped in the pores of the old building. There was a small stage on the north end facing the main room. The floor was cluttered with discarded church pews and folding metal chairs. There was no ceiling. Exposed vertical and horizonal beams tied the building together. Beyond the beams the room was open to the roof. A light fixture with a broken light bulb and a long cord hung from one of the wood rafters. The rafters were painted white, but the paint was faded and dull. The wood floor was made of wide planks. The sheen, if there ever was one, had been bleached by sunlight and the wood was now bare. There were two wide entry doors that closed in the middle. The wide opening allowed people, two or three abreast, to enter or exit at the same time. Off to one side of the entry doors was a small galley kitchen. Looking as if they had come from a lake cabin, a row of empty knotty pine cabinets hung over a yellow Formica countertop. It was an odd combination. On the counter was an electric heating unit used to keep coffee or water hot. There was a cast iron sink with a missing faucet. It looked as though someone had tried to take it out but had given up in the middle of the plumbing repair. There were two floor-to-ceiling storage cabinets on either side of an electric stove. The walls were painted different colors. One cabinet was painted white to match the white wall. The other cabinet was painted dark blue to match the dark blue wall. A cabinet door was open, exposing bare shelves covered with paper. Eddie swung the other doors open only to find dusty shelves, a stack of empty paper cups, and paper plates. The floor was made of sturdy tongue and groove planks. It was a mishmash; some boards were stained a light oak while others were stained dark walnut. The board edges were cupped, making the floor uneven. To the artistic observer, the kitchen looked as if it were built by different designers with strong opinions.

"There's nothing here. The place is empty," said Spud.

"All that's in here is old furniture, cobwebs, and dust," added Kermit.

"Let's lay out the bags. It's late and I'm hungry," said Eddie.

"You sure we don't want to go back outside and sleep on the ground? This place gives me the creeps," said Kermit.

"Naw, then we lose the bet and Tub will call us chicken," countered Spud.

Kermit flopped down in one of the church pews, "Right now, I don't care much about what Tub calls us."

"It'll be okay. Let's play cards. My flashlight has new batteries. We can play while we wait for that woman ghost," said Eddie.

Kermit looked up toward the balcony and then at the small circular stage; he hoped the night would be quiet but had a lingering suspicion that wouldn't be the case.

"Spud, you awake?" whispered Eddie.

"How can you sleep; this floor is hard as a rock and I keep hearing cricks and groans."

"Kermit, you awake?"

"Never went to sleep," he moaned.

"What time is it?" asked Spud.

Kermit was the only one with a watch. He found his flashlight and shined it on the face. "It's two o'clock. We went to bed an hour ago."

Somewhat nervous, Eddie said, "I keep hearing things."

"I suppose it's that ghost you ain't afraid of," said Spud.

"You're the one who said he wasn't afraid of ghosts."

"Well, I ain't."

There's Money on the Edge

Kermit pointed his flashlight toward the ceiling.

"Hey, don't do that," said Eddie. "Do lights attract or scare away ghosts?" he asked with a nervous giggle.

"I don't think they like the light. If they did, why do they always come out after dark?" asked Spud, wiping his mouth. "I'm thirsty."

"There's no running water; take a drink of your pop."

"I drank it all."

"The sink doesn't have a faucet. I remember seeing a hand pump for the well, but it's outside. After all these years, the well is probably dry. The pump may be frozen up. It probably doesn't work anyway," said Kermit.

"Do you think it's worth a try?" asked Spud.

"Yep. There's only one way to find out if there's water," Eddie said.

The boys, full of nervous energy and looking for a way to expend it, crawled out of their sleeping bags and fell in line behind Kermit. He led the way with the flashlight. The light cast an eerie shadow against the hollow interior. The old hall was a lot spookier with shadows rather than just the darkness. As they entered the kitchen, there was a loud crash. They froze.

"What was that?" Spud asked as he ran into Kermit.

"It sounded like a chair fell over," answered Eddie.

"It was upstairs in the balcony. I went up there earlier and there is nothing up there. It's just an open area overlooking the main floor. It was probably used when the place got too crowded and they needed more space."

"We have to go up there," said Spud.

Kermit stopped and turned the flashlight off.

"Why did you do that?" asked Spud.

Kermit responded matter-of-factly. "If there's somebody up there, don't you think they've seen or heard us by now?"

"Yeah, but we can't see them."

"It might be better if we don't see them, and they don't see us," Kermit replied.

Eddie crept forward. He found the narrow set of steep steps that led up to the balcony. "We have to find out if somebody is up there or what made that noise."

"I would just as soon leave the place to the ghosts," said Kermit.

Spud pushed boldly past Eddie, "Com'on, there are three of us and only one of them."

"I think one ghost can take us," said Kermit.

As Spud led the way, they slowly climbed the steps, trying to be as quiet as possible. Eddie and Kermit kept close to Spud. It was dark, except for streaks of moonlight radiating through a round window with square wood mullions. The light came from behind and above, at the very top of the roof peak. The moon's location determined where the light beam hit the main floor. On this night, the moon was at the proper angle to illuminate center stage.

The boys crawled from the steps onto the balcony floor. The semi-circle balcony was empty. There was a waist-high, half-wall that served as a protective barrier preventing the absent-minded from falling to the first floor. The boys crawled to the wall and, from their knees, peeked over the edge and looked down onto the stage. At center stage was a folding chair. The chair was upright and empty. The moonlight had become a spotlight shining brightly on the chair.

"That chair wasn't there," whispered Kermit.

"I don't remember it either," answered Eddie.

Absently, Spud asked, "Where did it come from?"

As they looked on, a wisp of wind blew through the open window, stirring the dust. When the breeze hit the moonlight, there were swirling sprinkles of light. The light swept in a whirlwind around center stage. The boys watched in silent amazement. As the whirlwind slowly twirled, they heard the distant, hardly perceptible, sound of music.

"What's that?" asked Spud.

"I couldn't tell. It kinda sounded like a flute," replied Kermit.

The music stopped as the light shifted off center stage. The boys turned and faced the back wall where the moon filtered through the window.

"That was weird," said Eddie.

"I think it was the ghost," said Kermit.

"I didn't see a ghost. All I saw was swirling wind and the soft sound of music. It was so distant that I couldn't tell for sure."

"If that wasn't a ghost, what was it?"

"I thought all ghosts were like Casper," said Eddie referring to the cartoon character on the television show, *Casper the Friendly Ghost*.

"I know one thing," said Kermit; "that wasn't normal. It wasn't scary though. The wind and the music sounded, I don't know, kind of sad."

"Well, at least whatever it was didn't go boo," Eddie joked.

"Maybe it was just the wind," offered Spud.

"I've never seen a wind like that. I wonder if the ghost, or the wind, was trying to tell us something?" wondered Kermit aloud.

"Why would you think that?"

"No particular reason. Doesn't there have to be a reason why ghosts appear?"

Spud and Eddie both shrugged but didn't respond.

"What should we do now?" asked Kermit.

"Whatever it was is gone. Let's go back downstairs and go to sleep."

"You think we should stay in here?" asked Kermit. "I'm not sure if I can sleep."

"It's too late to walk home. We can sleep outside, but there's only a couple of hours before morning. Then we can go to Kermit's place."

"We camped out to meet up with the other guys to play baseball. I'm going to play," said Eddie.

Spud stood up and leaned on the wood railing. "I think we should stay here again. I want to see if the same thing would happen."

"The moonlight is really the reflection of the sunlight off the moon. The moon doesn't have light. It may be next month before the light hits that window exactly at the same spot. Then it has to be a clear night with no clouds. I'll look at the almanac and check the weather," said Kermit.

Eddie stood beside Spud. He used Kermit's flashlight to scan the bottom floor. "It's weird, but I thought I saw a figure. It was hazy, but it looked like a woman. It was kinda eerie."

"Maybe we should just let that ghost go on its merry way," offered Spud.

"I have always heard this place was haunted, but I thought it was just talk. Now we know it might be. We have to come back. If that happens again, then we know for sure there's a ghost," Kermit said determined.

"Okay, it's settled; we come back. We'll bring anybody on the team who wants to come. We have to find out before they tear this place down."

Chapter 8

"Is he dead?" asked Spud.

"Last night, we saw a ghost and now there's a dead body. Maybe it's the curse," commented Kermit.

"How do you play baseball with ghosts and curses all over the place?" grumbled Eddie.

Kermit studied the body laying over first base, "I think so...I think he's dead. He ain't movin' and he smells. What should we do?"

"Wave down a passing car and have them call the cops," suggested Spud.

"Go shake him first to make sure he's dead," said Eddie.

Spud recoiled and stepped back, "I'm not touching a dead body. You do it. It's your turn."

Eddie shook his head, exhibiting a great deal of resistance. "How's it my turn?"

Spud pointed back toward the community building, "Because I crawled into the meeting hall. I was first."

"That was nothing; you jumped onto the ladder first," retorted Eddie.

"It's your turn."

Kermit raised his hand, "Hold it! We've got to do something. By the time you two stop arguing, rigor mortis might set in, if it hasn't already."

Eddie, skeptical, rolled his eyes and then bravely approached the body.

Eddie called, "Hey. Hey, mister."

Carefully, Eddie crept closer. Bending down, he extended his arm and touched the man's back shoulder. The side of his face was covered with dirt. Some of the dirt around his mouth was wet. His body odor, a combination of sweat, alcohol, and cigarettes, was powerful. Eddie pinched his nose and backed away.

"He stinks."

Spud backed up and took a deep breath. "I know. I can smell him from here. Is he dead?"

"I think he's breathing."

"What do you mean, you think?" asked Spud.

Eddie kept his eyes on the body. "I can't tell for sure, but I think his chest is moving up and down."

"Shake him," suggested Spud.

Eddie snapped, "You're a big talker. You shake him."

"I ain't afraid," said Spud as he inched forward and knelt on his right knee. Extending his hand, he shook the man's shoulder. "Hey, mister, are you okay?"

Nance woke with a start. He felt a touch on his shoulder and reflectively reacted with a jerk. He raised his head, the movement too quick. Sharp electrical shards scrambled his brain. His head started to spin.

Dizzy, he collapsed onto the ground. Rolling on his side, he forced his matted eyes open. It was hard to see. He tried to focus on the three shadowy figures scrambling away. Where was he? The bright morning light made him squint. He pushed his body up into a sitting position. He pressed his two index fingers against his temples and shook his head.

Startled, Spud fell back, knocking Eddie to the ground. "Run!" he screamed.

Eddie scrambled to his feet and ran, stumbling toward the pitcher's mound. Spud sprinted past him. Kermit tripped and fell on his stomach. In a flash, he was on his hands and knees, crawling as fast as they would take him. He tried to scream but the only sound that came from his throat was a loud grunt.

"Wait. Don't run," Nance said as he brushed the front of his shirt. Engulfed in a small dust cloud, he tried to focus.

Safely away, Spud and Eddie stopped. They quickly turned to gaze, warily, at the man who was still sitting on the ground. Kermit didn't stop until he reached third base.

"Hey mister, we thought you were dead," said Eddie.

"I feel like it," groaned Nance.

"What are you doing here?" asked Spud.

Holding his head, Nance responded, "I needed to take a nap."

Eddie, somewhat miffed, tilted his head and asked, "On first base?"

"It's as good a place as any," Nance said, standing up and brushing the rest of the dust and dirt off his clothes. "What are you boys doing here? It's too early to play baseball."

"It's never too early. Sometimes we play in the morning because it's the only time we have. We're meeting some guys for a game," said Eddie.

"Don't you boys work?"

"It's Saturday. We work all week," answered Spud. "If we can, on Saturday mornings, we play baseball. We can't play on Sunday because most of the guys go to church. Most of the team comes to play. Sometimes a few older guys come too. We play against them, but they're not very good. We beat them most of the time."

Nance chuckled, "I guess you don't have to be good to like to play the game."

"My dad gave me the morning off to play ball," said Eddie.

"I've seen you boys play ball. I watch from over there," Nance said as he pointed to a thick hedge of arborvitaes in right field. "I like to lean against that maple tree."

"Why don't you sit in the bleachers?" asked Spud.

"Your parents probably wouldn't like that."

Eddie was respectful of his elders, but from the man's appearance and smell, he could understand why.

Kermit pointed, "I've never seen you out there."

"Let's just say I'm a new fan. I played some ball myself," said Nance as he stretched. "I used to play on a country field just like this."

Spud studied him and wondered how an older man who looked like he did and slept in the dirt could be a baseball player. "You must really love the game to sleep on first base," he said.

Nance laughed and grabbed his head, "I guess I must."

"What did you play? Infield or outfield?" queried Spud.

"Played infield. Pitched some. Toward the end, I was mostly a pitcher."

"When did you play?" asked Spud.

Nance shuffled over to the grandstand and sat in the first row. The wood plank was hard but more comfortable than sitting on the ground. Spud and Eddie, now curious, followed but kept their distance. The man had a hard look. His face was a deep color of red, like a man who drank way too much wine or had spent too much time in a cold, harsh climate. His nose was wide and flat, like a boxer who had his nose broken too many times. Creases, like miniature black canyons, cut from the top of his nose and over his nostrils. The eyes were sad but not unfriendly. His hands didn't match his face. They were blistered and swollen, not hands used to hard work. His hands were more like those of a salesman or banker. His fingers were locked in a semi-circle, as if a ball had been pried from them. His shoulders were worn down to a slope. A small narrow scar ran across his cheek. The top three buttons of his shirt were unbuttoned. Underneath, he wore a flannel T-shirt with buttons down the front. He was neither fat nor skinny. A wide black leather belt held up his pants. There were grease spots on both pant legs.

"I played, but it was a long time ago. I started when I was about your age. I don't play anymore, but I follow the game really close."

"Do you live around here?" asked Eddie.

"I'm not from here. I follow the crops. Sometimes I live here, sometimes there. Like I said, I've watched you boys play. You're pretty good. Do you play on a team?"

There's Money on the Edge

"Lone Elder," said Spud, pointing to his hat from last year.

"We don't have our new uniforms yet. The first year the uniforms included shirts and pants. Last year, we wore jeans with a jersey," added Kermit.

"I guess it doesn't matter as long as you're playing," said Nance.

"We don't have a coach yet, so we don't have uniforms," replied Kermit.

"When does the season start?"

"Pretty soon if we can find a coach. Our coach from last year went to the Cubs. His son, Tommy, played on our team last year. He was a good player," said Kermit.

"Ah, the Cubs," replied Nance with a hint of recognition. "And where do these Cubs play?"

"In town," Spud said, referring to the nearby town of Canby. They're the best team around, but we almost beat them last year. We'll beat them this year."

"Sounds like the Cubs are your rivals," Nance observed.

"I guess so. We go to school with most of those guys."

"Well, you boys keep playing. Have a good season," said Nance.

"You going to be around?" asked Spud.

"Oh, I'll be around. I have some unfinished business to take care of. Maybe I'll see you again," he said and then started to walk toward the tall hedge in right field.

"Hey mister, do you want to coach?" asked Eddie.

"No, but I'll keep an eye on things and help out when I can. You boys have fun," he said as he walked between two tall arborvitae bushes and disappeared.

"Think we'll ever see him again?" asked Eddie.

"I don't know. If we do, maybe he can help out. Hey, here comes Tub and some of the other guys. Let's play some ball," yelled Spud.

Chapter 9

"Name's Charlie. Charlie Pierce."

Rebecca Flynn looked up from behind the counter. She observed the man who appeared to be about her age. She held her finger on the ledger with the sales numbers so she wouldn't lose her place.

"I'm Rebecca," she said curtly and then returned to her work.

Charlie wondered if that was how the woman greeted all her customers.

"Good to meet you, Rebecca."

"What happened to your arm?" she asked.

"Hurt it in a logging accident."

"Dangerous job. We don't get too many loggers around here; mostly farmers, but there are a few."

"I guess I'm one of the few. I'm living up the road with the Long family while I recover."

"My mom is friends with the Longs. Karen used to work here before she met Pete. How long are you going to be laid up?"

"Doc says two or three months. We'll see how it goes."

"What brings you to the store?"

"Do you own the place?"

"My mother does."

Charlie was suddenly uneasy about asking the young woman for a job. He was a bit intimidated by her beauty. Her hair was pulled back into a ponytail and she wore no makeup, but she was as pretty as any of the young women he had seen at the baseball games in San Francisco. He hesitated and then manned up.

"I was looking for something to do. I wondered if you needed some help?"

"You can't pump gas and wash windshields with that arm."

"I have a good right arm. I can use it."

"We don't need anybody to do that. Odell and Benny have been with us for years. Odell works the morning shift and Benny works until we close the station at seven. Sometimes they do go fishing, but I can fill in."

From a side entrance Charlie saw an older woman enter the store. Her hair was about the same color as the younger woman behind the counter, except a bit darker. They both had light complexions that matched. They were pretty and the only difference he could see was their age. With one quick glance, he could tell this was the mother, and more importantly, the owner.

"I'm Nell Flynn," the woman said before Charlie had a chance to introduce himself.

"I'm Charlie Pierce."

"Oh sure. Karen Long mentioned that you were staying with them until your arm heals. She said you were lucky."

Charlie smiled, "That's what they say. There were a few logs flying; I just ducked."

"Logging is dangerous. Karen doesn't like Pete logging, but he loves it. Likes the woods and the freedom of it all. Can you pour a beer?" Nell inquired.

Rebecca's shoulders sagged. "Mother. We don't need anybody."

"Now Rebecca, I'm sure you didn't mean it that way," Nell scolded.

"I'm sorry," she said to Charlie. "It's just that, well, we already have Jim."

"Jim can always use a hand," said Nell. "I don't have time to help him, do you?"

"I can lift the glass with my good hand and pull the tap lever with my cast. If you really need the help, it sure would be appreciated. I'm no good at sitting around. If you don't really need any help like Rebecca said, maybe you can direct me to a company that needs some."

"Nonsense. The crowd starts to pick up around five o'clock. Come in then and Jim will show you the ropes. Having a young man around will probably help pull in some young women."

Charlie felt his face redden.

"Mother!" exclaimed Rebecca.

"Oh, I'm just kidding. Young people are too thin-skinned. He's good looking, don't you think?" Nell asked Rebecca.

It was Rebecca's turn to blush. She looked away but didn't answer.

Charlie chuckled, "Well, I don't know if I'll help with the female traffic, but I'll be there."

"See you at five."

"I'll be here earlier. Thanks again," said Charlie.

He extended his right hand. Nell shook it briskly. Charlie nodded at Rebecca. She gave the slightest of nods and quickly looked away. Rebecca, he thought, would at least make coming to work worthwhile.

Never believing that being on time for a new job was the right move, Charlie was ten minutes early. He had been at the tavern a few times before with Pete. They had a couple of beers and played some shuffleboard. The tavern attracted a good mix of people; mostly farmers, factory workers, and loggers with a few professionals mixed in. Nell's Lone Elder Tavern was the kind of place where people left their occupations and egos at the front door and just became part of the family. They were good hard-working people who, after a long day of work, liked to have a cold beer and listen to country music on the jukebox. The tavern was popular because of its relaxed atmosphere and because it had the coldest beer in the county. Fights were strictly forbidden. Nell had learned from her husband that, if you wanted a family-type atmosphere, where women felt comfortable, fights could not be allowed.

Charlie was familiar with Nell's bartender, Jim Davis. He was an ex-Marine who spent ten years working in the Portland shipyards as a welder. A true-blue union man, Davis was built like a slab of steel. Unfortunately, even steel had limitations. Jim's was his lungs. Years of smoking and the smoke from welding eight to ten hours a day, six days a week finally caught up with him. His doctor said, "Quit smoking and find another

There's Money on the Edge

job, or die." Luckily, Jim was a boxing enthusiast and taught Portland street kids how to box. He met Gene Flynn at a neighborhood gym on the lower southeast side of town. They became friends and when Davis could no longer work in the shipyards, Flynn offered him a job. After Flynn died, Nell relied on Davis to run the tavern. To ensure he stayed, Nell rewarded Davis with a twenty-five percent ownership position. Nell, always the businesswoman, offered Davis a stake at fair market value. Davis was firm, liked a good joke, and treated every customer like he was the first, and the only one. With a bald head, thick mustache, arms the size of most men's legs, the few who did challenge him felt the effects for days after.

"I heard about the accident. Lucky you or Pete didn't get killed," said Davis.

"I guess; it just wasn't our day."

"Will you be able to pitch again?"

"That I don't know, but I wasn't planning on going back. I think my playing days are over."

"Well, I hope you change your mind. We don't get too many people in these parts who are good enough to make it to the big leagues."

Charlie wasn't sure how to take what Jim had said. He appreciated the support, but he wasn't from Oregon. Maybe they had adopted him. It didn't matter. Pitching, especially now with his injury, was not something he seriously thought about.

Jim turned out to be a good teacher and in a short amount of time, Charlie was pouring beer and manning the bar like an old pro. Nell was right; when word got around that a young good looking man was behind the bar at Nell's place, there was an uptick in the female clientele. Rebecca noticed but didn't seem to care. Mostly, she ignored the tavern, and Charlie.

Charlie went about the business of taking care of customers. He grew accustomed to patrons engaging in serious conversations. Most of the time, out of common courtesy, he ignored them, or at least tried to. On this particularly slow night, he noted that two regulars were at the very end of the bar having an in-depth conversation. He knew the men, but not well. Jack Wagner worked at one of the lumber mills in Molalla. His hands were cobbled and he wore his hair in a crewcut. Bill Cooper owned one of the area's larger farms. He grew wheat, corn, and raised cattle. He was about Charlie's height and always wore bib overalls with a blue work shirt. It was tough not to overhear them as they sipped Olympia beer, Oly to its drinkers.

"I can't do it," commented Wagner. "I'm working six days a week and sometimes double shifts."

"Last year, I helped, but I don't think I can this year. The farm takes all my time. Spring and summer are my busiest times. I'm not a head coach anyway," said Cooper.

"Isn't there anybody else to take the team?" asked Wagner.

"Not that I've heard of. We asked everybody and they either don't want to or are too busy. I didn't like Mike Walls, but at least he coached the team," said Cooper.

Wagner took a long drink, "Good riddance to him. If he wants to take his kid to play for the Cubs, it's a free country. It's the way he did it that I don't like. You can't tell me he didn't thumb his nose at us by leaving us without a coach less than a month before the season starts. He had it planned all the time. He always thought his son was the star. He didn't coach the other kids; it was all about his kid."

"With his son leaving and two of the boys moving up because of age, we only have nine players. We really need twelve or thirteen boys to field a team with vacations and other things that come up," said Cooper.

Wagner slightly bowed his head and sighed, "I don't know. Maybe another season wasn't meant to be. The death of Jason Larson was a hard shot to the gut."

"That was a terrible blow to his family and this community. How's Rich?"

"You lose a son in a tractor accident on the farm, I don't know. I do know he blames himself. He loved that kid," said Wagner.

"That could have happened to anybody. There are so many kids around here working the fields using tractors it's surprising these accidents don't happen more often."

"You put kids around equipment and things are bound to happen."

"Besides the Stump kid, and with the Walls kid leaving, Jason was our only other pitcher. We may not have enough players. The Dempsey, Stump, and Adams boys can play for the town teams. There might be a couple of others who might make it too, but that leaves four or five boys out."

"My son won't play. We just don't have time to run him to town. Eats at me because he loves to play, and I like to watch him. I think with a little coaching and a little more time he might become a decent ballplayer," said Wagner.

Charlie was now fully engaged and listening to the conversation.

"Excuse me, but I couldn't help from overhearing. Aren't there other teams around where the boys can play?" Charlie asked.

"There are teams, but we thought we had something special here. Once the boys are older, they generally go play for one of the teams in the bigger towns. We started the team because too many of the boys were left out. There weren't enough teams in town and then you had the politics of it. The kids in town will always get the spots over the kids on the farm unless they are really special. We started the team to give more kids a chance. The team is made up of local kids, but other kids from nearby towns can play here. The Stump and Dempsey kids live in Canby, but they like to play here because their friends do. Lone Elder gives the parents another option. Most of the parents like it because it's not as political. They think it's better for their sons."

"We were good the first year under McCoy but then he quit. That's what happens when you win; everybody wants to be part of a winner. Then Mike Walls started playing politics. He wanted to be the coach and forced McCoy out. Too bad we lost McCoy. We didn't appreciate him enough. Walls won, but he seemed to forget there were other kids on the team. He coached for his kid," said Cooper.

Wagner motioned for another beer, "Walls took his kid and went to the Cubs, the number one team in town."

"I don't mind seeing him go, but now we don't have a coach and not enough players," said Cooper.

"Can you get McCoy back?" asked Charlie.

"He turned us down. We were stupid and didn't back him up. We lost him and it was our fault," said Cooper.

"You interested?" asked Wagner.

"I don't know. I have some time," said Charlie motioning to his arm, "but I've never coached kids."

"You were a ballplayer. The kids would benefit from having you coach," said Cooper.

"Being a player and coaching a bunch of kids are two completely different things. Being a good ballplayer doesn't translate into being a good coach. I know what that looks like," replied Charlie.

Cooper wasn't sure what Charlie meant but was suddenly eager at the prospect of finding a coach. He understood the necessity of laying out what Charlie was getting into.

"A lot of the leg work is done. We've already registered the team with the league and there's a good group of parents to help out."

Charlie realized he may have gone too far and started to hedge. "Isn't there a dad to take the team?"

"You're talking about farmers and people who work at local mills. It's hard for them to find the time," said Wagner.

Cooper put his palms up, "Most men just don't want to get involved. It's never easy to coach kids. I don't think you'll have too much trouble with the parents, but parents are parents. I guess I could fall into this category; everybody thinks Johnny will be a big leaguer and don't like it when you sit him on the bench."

"What are you saying? The parents will help as long as their kids get preferential treatment?" asked Charlie.

"No. That's not it. Most parents aren't like that. Most of us just want the kids to have a good experience. As a player, the kids will look up to you. The good thing about you is that you have *no skin in the game*. You don't have a kid on the team. If you're fair, you won't have any trouble. We'll make sure of it," said Cooper.

"You do it for the kids. I helped last year and will help you; I just don't have the time to be the head man. Made me feel good when the kids did well. Most of these kids won't play that long. To give them a feel for the game, that's what this is about. It's a great game and we want them to like it," said Wagner.

"I'll help too in any way I can. I'd just be thankful my kid has a place to play," added Cooper.

Charlie leaned his back against the bar counter, "I'll give it some thought," he said.

"I'd like to say we have time, but we're going to have to give the parents a yes or no. We have to give the boys time to join other teams. It wouldn't be fair to them."

"If you have a mind to do it, you might talk to Nell. She helps. She helps buy the uniforms. We put LE on the jersey and she gets some free advertising. Smart businesswoman, that Nell. She also owns the property the field is on. She was going to put a building on it until we started the team."

"I'll talk to Nell and let you know tomorrow," said Charlie, unsure of what he was getting in to.

Chapter 10

Nell dabbed her eyes with a linen handkerchief, "It was tragic. I've known the Larson family for years. They're longtime residents. Jason used to come into the store to buy Snickers candy bars. He was a great kid and a fine baseball player."

"Had to be hard on the family and the team," said Charlie.

"A loss of a child is always devastating to a community. It's the worst thing that can happen to a parent. Even if it's not your kid, you still feel it. He was well liked by the other boys. I'm sure it was hard for the kids, but they're resilient; they'll come back."

"I'm surprised the team stayed together."

"They almost didn't. After Walls left, some people wanted to disband the team."

"Why didn't they?"

"Jason's father, Tom, stepped in. He came to what many thought was going to be the last board meeting. He gave a tearful speech. Said if the parents quit the kids, it would be an affront to Jason's memory. He had brave men, men who fought in World War II and Korea, crying like babies. Like I said, the loss of a child has a huge impact on the community."

"But Walls left."

"Yeah, he did. He never really cared about the team. He brought his kid out here to coach him. He played him all the time. If an article went into the paper, his kid was always mentioned, even if the other kids played better. Looking back on it, I think it would have been better to keep McCoy. He's a good man. I think it hurt him that the parents weren't more supportive. They let the smooth-talking Mike Walls convince them that McCoy didn't know enough about the game to take the boys to the next level."

"Some of my best coaches weren't super tacticians, but they were good with people. They surrounded themselves with people who knew the game. Does Mr. McCoy still live around here?"

"Nope, he retired and moved to Arizona for his arthritis. Jim tells me that you played some baseball."

"I did. Played for the Giants."

"What happened?"

Charlie, like many other people, felt comfortable talking to Nell. Thoughtful and a good listener, without saying it, people knew she was trustworthy and could keep a private conversation, private.

"Got frustrated with my game. Walked away."

"I bet that was hard to do if you loved playing."

"I'm not sure I understood it then. I've had second thoughts. I guess that's to be expected."

"I think my husband, Gene, thought that when he left boxing the first time. He made some money and then gave it up. He had to go back because he spent all his money, but he missed being in the ring too. He probably shouldn't have returned, but he said if he wouldn't have gone back, he would have always second-guessed his decision to quit. Sometimes it's hard to step away; you have to be sure."

"I'm not sure but the accident may have made the decision for me. I try not to think about it now. Being a player is hard; being a coach may be as equally difficult. I'm not sure I can coach kids."

"Well, given that we don't have a coach, this is as good a time as any to find out. I'd say you'll never know until you give it a shot. Heck, you might like it."

"I'm not used to dealing with parents."

"You'll find that most of these folks are very reasonable. Sure, they want the best for their kids, but most are realistic. I'd say that most of them would rather have their kids excel in school and go to college rather than become major league ballplayers. They talk about their kids becoming the next generation of lawyers, doctors, teachers, or farmers. I've never heard one say they expected their kid to be a professional baseball player, except for maybe Walls. How often does that turn out? I don't think most parent's expectations are too high; they just want their kids to play and have fun."

Charlie thought for a few seconds and then said, "If I decided to coach, how about working at the tavern? Practice and games may cause some conflicts. I don't like to make a commitment and then back off it."

"You take the team and we'll work around your hours. The season only lasts a couple of months. By the time it's over your arm will have healed. Then you'll be going back to the woods."

"Mr. Cooper and Mr. Wagner said we may not be able to find enough players."

"Once the word gets out, I'm sure we can come up with two or three kids."

"What do I have to do?"

"First, you have to come to the board meeting. Then get the kids together. We had better act fast before we lose more kids."

"Is this the last year for the team?"

"I don't know. Once they get older, there are fewer players and it takes the combined teams from Canby, Lone Elder, and some of the surrounding areas to field a team. Kids quit because they have other interests or have to work."

Charlie nodded in agreement, "It's a very hard sport to play. Only those kids who have played the sport know how hard it really is."

"How about it? Will you be the coach?"

"If you're okay with me having flexible hours, yes I will."

"Then we have a deal," said Nell with a big smile.

The Lone Elder board meetings were held in a room in the back of the tavern. The room was big enough for a u-shaped table seating fifteen people. There were chairs for another ten attendees. Word had spread about the new baseball coach and tonight all the seats were taken; it was standing room only. Lone Elder baseball was big news.

Nell rented the room out for meetings of all types. Once a month, the room was taken by a local quilting group. Twice a month, farmers gathered to listen to speakers discuss all types of subjects from the latest in fertilizer to how to increase yields with engineered crops. The meeting room was used so often that Nell recognized an immediate need for more space to accommodate larger groups. The community center across the street had served that function until a leaky roof and a combination of electrical and plumbing problems forced the county to declare the structure off-limits. Nell planned to tear the old meeting hall down and build a modern combination office and warehouse in its place. Until she did, the room in the back of the tavern was valuable space.

Introduced by Nell, Charlie stood to address the five-member Lone Elder board, parents, and interested third parties. Jack Wagner and Bill Cooper, the two men he overheard talking at the tavern, were members of the board. Nell was a member because she owned the baseball field and had a vested interest in what went on. Helen Sharp, a grandmotherly woman with a big smile and Kermit's mother, was the treasurer. The last member was Ron Lacy, the team's representative to the league. Lacy liked to tell jokes, wore white shirts with the two top buttons undone, and had a *green thumb* when it came to growing the best strawberries and beans in the immediate vicinity if not the whole Willamette Valley. Spud's mother, Louise, and Eddie's parents, Rowland and Emily, were there to offer support.

Charlie started slow. He was a bit nervous. Unusual since he had been in front of crowds many times as a professional.

"I've never been a coach, but I've played some ball. When I think back on my years playing little league baseball, I only remember a few wins and losses, but I do recall fond memories of my teammates and having fun. What kids really like to do is play. All the kids that play for me will play. It's my opinion that practice, lots of it, is the way you improve. If we practice hard, the kids will naturally improve, and that will translate into better ballplayers. Better ballplayers win, but that's not as important as the kids learning how to play a great game. It's not that I don't like winning; I do. It's just that at this age, it's more important for the kids to learn how to play well. If we do that," Charlie emphasized *we*, "we'll be successful. I know you're all busy, which is the reason I'm standing here, but the teams that have the most fun have parent involvement. I only have the boys for a couple of practices and two games a week. I need your help to work with the boys. Even playing catch for ten to twenty minutes will help them improve. Your participation can mean the difference in how well your son plays and, more importantly, will help build his confidence. This doesn't just apply to the men in the room. When I was young, my dad was gone most of the time because of his job. It was my mom who took me out and played catch with me. Believe me, it wasn't a natural thing for her to do. At first, she was afraid of getting hit by the ball, but she never told me because she thought that would make me afraid too. We both learned how to play catch together. She was proud of that. She, and my dad, were the reasons why I played. If not for them, I would have never made it to the majors. I'm not saying playing catch will be the ticket for your boys to make it to the pros, but you never know. The time you spend will help them become better ballplayers and leave them with an experience they will remember. Baseball is one of those games where the better you get, the more fun you have." Charlie paused, "That's about it. Are there any questions?"

Nell had a big smile on her face, "I'll get my mitt."

The board members and the parents nodded in agreement. There was an immediate sense that they had found their coach. Now relieved, they quickly got down to the business of planning the season. A Jamboree, picnics, a team campout, along with other activities were discussed and responsibilities assigned. There was a unanimous agreement that the season would be dedicated to Jason Larson. The community would move on, but they would never forget.

Chapter 11

The morning sun was unusually hot for late April. Charlie's arm itched. He found a long thin twig and worked it down his cast to scratch his forearm skin. He thought the itch was a sign his arm was healing and looked forward to the time when the doctors would remove his cast.

He surveyed the infield. It was all dirt and rough. The kids had removed the larger rocks and the clumps of grass. There remained enough smaller rocks and pebbles to cause a bad hop. He had played on worse fields, but they were mostly sandlot diamonds used for pickup games with neighborhood kids. Even in the majors, he had seen a bad hop caused by a small rock kick the baseball left or right and cause an error. Errors were part of the game, but reducing the chance they could happen made sense. A ball hitting one of the kids in the chest, chin, or nose was sometimes hard for a young infielder to get over. He jotted down a note to bring a rake and shovel to smooth the dirt.

The infield was larger than normal for ten to twelve-year-old kids. The pitcher's mound was flat, he assumed, to conform to league rules. The backstop was a series of poles in a semi-circle. One of the parents who raised chickens had removed the old, rusted-out mesh, replacing it with new poultry netting. The infield dirt extended well beyond the normal cut, making it necessary for the outfielders to know how to field balls on both dirt and grass. Charlie made a mental note to include the outfielders in infield drills. He would have preferred a grass outfield because he knew a hard-hit ground ball on dirt would skip past a young outfielder before he could react. There was no home run fence. A hard-hit ball could roll past the outfielders in left and center and end up in a potato field. To the right, the ball could end up in the arborvitaes. The field had some quirks.

Charlie giggled weakly and said aloud, "If a ball is hit past the center fielder it could conceivably roll forever."

He made another note to put a fast kid with a strong arm in center field. Defense would be a priority. That was, he thought, not necessarily a bad thing. Teams could win with pitching and defense. At least his players would be used to the field while the visiting teams may have difficulty with it. Lone Elder field would be a competitive advantage.

Charlie shook his head in disgust. What he was thinking didn't sound like a coach who wanted the boys to just have fun. He was a coach strategizing to win. He constantly had to remind himself that this was *youth* baseball.

He emptied the equipment bag. There was a set of shin guards, a chest protector, and a catcher's mask all looking as if they were hand-me-downs, dusty and well used. There were five wood bats with different weights in ounces burned into the knobs. On the bat label was the manufacturer's name, Louisville Slugger. Two of the bats looked okay; the others were chipped as if the boys had used them to hit rocks. Hitting rocks with a wood bat was not a bad idea for eye-hand coordination, but it made the bat barrel look like a rough minefield. His first request from the board would be for new bats. There were two batting helmets without the protective ear flaps. He tossed those aside. The league required players to use helmets and protective ear flaps. He had seen helmets with molded ear flaps being tested. A few major and minor leaguers were already using them. He would buy those if they were available. If not, the boys would be required to wear a combination of helmet and ear protection to prevent serious injury.

"The equipment doesn't look that good, but you can make it work," said Owen Nance after he strolled over from his usual spot under the maple tree.

Charlie was so focused on the equipment that he didn't hear the man walk up from behind. A bit startled, he quickly regained his composure.

"I've seen worse. At least we have some equipment to play with."

"I'm Owen Nance. People just call me Nance," he said as he extended his hand.

Charlie was cautious. He did a quick scan and wasn't sure how much of a conversation he wanted to have with the rough-looking man. He did notice that he wore an old baseball hat and had a friendly smile.

"I'm Charlie. Charlie Pierce."

"I know."

"Have we met?" asked Charlie.

"No, but I follow baseball. I watched you play and was a bit disappointed when you quit."

"Where did you see me play?"

"I saw you pitch in Eugene for the Emeralds and then for the Tacoma Giants. I was in San Francisco when you were called up. You had one heck of a curveball. I've never seen one drop that sharply except for Kofax. You have a 12 to 6 drop. That's a hard pitch to hit, especially when you mix it in with a fastball. Your changeup was nasty too."

"It didn't work out."

Nance took a seat on the bench. "It happens all the time, but you had real potential. What happened to the arm?"

Charlie raised his arm, "Hurt it in a logging accident."

Nance shook his head in disbelief. "Will you be able to pitch again?"

"I don't know. We'll see in a couple of months."

"You gonna give the majors another try?"

"Nah. Like I said, it didn't work out," Charlie answered with mild annoyance.

Nance pressed, "Not too many pitchers like you. I hope you do. They should have never hired Billy Stanton to manage the Giants. He could never relate to kids. Killed a lot of careers," Nance said as he picked up a bat.

"I can't blame my problems on him. I just couldn't seem to find the plate. Do you live around here? I don't think I've seen you around," said Charlie.

"I travel around a bit. I work when I can get it. Played some ball. It didn't amount to much. Love the game though. Tried my hand at sports reporting but lost my job. I might give it another try some day."

"Did you cover baseball?"

"Yes, that was my main sport, but I also covered the 49ers," Nance said referring to the San Francisco football team."

"Then you worked for the Chronicle?" asked Charlie.

"No. The *Sacramento Bee*."

"What happened? Why aren't you still reporting?"

"I guess you could say, the bosses and I didn't get along too well, so I left. Kind of like you, I guess. Now I watch games. You could say my hobby is looking for talent."

A slight breeze blew a whiff of Nance. There was the pungent smell of sweat and a hint of alcohol. Charlie's uncle died from alcoholism. He knew the terrible effects the disease could have on a person's mind and body. He guessed there might be more to the man's story but didn't want to pry into his business. He guessed that alcohol may have a great deal to do with Nance losing his job.

"Well, I could probably use some players."

"It's good that you took the team," said Nance.

"I can't work in the woods. I'll have the time."

"Don't you have enough boys?"

Charlie tilted his head and gazed at Nance quizzically. "Why do you ask? Do you know one of the parents?"

"I work for a man down the road a piece. One of his friends has a son that plays on the team. That's how I know you took the coaching job. He told me you played in the big leagues and who you were."

"Really. What's his name?"

"I think he said the boy's name was Lacy. Ron Lacy."

"I saw the name."

"Baseball is big around here and these kids are like local heroes. I've watched the boys a couple of times."

"We could use a couple of players. One of the kids was killed in a farming accident a few months ago. The coach quit and took his kid, one of the team's best players, to another team."

"I heard; the dreaded Cubs. Too bad about that young boy getting killed. I hope he left something behind."

Not sure what he meant, Charlie asked, "Left something behind?"

"You know, when you die, you want to leave something behind."

"I guess, but he was just a kid," Charlie responded, a bit confused.

"He left a hard lesson the boys probably don't understand, but the parents do. It can be over at any time. In an instant, your life can change, and for no fault of your own. You, for example, can be a big influence on these boys. Coaches can have a real impact on a boy's life."

Charlie thought Nance was starting to sound like a philosopher. "Well, I'll do the best I can."

"Maybe I can help."

"How? Do you want to coach?"

"I'd like to, but you probably don't want somebody like me around the kids."

Charlie didn't address Nance's appearance but knew he was right. "Parents can be kind of finicky, but I can use the help."

There's Money on the Edge

"I understand. I do know a couple of players who might help the team."

"Really? How do you know them?" Charlie asked, not sure of what he was getting in to.

"There's a kid, a black kid, who's a pretty good pitcher. He lives south of Canby in a small area known as Barlow. He should be about the right age."

"Why isn't he playing?"

"He might be. I don't know for sure. I saw his dad. I'm betting he works for the railroad. There aren't too many black families in this area. Maybe he doesn't think his son would be welcomed. Kid has a heck of an arm."

"How do you know?"

"I saw him throwing rocks."

"Rocks? I'm not sure throwing rocks translates into throwing a baseball."

"Oh, I saw him throw a baseball too. He has a wash bucket attached to a shed behind his house. Throws an old baseball against it. Has to keep moving the bucket because he tears up the wood."

"Do you know him?"

"Nope. I was riding the train and happened to see him when we stopped. I hopped off and watched him for a while. He's rough but has natural ability. Not too many naturals around," Nance said as he chewed a blade of straw.

"Why would he play for Lone Elder? I'd think if he were going to play, he'd play in town."

"Maybe. Maybe not."

"If his dad was going to let him play, I'd think he'd have done it by now. I'm a nobody around here. If he did agree to let his son play, I doubt that he'd take the chance on me and a country team."

"Don't be too sure. You're an ex-pro and that comes with some clout. You know, being a coach comes with some responsibility beyond just coaching the game. Motivating kids to play is important. Lots of kids would quit sports if parents or coaches let them."

Charlie didn't respond at first. He had witnessed a high school coach talk one of the players on his baseball team into playing his senior year. He thought what the coach had done was noble, because the year before he told the kid he wasn't going to play varsity without a tryout. The kid quit but played summer ball. He was one of the stars on a very good team. Most coaches would have never admitted they were wrong, but he did. The kid agreed to play his senior year and the team went to the state playoffs.

"Never thought of it that way."

"There's another kid. He lives close by. His parents were migrant workers. They followed the crops. Then, the mom got sick and they settled in Woodburn. The dad got a job working at the egg processing plant. The family just moved to Lone Elder."

"How do you know all this stuff about these kids?"

"I was a reporter. I watch things. I guess I have a reporter's eye for a story. The family also happens to live down the road from where I work."

"He works for Nell?"

"You mean the Nell who owns the store and tavern?"

"Yes, I don't know how your reporter's nose missed this one. She owns the egg processing plant, this field, and about everything else around here. I work for her at the tavern."

"Then he works for this Nell. The man's name is Lopez. His son is Jose. Kid's an excellent infielder. Best hands I've seen on a young kid. One of those kids who can play any position. Needs some help hitting. Hasn't done it much."

"Have you worked with this kid?"

"Nope, but I watched him play catch with his dad. Kid's good."

"Why doesn't he just sign up?"

"Mr. Lopez doesn't believe in anything but work. They don't have much money, and doctors are expensive. He wants the boy to contribute to the family."

"How about school?"

"Goes because he has to. He'll help your team, but you've got to talk the dad into it."

"I'm not sure I can do that."

"You're the coach. Kid could be a real star. You've got a couple of stars. I met the Stump and Dempsey boys. The Adams kid is good too. They'll need help. There are a couple of other kids who could be good solid players."

"How did you meet them?"

"Like I said, I watch the kids play. I watched them play in a couple of pickup games."

Charlie wasn't sure Nance should be around children. He seemed okay, but his dress and smell would cause people to be wary. He suddenly wanted to end the conversation and digest what Nance had told him.

"I'll ask around. Thanks for the leads."

"You bet. I'd check those boys out. I'll be seeing you around," said Nance as he turned and walked toward right field.

Charlie watched him go and thought how odd that exchange was. Who was this guy? An ex-sportswriter for the *Bee*? During the time he played in the minors and for his short stint in the majors, he thought he had met most of the writers, but that didn't mean he knew them all. He decided to let it go for now. He would keep an eye on Nance and make some calls to a few of his old teammates. He would also check on the two boys. He had been a coach for less than a week and there was already intrigue.

Chapter 12

As Nance told him, the Washington residence was located south of Canby in a hamlet called Barlow. The family lived on a dirt road off the main street. Theirs was the last house in a row of five that faced the railroad tracks. The boys on the team knew Darnell because they were classmates. They had known him since his family moved to the area two years earlier. The boys said Darnell was a very good athlete, but he didn't play for any of the school teams. They also said he was smart like their friend, Kermit.

Charlie had played with many black ballplayers. Because of their shared experiences, there were a few he called close friends. He knew of their struggles. The challenges they faced were far beyond just playing baseball. A tad uneasy about talking to the Washingtons, he thought about calling one of his ex-teammates to be his front-man. Thinking it might be viewed as weak or applying too much pressure, Charlie decided to meet Darnell's dad, Ed, first.

He approached the house feeling a bit uneasy. Knocking on the front door unannounced seemed like a solicitation. He noted how meticulous the Washingtons kept their yard. The house was painted bright white with green trim. A white picket fence surrounded the yard and house. He opened the gate. The lawn was mowed and edged. Not a blade of grass was longer than another. There were no weeds to be found. Flowers lined the concrete sidewalk leading to the front porch. There were clay pots full of flowers on the edge of each step. A little girl, he guessed about five, was sitting on the front porch playing with a doll.

"Hello," said Charlie. "What's your name?"

"Hello," the little girl replied as she fussed with the doll's dress. "My mom's in the house."

"What's your doll's name?"

"Matty."

"Matty is very pretty."

"She has a new dress."

"It's pretty, like your doll. What's your name?"

"I'm not supposed to talk to strangers," confirmed the little girl with a determined look.

Charlie smiled and shook his head in agreement. "I'll just knock on the door and talk to your mom."

"My daddy's working. He's always working."

"He sounds like a real hard worker."

"My mom says he works too much. She says he needs to spend more time with the family."

Charlie chuckled as he stepped around the little girl to knock on the front door. After a few seconds, a woman slowly opened the door. She forced a smile. Charlie sensed she was a bit uneasy. She had on a pink cotton dress. Over her dress, she wore a light blue apron with an image of a poodle in front. Her hair was short and her active eyes appealing. If she wore makeup, Charlie couldn't tell. Her complexion was that of a much younger woman.

"Hello, my name is Charlie Pierce. Is Mr. Washington at home?"

"What's this about?"

"I'd like to talk to him about Darnell."

The woman wiped her hands on the apron. She stiffened. Charlie worried that she had become defensive. She tilted her head slightly and her lips tightened.

Before she could respond, Charlie said, "I'm sorry. I should have introduced myself better. I'm the coach of the Lone Elder baseball team and wondered if I could talk to you about Darnell playing for us."

"Oh," she said. The tightness in the woman's face turned into a slight smile, her relief apparent. "I'm sorry, you kind of took me by surprise. I'm Barbara. Come in," she said, opening the door.

Charlie stepped inside. The house smelled of freshly baked bread. The aroma reminded him of growing up on his parents' farm outside of Modesto in California's Central Valley. The Washington home was as clean on the inside as it was on the outside.

"Darnell!" Barbara Washington yelled. "There's a man to see you. He just finished his chores and was upstairs reading a book."

"Does he take care of the lawn?"

"Oh yes. That's part of Darnell's chores. He has to complete his chores before he can play. With his dad gone all the time, he must help around the house. He also helps take care of his sister, although most of the time I think she takes care of Darnell."

"I'm impressed. The yard looks great."

"Thank you. I know he's proud of it."

"Yes, mom," said Darnell as he stepped into the living room.

The first thing Charlie noticed about Darnell was his height. He was about the same height as Eddie Stump. His hands were large, which Charlie recognized as being helpful when pitching a baseball. His jaw was square and his shoulders broad. If Darnell Washington wasn't an athlete, he at least looked like one.

He was a bit on guard but extended his hand. He looked Charlie in the eye and gripped his hand firmly. Charlie was impressed, not only with Darnell, but with his parents who had taught him well.

"I'm Darnell."

"I'm Charlie Pierce, the baseball coach for Lone Elder. I heard you might be a pretty good pitcher," Charlie speculated. Before Darnell could respond, he added, "A couple of the boys on the team, Spud Dempsey and Eddie Stump, said you were good at sports and might be interested in playing."

"I've never played much baseball. Sometimes I throw with my dad or against the shed. I don't know if I'm any good. I've never played."

"Our poor shed," appraised Barbara.

Charlie smiled. He also took note; what Nance had said was true. "Would you be interested in giving it a try?"

"I don't know. You'll have to talk to my dad."

"Ed, my husband," Barbara interjected, "isn't much for sports. He

There's Money on the Edge

thinks it takes away from Darnell's studies and his chores."

"We have a couple of openings on the team and the boys speak highly of Darnell. The season only lasts a couple of months and it might be a way for Darnell to be around other boys his own age, especially after school ends for the summer."

"I'm always worried about Darnell having other boys around during the summer. He's a hard-working boy, but he needs to have some fun too," said Barbara. "I don't know much about Lone Elder."

"I know about it, mom," said Darnell. "It's another team besides the ones in town. Kermit Sharp plays on the team. Kermit and I are good friends."

Charlie resisted a smile; he had scored a small win. "Yes, Kermit plays for the team." Charlie turned toward Barbara, "Do you think Mr. Washington will let Darnell play if he wants to?"

"I don't know, but I'll talk to him. I think being on a team would be good for Darnell."

Two wins. "When will Mr. Washington be home?"

"This Friday night. He's on the Portland to San Francisco run. He's the engineer on a freight train."

"Do you think it would be okay to talk to him on Saturday?"

"Come around noon. That will give Ed some time to rest up and play with the kids."

"I'll be here. One more thing. Darnell would you be interested in playing some catch?"

"I'll get my mitt," he said, quickly disappearing.

"You don't mind, do you?" Charlie asked Barbara.

"Heavens no, but how are you going to throw with just one arm?"

"I can catch with my right hand and toss it back. I just want to see how he can throw and what we have to work on."

"Go ahead. He needs to get out of the house. We have a field out back where you can play."

"I'll get my mitt," said Charlie.

Charlie met Darnell behind the house. Darnell had a mitt Charlie was certain had been used at the turn of the century. The glove had a thumb and four individual fingers. Darnell would need a mitt. Not a big deal except it could give the father another reason why his son couldn't play. From the looks of the house and Mr. Washington's work ethic, he doubted an offer to buy Darnell a glove would be well received. People with pride didn't like charity, even if it wasn't. Charlie decided to cross that bridge when he came to it.

"You're right-handed?"

"Mostly," replied Darnell.

"Do you bat right-handed?"

"I don't know. I've never batted except to play softball. Then I hit left-handed. It felt more natural."

"Okay. Just throw some easy ones to warm up. Then we'll back up and play longer catch."

Charlie could tell by the way Darnell caught the ball, not real smooth, that he would need a lot of work. But he also saw a natural fluid motion when he threw. After a few tosses, they backed up a few paces. And then

Charlie backed up again. Darnell had no trouble with any distance. As he warmed up and his arm became loose, his throws grew harder and harder. Nance was right; Darnell Washington had a wonderful, maybe even gifted, ability to throw a baseball. He would be a project, but the thought of having Eddie and Darnell on the same team excited him. The combination would make Lone Elder competitive. All he had to do was convince Ed Washington to let him play. He would have to decide quickly. The deadline for players to sign up was less than one week away.

Chapter 13

"Eddie, do you think that man, Nance, could be Carl the ghost," asked Spud.

"He was a little too alive to be Carl," answered Eddie as he took careful aim with his Daisy Red Ryder BB gun.

"Well, he's not from around here. Nobody seems to know who he is," added Kermit.

"I hit it," exclaimed Eddie. The boys had set up tin cans on a flat boulder beyond a narrow creek. They took turns shooting Eddie's Daisy Red Ryder and Kermit's model 25 pump action BB guns. Spud's mother, a single mom after his dad was killed in a logging accident, wasn't comfortable with him having a BB gun. She said he could have one when he was a year older. Owning a BB gun was on the top of Spud's want list, but until then he used Eddie's. Kermit's was a vintage Daisy that was also fun to shoot.

Without a BB gun, Spud became an expert at making slingshots. He cut a Y-shaped branch from a willow or other bush sturdy enough to hold up under the tension of stretching the rubber strips to arm's length. He used two strips of rubber from an old truck's inner tube for the bands.

He cut a square piece of leather for the pocket. Then he tied the rubber strips to each side of the pocket and Y. For ammunition, Spud used BBs, small rocks, or other projectiles that comfortably fit into the pocket. On a shooting expedition, they shot at old tin cans, thin tree branches, and other targets providing a challenge, excluding birds. Kermit was an avid bird watcher. He studied them and even wrote his congressman about legislation banning farm chemicals that could harm them.

Kermit pumped his 25 and fired at the can next to the one that Eddie had hit. He hit the bottom, flipping it into the air.

"I've never seen him until the morning we saw him sleeping on first base. I know almost everybody who lives around here. He just kinda appeared out of nowhere."

"The man said he followed the crops. That could explain why you've never seen him," said Spud as he fired again, missing the can. "I work with people who travel around all the time when I'm picking berries and beans. They come to Oregon in the summer and then head back south to California and Arizona."

"He knows a lot about baseball," observed Kermit.

Spud stretched his slingshot to the maximum extent of the rubber straps and let fly a quarter-inch rock. He hit the can Eddie had missed dead center. He threw his chest out and laughed. Eddie handed him his BB gun in apt surrender.

"Nice shot," Eddie acknowledged.

He took the slingshot from Spud. He wasn't as good with the slingshot as he was with his BB gun, but after a few attempts, he hit a can.

"I think he might be Carl. It's weird he shows up the next morning after we saw the ghost," said Spud.

"Maybe it's a coincidence. We need to talk to him again," said Kermit.

"About what? You're gonna ask him if he's a ghost?" asked Eddie.

Spud took a shot at the can, missed, and handed the air gun back to Eddie. He grabbed his canteen and sat back against the trunk of a Douglas fir tree. "Well, if he's Carl, we want him on our side. If we get to know him, he might not put a hex on us. If he ain't Carl, maybe he can help us figure out if there is a curse and how to make it go away."

"What kinda season is this going to be? Ghosts, curses, and all kinds of crazy stuff and the season hasn't even started," moaned Eddie.

"I wish Jason was still alive," said Kermit about one of his good friends.

"If there's a curse, he has to be part of it because he played baseball on the field," said Spud.

"I didn't think it was that kind of curse. I thought the curse had more to do with playing bad baseball. You know, making errors and striking out," added Eddie.

"My mom said, *when it's your time, it's your time*," said Spud.

Kermit aimed the no. 25. "There is no sense rushing it either. If we solve the curse, then we won't have to worry about it."

"How do you propose we do that?" asked Eddie.

"Find out why it happened," said Spud.

"I'm not sure how we do that," replied Eddie.

Kermit pulled the trigger. "We'll have to go back and see the ghost."

Spud didn't immediately reply, but then said, "I think we should honor

Jason by becoming the Lone Elder Oaks."

The season before, Jason Larson mistakenly thought the maple tree off the first base line was an oak tree. He suggested the team be called the Oaks until Kermit reminded him the tree was a maple. Nobody liked being called the maples, so the team was just Lone Elder.

"I second it. We'll put it up for a team vote," said Eddie.

"I like it. We're the Lone Elder Oaks.

"I think Jason would have liked that," replied Kermit.

Chapter 14

"Nell, do you know a Hector Lopez?" Charlie asked.

"I do. The plant foreman tells me he's a hard worker. He started at the plant about six months ago."

"What does he do?"

"I think he works in packaging, but I'd have to ask. Why do you want to know?"

"He has a son who I hear is a pretty good ballplayer. We need players to fill out the roster."

"He works the day shift. The shift is over at three-thirty if you want to talk to him. If I remember right, his English isn't that good. You might have to take Rebecca with you. She's fluent in Spanish."

"Is she here?"

"She's out front manning the store," said Nell.

Since their first meeting, Nell had sensed tension between Charlie and Rebecca. She thought they may have both realized there was a natural attraction and were resisting it. It was as if they were two adversaries circling, afraid to make the first move.

"I'll watch the bar. Go see if she'll help you."

Charlie was hesitant.

With a slight smirk on her face, Nell said, "I don't think she'll bite."

"Are you sure?" asked Charlie with a big smile.

Charlie walked up the back steps leading to the main store. Rebecca was at her usual spot behind the counter. He hadn't seen her much because she was spending more time working at the plant. Increasingly, she filled in at the store only when someone was sick, on vacation, or needed a little time off. It was late afternoon and the store was empty.

"How's the arm?" she asked.

"I'm looking forward to getting the cast off," answered Charlie.

Although he didn't want to admit it, he missed seeing Rebecca. Naturally a bit shy, especially with women, Rebecca presented a different kind of challenge. It wasn't that she made him nervous, or at least he told himself that, but rather because she was Nell's daughter. Nell had been good to him. Fraternizing with her daughter didn't seem right, or at least he didn't think so. At times he sensed that Nell wanted him to know his daughter better, but that's just what it was; a perception and one without foundation. Charlie knew Nell wanted a better life for Rebecca. She was smart and had a future and he...well, he was a washed-up baseball player who now occupied the lowest rung on the logging crew ladder. There was nothing wrong with a man being a logger. Logging was a good occupation for him, but for a woman with aspirations like Rebecca, probably not what she would be interested in for a boyfriend or husband. She was the kind of woman who had goals, and that probably included a certain type of man.

No matter how much he tried to avoid it, Charlie found it hard not to look at her. Her beauty was well beyond country wholesome. Her clothing was stylish and hinted at her shapely figure without revealing it. Her cheeks told the story. Today, they were neutral, but they could quickly turn to shades of crimson depending on whether she was happy or upset. Her smile was warm and engaging. Her teeth were straight, sparkled, and looked as if they had never been used. Her intelligence was multi-faceted and included a good deal of common sense. Like her mother, she held strong convictions, but only those closest to her knew what they were.

Charlie realized Rebecca was a reach for a man with an uncertain future. With him, there were no guarantees. She, on the other hand, was destined to be somebody. At the very least, she would be a businesswoman running her mother's operation. He didn't feel like she was above his station, but he also couldn't explain what it was that kept him from pursuing her, other than she was difficult to read and had a sign around her neck that said: *proceed with caution.* What made his condition worse was a lingering suspicion that he was just weak and feared rejection.

"What will you do when the cast is off?"

"I'm not sure yet. Probably go back to logging."

"After what happened, I'd think you'd stay away from the woods."

"I have to make a living. Being Lone Elder's baseball coach doesn't pay much."

"I also see no reason to tempt fate. You may not get paid to be the coach, but I would think the payment for being a coach goes well beyond financial."

"Well, you can't live on feel good compensation. I have to get on with life."

"My mom will be sad to see you go. I think the boys on the baseball team will too."

Charlie noted the omission. Rebecca did not mention that she would miss him. It was a telling exclusion and it hit him harder than he had expected.

"That's a way off. I won't be able to work in the woods for a few more weeks. The baseball season will be over by that time. I'm going to finish what I've started. Those boys have already been through some tough times, I don't want to make it worse. That's why I came in here. I need your help."

"I hope you don't want me to pitch."

Caught a bit off guard, Charlie laughed loudly.

"What's so funny? I can throw a baseball."

"I'm sure you can, but I don't need you to pitch. But I do need an interpreter."

"Interpreter?"

"I need to talk to Hector Lopez. Hector has a son, Jose, who I've heard, happens to be a pretty good ballplayer. The guy that told me about him thinks he's a natural. Jose is a shortstop and we need one."

"Who told you about Jose?"

"Nance."

"Who's Nance?"

Charlie scratched his head, "Frankly, I don't know for sure. I met him at the field. He said he used to be a sports columnist and follows baseball real close. He's kind of rough-looking, like he's been through some hard times. He just showed up at the field. Told me about Lopez and another kid, a pitcher. Haven't seen him since. I figure he'll show up again."

Rebecca touched her chin with her delicate fingers, "I've never seen or heard of a man named Nance."

"He's kind of mysterious, but he sure seems to know baseball. The young pitcher he told me about has great potential. From what I've seen, he's right on the mark. That's why I want to talk to Hector Lopez. Your mom said he worked the first shift."

"That's over in thirty minutes. Let's go talk to him. I'll have Odell watch the store. It's not too busy this time of day and he should be able to handle it."

The egg processing plant was a long rectangular building with aluminum siding and a green corrugated metal roof. On the north end were the business offices. In the middle of the building were two swinging doors. Rebecca told Charlie to stop in front of the two doors.

"He'll be leaving by the employee entrance," said Rebecca.

"We don't want to alarm him. He probably knows you're the boss and may be somewhat nervous being singled out."

"I'm not the boss. We have managers to run the plant. I don't get involved directly, except to help mom with oversight."

"I bet your workers know who you are."

Rebecca shrugged, "There are only a few Mexicans working for us, but they're a growing part of our workforce. Once they decide to settle here permanently, we hire them. They're good workers."

"I've played ball with a number of players from Mexico and Cuba; they love the game and work hard at it."

Rebecca was going to ask Charlie if he had any desire to give baseball another try but decided he was asked that all the time and let it drop.

"There he is. Mr. Lopez," Rebecca said raising her hand to signal him.

Charlie immediately waved him over and extended his hand. Lopez, cautious at first, acknowledged Rebecca with a smile and shook Charlie's hand.

"I in trouble," Lopez said in broken English.

"No. Oh, no," said Charlie with a warm smile.

Lopez didn't say anything but smiled back, looking relieved.

"I'm here about your son."

"Is he in trouble? What did he do?"

"Nothing. Oh, no, he did nothing wrong. Can we sit down?"

Lopez nodded and followed Charlie to an outside picnic table the workers used for lunch on nice days. Charlie opened his hand, motioning for him to sit. Rebecca joined them.

Hector Lopez's broad smile exposed a mouth full of teeth and deep dimples. He wore a white tee-shirt with the short sleeves rolled to his shoulders, a pair of Levi jeans, and work boots. His skin, weathered and creased, was as hard as the desert from spending long hours in the sun. He was probably around forty but would look the same at sixty.

"How's your wife?" asked Charlie.

Rebecca translated in case Lopez didn't understand.

Lopez shook his head and smiled, "She's good," he said in English determined to use the language.

"That's good news," said Charlie.

"We were able to get his wife medical help," said Rebecca, remembering what she had heard at the office. "Mom said she's made a complete recovery."

Charlie didn't ask about her illness, thinking it was impolite and none of his business anyway.

"I heard that you just moved into the Lone Elder area from Woodburn."

Once again, Rebecca translated. But before she could finish, Hector responded.

"We like it here. Good community."

"Has Jose enrolled in school?" Charlie asked.

"Yes. He started. Jose is in the fifth grade."

"Has he gotten to know some of the boys?"

"Oh, yes. He's happy."

Charlie had to verify Jose's age to make sure he could play on the team. The boys told him Jose was in their class, a good bet he was of the right age. He decided to hold off until Hector said he could play.

"The reason we're here," said Charlie, motioning toward Rebecca, "is to see if Jose would be interested in playing baseball on the Lone Elder team. He would be playing ball with many of the kids he goes to school with."

There's Money on the Edge

"Baseball?" asked Hector as if he'd never heard of the sport.

"Yes. We play right here in Lone Elder and we are looking for boys to play. We heard that Jose is a very good ballplayer."

Rebecca translated again. Hector let her finish this time, not because he didn't understand, but because he was mulling over what Charlie had asked.

After a brief period of silence, he responded, "Jose has never played on a team. We need him to work and make money."

"A couple of the boys have just started playing, so he would fit right in. Has he played just for fun?"

"Oh, yes. We play catch. On Sundays, we play baseball and soccer."

"There are two games a week. One on Tuesday and one on Saturday. We practice on Mondays and Thursdays. The games are at six o'clock and practice is at the same time. The parents have to have time to get home from work. Most of the boys work on farms or in the fields. We have to give them time to get home and rest up."

"I don't know. Jose picks berries and beans. When he's done, he helps his mother with chores. Summers are pretty busy. I don't know," he replied, unsure.

"How about if Jose went to work at the plant. He could come to work with you," said Rebecca.

Charlie was surprised by the offer from Rebecca but smiled at her appreciatively.

"Can he do that? He's young?" asked Hector.

"We hire other local boys to do odd jobs. I'm sure we can find a job for him."

"I don't know. Let me talk to his mother. Maybe he can play. How long is the season?"

"About two months. It's a short season. At his age they keep it short. We have to give people time to go on vacation before school starts. Even with playoffs, if we make them, no later than the first of July."

"I have to think about it. We'll have to get him to games and practice. I won't say yes unless we are sure he can make it. If we say yes, Jose will be there."

Charlie nodded at Rebecca. He respected what Hector said. Too many times kids joined teams and then skipped practice, missed games, or even quit in the middle of the season. Playing sports, he thought, was about teaching good lessons, not bad ones. He was always taught that if you made a commitment, you stuck to it. Most parents felt the same way and he was happy to hear Hector say it. It told him a lot about what to expect from Jose and his parents.

"Thank you, Hector. All we ask is that you consider it. I'm the coach and I promise we'll have fun and Jose will learn the game," said Charlie.

Hector extended a handshake to Charlie and Rebecca and then walked to his car.

"What do you think?" Rebecca asked.

"He could go either way. A lot depends on how healthy the mother is. If she's healthy, she may feel a bit obligated to let Jose play after what Nell did for them. Having you here helped out in that regard."

"Do you think so?"

Charlie glanced across the picnic table. In the late afternoon sun, Rebecca's skin was fresh and alive, her lips full and tempting, her Irish blue eyes engaging. He hoped she didn't look at him too long; he didn't want to appear interested.

He uttered, "I'm sure of it. Thank you. You were a big help."

"I didn't do much. You've kind of gotten into coaching this team, haven't you?"

"You know, I guess I have. It brings back memories of playing when I was a kid. I'd be letting the kids down if I didn't field a team and give it my best shot."

What Rebecca wasn't going to ask, she did, "Do you have any regrets?"

"Every day."

"Isn't it the dream of every kid to make it to the pros?"

"It was mine. I don't know why I quit. It was just too much pressure. I guess I wasn't ready. I'm not sure if I'll ever be, and now with my arm, who knows."

"Well, it's none of my business. I heard a couple of the men talking and they said you could've been the next big star."

"No pressure there."

"I think they meant it was sad to see a great talent give it up. Anyway, like I said, it's none of my business."

Charlie didn't mind Rebecca asking, but he felt a hint of shame when she said, "*give up.*"

"Would you like to help with the team?"

"Heavens, what would I do? I ran track and played tennis. I don't know the first thing about baseball."

"You could keep score and help me organize things. I've never done this before. There are a lot of things I'll have to do besides coach."

"I'll think about it."

"Boy, I sure wish people would quit thinking about things. I'm going to have a small get-together. The boys and their families. A fun thing. We'll have a cookout and then the boys will play the parents."

"Are you sure parents should play their kids? They could get killed."

"The kids or the parents? I'm hoping the parents realize they aren't playing to win."

"I wouldn't bet on that."

"I'll have a talk with them before we start. No yelling at the umpires, no fighting, and no taunting the other players. Satisfied?"

"If you are, I am too."

"Like I told Hector, I want the kids to learn the game and have fun. Baseball, like all sports for kids, should be fun. I want the boys to win, but it's more important they like the game."

"Well, you sound like a coach. I guess I can help. What would you like me to do?"

"Help me contact all the parents and then put the thing together. I don't think I'm very good at it."

Rebecca nodded. She had let her guard down and wondered what she had gotten into. She was starting to see Charlie Pierce in a new light. Or, maybe she had never given him a chance. It didn't matter now. It scared her a bit that she was starting to like him.

Chapter 15

At twelve o'clock on Saturday, Charlie, as he had committed, was knocking on the Washingtons' front door. After the second knock, the door swung open and behind it was Darnell. His smile was gone. In its place was a look of sadness. His head drooped and he stared at the floor.

"Hi, Darnell. You look sad. What's the matter?"

"You should talk to my dad. He's upstairs. I'll get him."

"Darnell, who is it?" Barbara Washington asked from the kitchen.

"It's me, Mrs. Washington. Charlie Pierce."

"Heavens, where did the day go? It's already noon. We were expecting you. I'm sorry, please come in."

"There's no need to be sorry," said Charlie although from Darnell's body language he expected bad news. Had he gotten his hopes up for them to be dashed?

Down the stairs from the second floor came Ed Washington. Broad and imposing, he looked like the train engines he operated. He wore a pair of striped overalls and a blue denim work shirt. A red handkerchief hung from his front pocket. Charlie thought he fit the image of a train engineer down to the last detail.

"Hello, I'm Ed Washington," he said in a baritone voice that seemed to rattle the walls.

"I'm Charlie Pierce."

"Mr. Pierce, would you like an iced tea? It's pretty hot today."

"That would be fine," he said, thinking he needed to stay cool.

"I'll get the iced tea," said Barbara.

"Why don't you and I sit on the front porch for a spell," said Ed.

Charlie nodded as Ed walked past. He followed him to a round wood table with two beefy-looking wood chairs. Ed sat down and motioned for Charlie to do the same.

"Now, what can I do for you, Mr. Pierce?"

Charlie got right to the point. "I'd like Darnell to play baseball for Lone Elder."

"Darnell has never played baseball; he's never played a sport. Why would you be interested in him?"

Charlie immediately understood from Ed Washington's demeanor that he needed to be straight with him.

"First, I heard he has a great arm and might be a pitcher. Second, we need two players to fill out our roster. I'm trying to field a team."

"Who told you he had a great arm?"

Charlie was caught a bit off guard, "Well, this man, he's an ex-sports reporter. He told me about Darnell. He told me that Darnell might make a good pitcher."

"Who's this fella?"

Charlie drew a blank, then quickly recovered. "His name is Nance.

There's Money on the Edge

I met him at Lone Elder. I really don't know him. He knew we needed players and gave me a tip on Darnell and another boy."

Ed persisted, "I wonder where he saw Darnell throw a baseball. Darnell has that old metal bucket attached to the shed. That would be the only place he would have seen him. Now you have me worried about somebody spying on my place. You see, I'm gone a lot."

"I assure you it wasn't that. He saw him as he was riding a train."

"Is he an engineer or conductor?"

"No sir, he was riding the train."

"A freeloader. We don't like freeloaders in the train business. They can get hurt or hurt other people. Is this man a coach?"

Charlie could feel sweat dripping down his back. "No sir, just a man I met at the ball field," Charlie rallied. "He's a bit down on his luck."

That seemed to satisfy Washington and he moved on.

"Playing for a team is a big commitment."

Charlie decided not to sugarcoat things. "Yes, we practice twice a week and have two games. Because Darnell hasn't ever played, he'll have to practice more, but I can give him drills that he can do after his chores are done. I played catch with him earlier this week and he has a natural throwing ability. It will take some time, but he's a good athlete. He'll quickly catch up to the other boys."

"I'm worried this will interfere with his schoolwork."

"The season starts in May and school will be about out for the summer. The boys tell me that Darnell is one of the smartest boys in school."

"He has to be. You see, Mr. Pierce, there aren't too many black people around here. Like it or not, my children need to work harder than the white kids. It's different for us."

"Mr. Washington, I would never say I understand what you have to deal with, but sports are a way to equalize things. To make Darnell part of a team will help him gain acceptance. He'll have shared experiences with the other boys."

"I don't know why we have to gain acceptance."

"Not just because Darnell has dark skin. Lots of kids who don't have a leg up on life use sports for recognition. Sports helped me. I'm from a poor background. Playing baseball got me through school. If it weren't for sports, I don't know where I'd be."

"Did you play baseball?"

"I did. Made it to the majors."

"I see you hurt your arm. Did you hurt it pitching?"

"This? No, I got hurt in a logging accident. That's the only reason I'm coaching. The team lost their coach and I happened to have some time," Charlie said grabbing his left arm.

"Logging? I did some of that before I got on with the railroad. That's hard work, but I loved the woods. I'd take my fishing pole and after work, I'd do some fishing. Love to fish."

Charlie relaxed, "I did the same thing. I like to fish too." He felt a connection and was cautiously optimistic.

"You know, I'm very careful with my children, this being a white area and all. Sometimes I feel like we can't make a mistake. If we do, all black people get labeled. I figure education is the best thing I can do for my kids. Education and hard work are a good combination. I tell my kids that you may not be as smart as someone, but if you work hard, you'll be successful."

Charlie decided to take a chance. "Good words to live by. I don't know how well Darnell will do, but he'll have fun. All work and no play aren't good either. The best part might be that he'll get to know the other boys better. Knowing someone is the best way to remove barriers."

Ed leaned back. His chair groaned. Charlie thought he saw it sag. He paused, not wanting to be the first one to talk; never a good idea when waiting for a decision. Ed didn't talk for a couple of minutes, which seemed like half the afternoon. He brought his hands together and interlocked his fingers. They looked like a round steel ball. He rested them on his stomach. Thankfully, Barbara opened the front screen door and delivered two tall ice teas. She set them on the table and went back into the house without saying a word.

"Well, I talked to you with the intention of saying no. Barbara and I had a discussion this morning. My wife can have strong opinions. I don't like to argue with my wife because it generally means she's not happy. You see, you've already caused me some trouble. She wants Darnell to play and my life is much better if she's happy. You married?"

"No, I haven't found the right girl."

"When you do, life is a whole lot easier when they ain't mad at you. Now, if I say no, my wife is unhappy. Then there's Darnell. He really wants to play."

Charlie sat up, "That's great news." Then he quickly sagged back into his chair.

"If I let Darnell play, that causes me some worry. I need to run them trains. I'm gone a lot and that means the misses will have to drive. She's a good driver, but I don't like her driving on those country roads."

Charlie thought he read a bit of concern in Ed's response beyond Barbara driving the car.

"I'll tell you what. If Mrs. Washington can get him to practice and the games during the week, I'll get Darnell home. If Barbara stays for the game, I'll make sure they get home safely. We don't play night games. We play a game every Saturday and hope you can make them."

"Mr. Pierce, you seem like a good man. Kids need to have experiences beyond family and work. I think playing baseball will be good for Darnell. I hope you don't expect too much from him."

"I think he has talent, but developing that talent will take some time. With patience and hard work, Darnell will do well."

Ed got a big smile on his face, "I think you're a good man to be Darnell's first coach. You play Saturdays?"

"We do."

"Sometimes I have to work on weekends, but if I'm home, I'll be there."

"I'd like to invite you and Mrs. Washington to a social event. It's a chance for the parents and kids to get to know each other."

Ed Washington extended his hand as if he were completing a deal, "I wouldn't miss it."

Chapter 16

The sun still hovered above the trees as Nance watched from the corner of the community center. Ronnie Samuels got out of his car and entered Lone Elder tavern. Even from a distance, he recognized Samuels' pole-like frame. He wasn't a man you would ever want to meet in a dark alley. There was nothing noteworthy about his height other than he was on the tall side. Nance guessed Samuels to be about six foot two or three. There was little definition to a chest devoid of muscles. The veins in his gooseneck were pronounced and appeared to be the only things holding up his head. When he swallowed, the sharp point of his Adam's apple was oddly captivating as it traveled up and down like an elevator. His face was narrow and boney with patches of whiskers on his chin and cheeks. His nose dropped in a sharp slope from eyes that could never be trusted.

Samuels was once again using his real name. While in Sacramento, Samuels went by Tom Williams. Waylon Webster was the name he used in Washington. There were others. Sometimes Samuels used his first name, Ronnie, and different last names. Nance didn't know for sure, but he assumed it was so that if he did run into someone and they called out his first name he would answer as if nothing was out of the ordinary. Or, maybe he just missed being Ronnie. He didn't know for sure. Whatever the name or the reason, Samuels was a killer. Nance now knew that he was the man responsible for attacking and killing the editor of the *Sacramento Bee*, Chester Marsh. It was a crime Nance was accused of committing. At first, he thought, Samuels killed Marsh during a robbery attempt, but the reason was far deeper. Marsh was a contract hit. Timed perfectly, he was now certain to point to him as the killer.

He and Marsh had gotten into an argument over what was a huge story. He had uncovered a conspiracy by a group of minor league baseball players to take bribes and throw games. At the time, the team was in last place and the season was about over. The players, to earn extra money, conspired to throw games, making in the process as much money as they made playing the whole season. The big leagues hadn't yet earned the status as a major entertainment industry. Players didn't command huge contracts like actors or singers. The pay at the minor league level was far worse. Many players subsisted on incomes just at or below the poverty line. Most had to have jobs during the off-season. To equalize the lack of income, players made errors on routine plays, struck out with men in scoring position, or served up fat, juicy hanging curveballs. Although not always foolproof, the men were able to throw most of the games their co-conspirators bet heavily on.

When Nance thought there were too many unusual occurrences, he started to investigate. He suspected something was amiss but could never prove it. Then he got a tip. A disgruntled teammate reported he overheard a group of ballplayers talking about fixing a game with a notorious gambler. The gambler was also reputed to be a member of the Los Angeles mob. Then, as suddenly as the player came forward, he changed his story. Sources told Nance that the man's family had been threatened. Fearful, he shut up and shortly after, quit the team.

When the Sacramento Golds, a double-A minor league team, lost all the games of a three-game series in what amounted to a level of play equal to high school or summer ball, Nance thought, even without having a whistleblower, he had his story. Except that, Marsh didn't buy it. He thought Nance was relying too much on circumstantial evidence. Nance knew that not all members of the team were involved. He was certain they would come forward to expose the conspirators once the story was published. Marsh didn't buy it. The informer had left the team, and there was no guarantee the other players would stand against the accused.

Nance thought it was a big story, reminiscent of the Black Sox Scandal when players of the Chicago White Sox conspired to throw the World Series against the Cincinnati Reds. What he didn't know at the time was that Marsh's family was involved. His brother-in-law, a compulsive gambler, mostly on horses, was in debt to the very men who were behind throwing the games. In a heavy-handed meeting, the mob threatened to expose the brother-in-law, or worse, unless Marsh killed the story. Marsh hated his brother-in-law but thought the impact on the family-owned newspaper would be devastating. Still, he was torn between protecting his family and publishing the truth. Marsh then made an honorable decision and a critical mistake. He relented and ran a story from another reporter about mob links to the Golds. Shortly after, Marsh was murdered. Nance suspected a mob hit but the police did not.

The police, with no solid leads, zeroed in on Nance as the most likely suspect. With motive and so much evidence against him, Nance fled. To investigators, leaving was as good as a confession. He ran, hid, and ran again, always one step ahead of the police. He eluded the law while seeking answers. Then he received a tip from a man who had underworld connections. He told him the killer was Samuels and that Marsh's death was a contract hit. Nobody knew who had put out the contract, but it was Samuels who had stabbed Marsh multiple times with a knife. Samuels disappeared.

After a series of false leads, bad tips, and hearsay, Nance tracked the increasingly paranoid Samuels to San Francisco and then Portland. Samuels lived in society's soft underbelly. After tracking him to Portland, Nance got a break. Using the public libraries, he scoured newspapers for arrests in hopes that Samuels had committed a crime. Luckily, while reading a local news section, he discovered a small article on one Ron Parker, alias Ronnie Samuels. The article linked Samuels to a series of robberies in Portland and Seattle. A few years earlier, Samuels was part of a gang that terrorized older rich women. The article said Samuels was apprehended in an elaborate sting operation. Convicted, he was sent to the Oregon penitentiary for five years. The most important piece of information was that Samuels was originally from Salem and had worked as a mechanic in Aurora. On a hunch that *"the chickens always come home to roost,"* Nance traveled to Aurora and located the garage where Samuels still worked. After a year of searching, he found Samuels running a rundown, one-stall, automotive repair shop.

Samuels, always the loner, laid low. He was like a snake who slithered out at night stalking prey. He lived alone and, for the most part, avoided people. When he did leave his trailer house, it was to have a beer at his favorite tavern, Lone Elder. Nance thought it was odd that Samuels drove the five miles to Lone Elder when there was a tavern in Aurora and others in Hubbard. Nothing about Samuels appeared to be normal. The man had unusual habits. He slept late and often worked into the early morning hours. He would sit outside his garage smoking cigarettes until he crawled into bed just before daylight.

Nance knew Samuels' routine but not what to do about it. He thought of confronting him but was fearful he might flee. Nance felt an uneasy pressure to do something. If Samuels fled, he may never find him again. He could turn him into the law, but as far as they knew, he had committed no crime. It would be his word against Samuels'. Unless he found a link or leverage to Marsh's murder, he would be an easy mark for the hardened criminal. The problem was, time was running out.

"Hey, mister," said Kermit.

Startled, Nance spun around to face the boys he had met on the baseball field. He was so focused on what to do about Samuels he hadn't heard them walk up from behind.

"Yes, boys. What are you doing here at this hour?"

Spud, like Eddie and Kermit, kept his distance, still somewhat unsure of Nance, especially since they thought he might be Carl the Lone Elder field ghost. "We were fishing in the creek on the other side of the potato field. We saw you walk behind the building."

"Did you catch anything?"

"Just a couple of small ones. We threw them back so they could grow up," said Spud.

"We were wondering if you knew about the curse?" asked Eddie.

"What curse?"

"The one put on the baseball field," answered Spud.

"What about it?" asked Nance as he kept a close watch on the tavern.

Eddie was surprised. "You know about it? You know about the curse?"

"Most major league baseball fields are cursed; that's why baseball players are all superstitious. Why do you think the pros stick to strict routines? You got to be careful not to upset the baseball gods," said Nance having some fun, but also knowing that many baseball players believed what he said.

"What do you mean, sir?" asked Kermit.

"Most pros have a routine. They follow the same routine before every game. Some wear the same clothes. Some eat the same food. Others warm-up the same way. You don't want to upset your cosmos," Nance said waving his hand around his head.

Interested, Kermit asked, "Cosmos?"

Realizing he was way too deep for kids, he clarified, "You know, like the imaginary space around you. Think of it like you're a planet. You don't want to upset your universe; you want tranquility. Some players step on the foul line when running onto the field. Others jump over it. It depends on your superstition. I knew a shortstop once who used the same glove from high school until he made it to the majors. Then he lost it, or somebody stole it, and he started making errors. He had disrupted his cosmos. Got sent down to the minor leagues. Then, luckily, he found his glove and worked his way back to the majors. You don't want to upset your universe."

"We don't want a hex put on the team. That's why we were wondering about the field being cursed," said Eddie.

Not wanting to scare the boys, Nance answered, "You boys might be too young for a curse to work. The baseball gods are still on your side."

"Odell, over at the store, said our field was cursed. What if that's true? What do we do?" asked Kermit.

"I don't rightly know."

"He said our field even has a ghost. His name is Carl. Did you know that?" Eddie inquired.

"No, can't say as I did. I wouldn't worry about this Carl too much. If you play good ball, he shouldn't be a problem."

"We camped out on the floor of this building and saw a ghost," Eddie said, pointing to the building.

Taking his eyes off the tavern, Nance moved around the corner.

"You boys don't believe in ghosts, do you?"

"We saw one. We think it was a woman," said Kermit.

"A woman?"

"Odell said a woman disappeared on her wedding night and ever since then the building has been haunted," answered Kermit.

"What was the woman doing?"

"She was on the stage. We thought she was playing an instrument," explained Eddie.

"I think it was a flute," said Kermit.

"A flute? Maybe it was just the wind," said Nance, mildly amused. How good would it be to be young and innocent? A haunted building with a ghost. The fun of it.

"The team is going to camp out the night before our Jamboree and team picnic. There will be a full moon. When there's a full moon, we'll be able to see her again," said Kermit pointing to the peak of the building.

"The light has to hit that window just right. The reflection lights up the stage. Then the ghost comes out. We tried on another night, but it was too cloudy. It has to be a clear night and the moon just right," said Spud.

Eddie noted Nance kept peeking around the corner of the building and looking at the tavern entrance across the street.

"Are you looking for someone?" he asked.

Nance deflected the question, "Just waiting for a friend."

"Are you coming to our Jamboree and picnic?" Spud asked.

"The picnic? No. I don't think that would be a good idea."

"What about the Jamboree?"

"What's a Jamboree?" asked Nance.

"It's the start of the season. It's Lone Elder's turn this year. All the teams come here. We play a two-inning game and then have a big picnic

There's Money on the Edge

with hot dogs. It's like opening day in the majors," said Spud.

"That sounds like fun. There's nothing like opening day in baseball."

"We've got two new players," said Kermit.

"Are they good?" asked Nance with a satisfied smile.

"They haven't played much," said Spud talking like an old pro.

"They'll be good. One kid is a pitcher. He throws hard. The other kid is a shortstop. We lost a kid who played shortstop and pitched last year. He went to the Cubs," said Eddie.

"That's what I heard."

Eddie kicked the dirt. "They're pretty good. We lost last year because we made too many errors."

"Even the best pros make errors," counseled Nance.

"We were wondering if it could have been Carl," said Spud.

"You never know, but I doubt it. If you boys play well, I don't think you have to worry about Carl."

Spud leaned over and whispered in Eddie's ear, "I don't think he's Carl."

Eddie shook his head in agreement. "You gonna come to our practices or games?"

"I just might. I met your coach."

"He's cool," said Spud.

"How's his arm?"

"He said the cast comes off in a few weeks. Got hurt logging."

"Dangerous job; too dangerous to risk a *golden arm*. If a man has a gift, he should use it," said Nance.

The boys stared at Nance not understanding his meaning. Then Spud asked, "What's a *Golden arm*?"

"If you can throw a baseball in the nineties, throw it where you want it to go, and get batters out, well, that's one definition of a *golden arm*. Your coach has a *golden arm*, or at least he had one. You should ask him about it sometime."

"How do you know?" asked Kermit.

"Let's just say our paths crossed a few years ago."

"Are you coming?" asked Eddie.

"I'll be there, but right now, I have to run along. You boys be careful of that ghost, and don't worry about Carl. Ghosts come in all sizes and from all dimensions. Just make sure you're brave enough to face them when they appear. There are good ones and bad ones; you just have to know the difference. Play well at your Jamboree," Nance said as he walked to his pickup truck.

Chapter 17

Once he was sure Samuels had settled in for a beer, Nance quickly got into the 1956 Chevrolet pickup truck he had borrowed from his employer, John Gains. His money had run out and he was lucky to find work. The owner of a dairy, Gains, provided a room above the milking barn. Even better, the job included one meal a day. Nance helped Gains milk cows, repair the barn, and perform other odd jobs. Gains, an older man, had lost his wife and ran the dairy by himself. He was happy to have help at five o'clock in the morning for the first milking. The best part about Gains was, he didn't ask questions.

From shadowing Samuels, he knew he would only stay at the tavern for an hour, maybe two at the most. He had to hurry, but in case he ran into the random cop who occasionally patrolled the country roads, he drove just above the speed limit. A ticket now would wreck his plans and most probably result in his arrest.

Samuels' house, if you could call his rundown travel trailer one, was located behind the garage where he rebuilt engines and repaired cars. He calculated it would take fifteen to twenty minutes to drive to Aurora. That gave him, to be safe, fifteen to thirty minutes to conduct a search.

Samuels' garage was located on a dirt driveway just off the 99-E highway. The main north, south artery, the 99-E Highway meandered through Canby, Aurora, Hubbard, Woodburn, and many other Willamette Valley towns and cities. The dirt drive was about one-quarter mile long with no possibility for a turn-a-round until you reached the garage. Believing it was too risky to park the pickup truck in front of the garage, Nance parked in a church lot in the central part of Aurora. He figured the pickup truck would be concealed because there were other cars parked there. The lot was used by shoppers who considered it safer than parking on the shoulder of the main highway.

From the church, he walked a short distance to a small park. The park was empty except for a rusted Ford pickup truck with a canopy. Resting on steel rods, front and back, was an aluminum fishing boat. The park offered convenient access for those wishing to fish the muddy Pudding River. A scattering of Douglas fir trees blocked the remaining sunlight. The dark shadows offered good concealment as he approached Samuels' trailer house from the rear. If, by chance, Samuels did return early, he had an escape route. He checked to make sure his flashlight worked.

As he anticipated, the trailer and garage were deserted. He expected Samuels to have security measures to protect the garage. Men who owned garages did their best to protect their tools from thieves. He saw the garage was secured by a heavy padlock. The door window was covered with heavy mesh wire. Thieves, Nance figured, knew how to keep other thieves out. Nance was interested in the garage but decided to start with the trailer house. It was a long shot, but he figured if there was evidence about the murder of Marsh, he might find it in the trailer. He hoped Samuels had gotten sloppy. If he didn't find anything, and he had the time, he would search the garage. Suddenly, he froze. From inside the garage came the loud, vicious snarl of a watch dog. He had met Samuels' security. Nance drew a quick breath. Fortunately, the garage door was locked and the dog penned in. He was safe but worried the dog's bark would alert neighbors. The closest house was at least a football field away, but the dog's bark resonated. Worse, he was jumping around and knocking things over, and in general, creating a ruckus. The noise could carry a long distance.

He stepped back and went to the garage door, "Easy boy, easy," he soothed.

Rather than calming him, the dog lunged against the door in a rage. Jumping high, he landed on the workbench, knocking off tools and car parts. He was causing such a racket; Nance was sure he would attract attention. He had to move quickly. He ran to the trailer and twisted the doorknob. The door was locked. He opened his set of wire pics. Using the skills he had learned working the crime beat in Sacramento, he picked the lock. The lockpickers had taught him well. He pushed the door open. What he found was a mess. There was a tiny kitchen sink piled with dirty dishes. Newspapers were stacked in one corner. In another was a trash can filled with beer and wine bottles. On the kitchen table were a coffee mug, mustard bottle, a box of sugar, and a Sony portable television with an antenna. Blankets covered the sofa. It looked as though Samuels lived and slept in the main living room. He wondered where to start. He understood that even the owners of clutter could tell if any part of their mess was out of place. The other problem was that he wasn't sure what to look for. He didn't expect to find an obvious clue. He hoped instead to find a potential lead or some small bit of evidence. It was nothing but hope. This was beyond a longshot, but what else could he do? Samuels would never admit to anything.

He studied every inch of the trailer. He opened a closet door. When he did, a pile of clothes fell out. After quickly going through them, he pushed them back in and slammed the door. Next, he went to a row of cabinet doors and slid the top drawer open. It was stuffed with bills. He scanned them, especially the telephone calls, but there were few numbers listed and they did not identify individual calls. He did find bills from parts houses for car parts. The electricity and water bills looked normal. He put them back, closed the drawer, and opened another. It was also full of more old bills. After checking the remaining drawers, he went through a narrow hallway to a bedroom. Clothes, towels, and other household items were stacked on the bed. To shift through everything would take hours; time he didn't have. He backed out of the bedroom and opened a door to the bathroom. It was empty, except for a toilet and a small sink. They didn't look as if they had been used. In the corner was a shower stall. It was dry. He wondered if Samuels took showers. The thought occurred to him that Samuels may have a bathroom in his garage. Hanging from the shower pipe was a string with a soap attached to it. Finding nothing of value, he closed the shower door. He took one final look around the bathroom. There was a metal medicine cabinet attached to the wall over a tiny round sink. He opened the mirror door. Behind the door were three shelves. There was a bottle of aspirin, half a tube of toothpaste, spray deodorant, and a dish of shaving soap on the first two shelves. On the top shelf was a harmonica. Odd, thought Nance. Why would Samuels have a harmonica in the bathroom unless, of course, he played it. It made little sense that he would store it in the cabinet. In such a small bathroom, there would be considerable moisture even if Samuels just used the sink and not the shower. He didn't give it any additional thought until it hit him. Marsh played the harmonica. It was a well-known joke among reporters that you could always tell Marsh's mood by his harmonica playing. In Marsh's case, there was only degrees of bad because he was a terrible harmonica player. Nobody seemed to know what he was playing. His staff was sure of one thing; it wasn't music. Rather, it was more like a primitive screech. Could it be possible?

Nance grabbed the instrument with the tips of two fingers to avoid leaving fingerprints on it. It was in bad shape. One side still had the wood cover, while the other cover was gone. He examined the wood. It was chipped and faded. The varnish was gone, and it looked as though the wood had been wet. That was understandable given the potential for moisture and humidity in the small bathroom. He turned the harmonica over and examined the metal reed plate. He recognized the harmonica could be Marsh's, but he wasn't positive. The obvious question was, why would a guy like Samuels have a harmonica? Was it a sorted souvenir of the killing? Or, did Samuels play harmonica? It didn't seem likely, but if he were confronted, he would surely claim he did.

Nance's instinct was to take the harmonica with him, but for what reason? If it were in his possession, and he was caught, it would be the nail in his coffin. There would no longer be an assumption of his guilt. It would be a damning piece of evidence that he had committed the crime. He put it back on the top shelf. It was the proof he was looking for; Samuels was Marsh's killer. Now, all he had to do was figure out a way to lead the police to Samuels. Nance looked around the trailer to make sure everything was as he found it. He exited to the sound of the watchdog's bark. As he made his way off the property, he assumed that if the dog had torn up the garage, Samuels would know somebody had been snooping around. How would he react? That was the big question. There was no sound reason why Samuels would think the attempted break-in was tied to anything but the planned robbery of his garage. He might be reassured that his watchdog had done his job and scared off the would-be thieves. If that were his reaction, Samuels would take additional precautions. He could also become paranoid and flee. There was no guarantee, but Nance had the uncomfortable sense that the time was growing short to prove Samuels was a killer.

Chapter 18

Tommy Walls clapped his hands together and patted his bicep. "Hey Darnell, wait until we play you. I'll hit the next one into the potato field."

As Tommy rounded third and trotted to home, he swept his hat from his head and spread his arms in an imaginary salute to the empty stands. Tommy, a spitting image of his father, cut his icy black hair short to the scalp on the sides while leaving it longer on top. Without his hat, his hair looked a bit like an unruly mohawk. He was about the same height as Darnell and Eddie, but his body was thick beyond his age. A showman, on the field he played to the girls; off the field, he wore tight pants and did everything he could to gain their attention. Tommy was a few months older and far more mature than the other boys. He was also the best baseball player in the area. The problem was, he knew it.

So did his father, Mike, who coached the Cubs. The Cubs were favorites to win the Mid-Willamette league title and maybe even win the state championship. Where Mike was bellicose, especially, when it came to his son, Tommy could be downright obnoxious.

"We're gonna win the championship this year, Tub," Tommy yelled from the bench.

As the boys from the area often did, they were playing a pickup baseball game. There was no supervision; just boys of the same general age meeting to play for the fun of it. There were no starters or bench players. Whoever showed up played until they became tired and went on to another activity. Sometimes they chose teams; other times, they just hit and fielded balls. Two, often older kids, rotated choosing players until all the kids were on a team. The teams were generally equal. On this day, most of the Cubs were on one team while most of the Oaks were on the other. Tub Adams was the only member of the Oaks who played with the Cubs.

"Nice hit," Tub said to Tommy. "We're not going to be very good."

"I told you, you should have played for the Cubs."

"I didn't want to play for the Oaks, but my dad said I had to because my cousin is on the team."

"Kermit?"

"Yeah, Kermit."

"He's lousy. He only got one hit last year, and it was really an error. You ain't gonna win with Kermit," laughed Tommy.

"I know, but dad said I had to play one more year with this bunch of farmers. Then I can join the Cubs."

Tommy pointed to Darnell. "With that kid and Kermit, you ain't gonna win many games."

Darnell watched as Tommy and Tub laughed at him. "I'm not very good."

"Don't listen to that loudmouth," said Eddie. "He talks that way to everybody. You got to ignore him."

"I don't think I want to pitch," replied Darnell.

"You can do it; besides, it doesn't make any difference," said Spud. "This isn't a real game. Just throw the ball over the plate. Hit my mitt."

"All you have to pitch to is one more batter, then I'll pitch to a couple," said Ron "Dinky" Lacy. Dinky, as his nickname implied, had a slight build and had front teeth much too large for his face. "Don't worry about striking them out. Let them hit. We're behind you. We can get them out."

"You think you're gonna win with Darnell pitching?" queried Tommy. "We're gonna bomb him. The only pitcher you got is Stump and he can't pitch every game. His arm will fall off."

"Shut up, Walls," said Spud. "I'm betting that Darnell will strike you out."

"You want to bet on that with real money?"

"A buck says he does it by the end of the season," challenged Spud. Dollars didn't come easy, but it was a risk worth taking. Then shaking his head to reinforce the bet, he said, "Yeah, a buck."

"Deal," replied Tommy with a confident smirk. "Who's the Mexican kid at short? Is that little Jose? If it ain't the little Mexican…I thought Mexicans went back to Mexico after the harvest. Better yet, I'm glad you didn't. All we got to do is hit a ball to you; you'll never catch it, and if you do, you'll never be able to throw it to first. Not with those skinny arms. I swing bats bigger than him."

Jose Lopez understood what the Walls kid was trying to do. It wasn't the degrading comments he made about him being of Mexican descent that bothered him. He was proud of his Mexican heritage; he was as American as Tommy Walls. Traveling around the west coast to harvest crops, he had often heard people toss racial insults. Calling him out because he didn't think his arm was strong enough to throw the ball to first base was what made him mad. He could make it to first, except if the ball was hit between third and short. Throwing from the *hole* was a long way and his arm wasn't strong enough to make it there. Tommy was right and it angered him. He committed to do something about it.

"Walls, you got a big mouth," said Eddie having enough. Eddie was slow to anger, but guys like Tommy sped the process.

"Yeah, what's the town drunk's kid going to do about it?"

The comment about his dad, a Korean War veteran, was the tipping point. Rowland Stump, a Marine, had seen some of the war's most savage fighting at Chosin Reservoir. His inability to cope with what he experienced drove him to the depths of alcoholism. His dad's problems were common knowledge around town. It was also well known that he had fought back and kicked the disease. He regained a large measure of respect by helping other veterans deal with their own post-war traumas. Operating a successful hardware store, along with his many other civic and personal responsibilities, left his father little time to help with the team. He took great pride in Eddie's activities and helped when he could. Although he kept it quiet, he also helped Nell with the costs associated with uniforms, equipment, and other team expenses. Rowland Stump did not want his son to get any special treatment.

Eddie threw down his mitt and started walking toward Tommy. Spud and other members of the Oaks fell in behind him. Tommy was followed by the other members of the Cubs.

"Take that back, Walls," demanded Eddie.

"Make me," said Tommy.

Spud confronted Tub, "Whose side are you on?"

"I ain't on anybody's side. Tommy's my friend."

"Then you're with the Cubs."

Jose stepped in front of Eddie, "You think I got a weak arm? How about I show you how weak it is?"

Jose threw a wild punch, but Tommy ducked.

Tommy pushed him aside. "Get out of my way, you punk."

Jose charged. He attempted to tackle Tommy by grabbing him around the legs. Tommy tried to throw Jose off, but he held on tight. Darnell, Spud, Dinky, and the rest of the Oaks joined the free-for-all. Members of the Cubs charged in to protect their star player even if they also thought he was a bit of a jerk. Tommy held Jose down. But before he could throw a punch, Eddie tackled him and threw him to the ground. Members of both teams piled on. The pushing and shoving had turned into a melee. With his considerable weight, Tub did a spread-eagle belly flop onto the growing pile of bodies. There were shouts and groans as elbows were thrown and punches met their marks. With the honor of both teams at stake, nobody was willing to give up.

Chapter 19

"How's the team?" Rebecca asked.

"I don't know yet. The first couple of practices were a bit rough."

"Rough?" she asked.

"We've got a couple of new players and it might take them a while to learn the game. They have raw talent. Then we have three really good players. We can build around them. The rest of the team just needs work. Some are good ballplayers; others just play for the love of it. It all depends on how they play. You have to have stars, but the supporting cast will make the difference."

"It sounds like any team."

"If the good players can carry us until the other kids come around, we might win a few games."

Rebecca admitted; she didn't like Charlie when they first met. Or at least, she thought so. He had, unknowingly, invaded her space and become a threat to her well-being. She tried to put up stop signs, but he just kept rolling through them. As much as she tried to resist, she liked him being around. She was adamant; she didn't have the time or desire for a relationship. But her defenses were weakening. The question was, why? For a woman who prided herself on her abilities to know and explain things; she really couldn't explain her attraction. He was likable; the tavern patrons attested to that. Not that she cared, but being an ex-professional baseball player came with a certain level of recognition. Fame always attracted people, even if it was fleeting. Maybe, she thought, it was his involvement with the kids. He was really good with them and they already looked up to their coach. Was it how he treated her? His treatment of her was neither bad nor good. Basically, he ignored her and she wasn't used to being ignored. There were some signs of him wanting to be friends, but so far, that hadn't translated into a date.

Then there was the way he looked. The hard work of logging had chiseled his frame. He was athletic. His smile was genuine and hard to resist. His eyes were the color of dark pine; penetrating, without the need to stare. A slight dimple in the middle of an oval-shaped jaw was one of many natural physical attractions. The recent influx of young women to the tavern was a testament to his looks, personality, and to a lesser extent, his fame. She noticed when she saw him pay attention to them. She tried to ignore what she thought were the dalliances of immature girls but couldn't. Was she jealous? No, she didn't think so. But if that were true, why did she even care what he did?

"I'm sure you will. Hey, what's going on over at the field?" Rebecca asked, pointing toward the baseball diamond.

Charlie turned to see a big pile of young bodies. At first, he thought they were playing a game, but then he heard yelling.

"Looks like we got ourselves a bit of a ruckus," he said as he ran to stop it.

"Should I call the police?" asked Rebecca.

"No. I think this might be teammates sticking up for teammates. I should be able to handle this one."

"Do you need help?"

"Better leave this between us guys."

By the time Charlie made it to the field, the boys were starting to separate. Spud, Jose, Darnell, and Eddie were facing off with Tommy and three of his buddies.

"Take it back," demanded Eddie.

"Make me," taunted Tommy.

"Okay, boys. That'll be enough. What's going on here?" Charlie demanded in a firm but not angry voice.

Eddie pointed at Tommy, "He started it. He said bad things to Darnell and Jose."

"What's the matter, Stump? Can't you take a little teasing?"

"I can take it; just don't say it to my teammates."

Charlie smiled under his breath. Nothing like a little wrestling match to bond a team together.

"You must be Tommy Walls?" Charlie quizzed.

"Yep. My dad coached out here last year. I'm playing for the Cubs," he said in a confident voice with his chest out.

Wanting to defuse the situation and not give Tommy Walls or the Cubs extra motivation, Charlie said, "I hear the Cubs have a very good team and that your dad is a really good coach."

"We're going to win the championship this year," Tommy boasted. "These guys just don't want to admit it."

Before Eddie could respond, Charlie said, "That's what I've heard. Well, best of luck to you. Now, I think you boys should get back to playing baseball. Fight's over," he declared.

"Com'on Cubs! We don't need to play ball at this lousy diamond. Let's go back to town and play on a good field. See you guys at the Jamboree. You coming, Tub?"

"Nah, you go ahead," Tub said without conviction.

"Hey Walls, anytime you want to play us, we'll be ready," yelled Spud.

"Yeah, Walls. Next time we won't be so easy on you guys," said Darnell.

"I hope you guys don't finish in last place. With Kermit, Jose, and Darnell on your team, you don't have much of a chance," Tommy retorted.

"We'll see about that, Walls," said Eddie.

Walls turned and raised a middle finger as he rode away, with the other members of the Cubs following behind.

"Is that your IQ?" asked Kermit. "Even if he is my cousin, he's an arrogant jerk."

"Okay, boys. Leave it alone. If you have something to prove, let's prove it on the baseball field. If we're going to beat the Cubs, you're going to have to work hard. As long as you're all here, how about we play some baseball?" said Charlie. The battle lines, if they weren't already there, were drawn by Tommy Walls. Charlie felt it, and by the way the Oaks took the field, they felt it too. The rivalry with the Cubs, already intense, had just been ratcheted up a notch.

Chapter 20

Ronnie Samuels petted his German Shepard, Brax, on the head. After calming him down, he grabbed a shop rag and wiped oil off the dog's thick brown chest hair. The garage was a mess. Something or someone had caused the dog to go into a frenzy. Brax had knocked over the tool chest and there were tools everywhere. A five-gallon can of used motor oil had tipped over. A main channel with multiple tributaries carried the oil in every direction. Most of the oil had been absorbed into a black dirt floor already saturated with grease and oil. A large oil puddle formed in a depression under the workbench. Brax had tracked oil into the small office. The tan shag carpet was thick with oil. It was destroyed as was the pillow that Brax slept on. To remove the oil from Brax's hair would take detergent and a warm water bath.

Ronnie could find no sign of a break-in. None of his tools or equipment had been stolen.

"Come here, Brax," Ronnie commanded.

Ronnie searched around the garage for footprints. The ground was cracked and hard. If there were human footprints, where the oil spilled, they would be easy to see. He checked the area around the garage and back doors. Then he got down on his hands and knees but didn't see any impressions. He hooked Brax up to his chain and walked into the woods. He assumed if somebody was after his tools, they would have used the highway and driven down his dirt driveway. A thief would need a car or pickup to haul away his tools and equipment. But this didn't seem like a robbery. Maybe, he thought, it was kids. Kids could have been snooping around and been scared off by Brax. A disgruntled customer was another maybe.

Ronnie went to the trailer and unlocked the door. Always cautious, he peeked his head into the doorway. He made a quick scan; everything seemed to be in order. He had put in place three security checkpoints. He made sure all the cabinet doors were closed tight; they were. The sofa blankets hadn't been disturbed by someone searching under the cushions. The heating grate covering the vent where he had stashed one thousand get-away dollars was still attached tight to the wall. The security checks were in order, but somebody had been inside; he could feel it. If there was a thief, he had to pick the door lock to get in. Would a kid pick a lock? He doubted it. If there was a thief, what was he after?

With the dog barking and raising a ruckus, the thief may have thought the trailer was a safer option than the garage. If true, it was a big mistake. Other than the get-away money that he used as a decoy, there was nothing of value in the trailer house. He was smart. He had spread his money around hoping that if one cache was uncovered, another might be safe. He kept most of his cash in a safety deposit box at the local bank. The stolen goods were kept in a water-proof metal chest in the garage backroom where he stored car parts. He figured if there was a break-in, Brax would be enough of a deterrent. As an added precaution, he hid stolen goods among the parts. Thieves, even professional ones, had to get past Brax and then spend time trying to find the stolen goods. There was nothing like trying to outwit another thief. It was professional gamesmanship. He was so close. He had taken great pains not to attract attention. He lived simply and worked hard. It was all a ruse—part of his plan. Still, he couldn't help but wonder if he had slipped up. If he did, who had found out? Did somebody, like an ex-inmate, figure out what he was up to? He grabbed a beer from the garage refrigerator, took a long drink, and then sat the can down on the picnic table behind his trailer.

"Come here, Brax," he called. "Who was here, fella? Who was here? Was it some kid snooping around or was it a thief? If you could talk, you would boy, wouldn't you?"

Ronnie sat back and took another long pull. He pondered his next move. Should he pack up and go south, to California? The frenzy caused by the murder of Chester Marsh had died down. He was sick of fixing cars and tired of living like a mole. He had enough money to live comfortably. If he needed a few extra bucks, he could take another contract job. There was always somebody trying to get even or looking to take advantage of someone else. Blackmailing more money out of his last employer, although risky, was another option. In hindsight, the hit on Marsh was worth far more than the agreed price. Ronnie heard his ex-employer had put out a contract on him. If, as he suspected, the hit was to tie up *loose-ends*, going back for more money was enticing, if for no other reason than to make the man sweat. Maybe, he was being paranoid. He had completed contract work before and there was never any problem. Why would there be a problem now?

He was getting way ahead of himself. Maybe there was nothing to the attempted break-in. There was no hard evidence; only his gut instinct. Brax could have gone crazy over a raccoon or possum. Still, he was an ex-con. You were always a suspect if you were one, and it didn't matter how straight you lived. The press had reported on the string of break-ins, but he had never been questioned. Had he been lucky? As an ex-con, he had to be on the list of primary suspects. He had been careful, but a mistake could happen. He planned one more hit, certain it would be a big payday. He had enough money; why did he feel the need for one more burglary? Was he being greedy? He didn't think so, but then why do it? One more, and then he would quit, or at least he told himself so. Why quit something you were good at? No, he would just be extra cautious. He'd start with double locks on the garage. At night, he planned to carry a gun and have one safely stored in the pickup truck. If the person came back, he would be ready. He would be ready for anything that happened. He had to be.

Chapter 21

"I don't know if I want my kid playing on a team with a Mexican and a black," said Steve Adams.

Charlie looked at Adams with a mix of scorn and disbelief. "I didn't think this was going to be a problem, and, it shouldn't be. As a parent, you should want your son to interact with all kids regardless of their color or heritage."

"What are you? A psychologist? This is just a small-town baseball team. We put this together for a few boys to have a chance to play."

"I thought that's what I was doing. If you remember, we didn't have enough kids to fill out the team. Without Darnell and Jose, we wouldn't have a full team. We're lucky to have them."

"Maybe that would've been better."

"You know, if Tub is going to play sports, he's going to have to interact with all kinds of kids. The beauty of sports is that it puts a bunch of kids together from different backgrounds and they get to know each other. Good for the kids and good for the community."

"I like this community because all the kids are from the same background," said Adams, a man with a flattop haircut, a white short-sleeve shirt, and a tie that crested the crown of his stomach.

Charlie didn't like to pigeonhole kids but thought Steve Adams had produced a chip-off-the-old-block in his son Tub. Their mannerisms and physical appearance were similar if not almost identical. The only difference was that Tub, after the recent melee between the Oaks and Cubs, had at least tried to accept Darnell and Jose. He had to. Tub was still on the outs with many of his Oaks teammates. The boys knew he was playing both sides of the fence. He wanted to stay on good terms with Tommy Walls so he could play for the Cubs next year. One thing the other boys recognized was loyalty, and Tub had shown very little of it to the team. Rather than Darnell or Jose, it was Tub who was looked on with a bit of distrust, if not scorn.

"Mr. Adams, both Jose and Darnell are part of this team. They are learning, but they can help us. Give them a chance."

"I don't want you to think I'm a racist; I'm not. I am concerned about who my son grows up with. I guess I'm a little afraid of the influences like I would be if he started to hang around kids who smoked. I want the best for my son and his friends."

"Exposing him to all types of people will help him grow as a person."

"I grew up with all types of kids. I'm from Los Angeles. I saw a whole lot of crime. Most of it came from the black and Hispanic areas. The violence was bad. I don't want my son exposed to that. I moved here to get away from it."

"I lived in California and have been in those communities too," said Charlie. "Most of the people are good, hardworking, law-abiding citizens.

Any time you have a concentration of people of any race, you're going to have a few bad ones. That doesn't mean the whole community is bad. We both know it's just a few who cause the trouble."

""It's the few I worry about. You just don't know where people are coming from. What they believe. What they think.""

Charlie suspected Adams was pointing a finger at the Washington family, and for no logical reason. "Have you met Darnell's parents?"

"I haven't. I've seen them around town a few times."

"They are just like you. First, they're very good people. Second, they are very good parents. They're hard workers. Ed works for the railroad and Barbara, his wife, is a stay-at-home mom who is dedicated to her kids. We both know there is no guarantee when it comes to kids, but they look like the typical family and the chances of Darnell being anything but a fine young man are very remote. Ask Tub. Darnell is a smart kid and I wouldn't be surprised if he were a successful businessman, lawyer, or doctor. You'll find that Jose's parents are very similar. Why shouldn't they have a chance to grow up and play baseball just like any other kid?"

Adams folded his hands and didn't immediately respond. Then looking up as if he were looking for divine guidance, he said, "Okay, I'll give it a chance. Maybe I've been a bit too rigid. I didn't mean to be. I just want what's best for my son and the rest of these boys."

"Just get to know the parents. I think you'll like them. They're fine people."

"I don't believe in meaningless talk. I mean to talk to Ed Washington and his wife. I will also introduce myself to Jose's parents."

"A good place to start is at the Jamboree picnic. They'll both be there."

"So will I."

Charlie watched as Steve Adams got into his car.

"It looked like you were in a serious conversation," said Rebecca as she opened the screen door to the store and poked her head out.

"I didn't think being a social worker came with coaching little kids."

"Jose and Darnell?" she asked knowingly.

"Yep."

"I hoped you wouldn't get any pushback. How bad was it?"

"I've seen far worse. At least, he'll think about it. He said he'd give it a try."

"Probably fear of the unknown more than anything else. Attitudes are changing. No matter what you might hear, I think most people agree there is inequality between whites and blacks."

"It will be a long hard fight. All I can do is what I think is right. I feel like the boys, especially Darnell and Jose, are my responsibility."

"How's the team coming along?" asked Rebecca.

After their rocky start, Rebecca had become a big help. As he requested, she helped organize the Jamboree picnic and was a friendly sounding board for the ideas or issues he was having as the team coach.

"I have some good players and others who need a little more coaching. We may have a tough time at the start of the year. But if all goes according to plan, we'll be okay."

"You have a plan?"

"Yep, you got'ta have a plan."

"Does your plan include dinner?"

"My plan always includes dinner."

"Good, then come to the house at six. I need a Guinea Pig for a new pasta recipe."

"I've never found a pasta I didn't like."

"Don't speak too soon. See you at six."

Chapter 22

"We can't all stay in there," said Spud.

"Yeah, our parents will find out and we'll get into trouble," said Dinky, his signature two front teeth protruding.

Short and thin with deep-set eyes, Dinky played second base and was an excellent fielder. He was the team's leadoff hitter because he rarely struck out and could get on base. His expertise was the walk. Dinky was also the team's chatterbox. He had taken the repetitious infielder's chatter, *hey batter, batter,* to what even his own teammates thought was an annoying level. There was no proof his continuous chatter threw hitters off, but it seemed to keep the nervous Dinky calm.

Rarely was anyone on the Oaks ever referred to by their real names. Some had nicknames while others answered to their last name only. Eddie was Eddie, unless he was Stump. Spud preferred to call him Stump. Spud, whose real name was Atwood, had always been Spud. He owed his nickname to his sister, Marilyn. She called him Spud because she saw him pull a raw potato from their grandparents' garden and eat it. Neither she nor Spud liked Atwood, a name passed down from previous generations. Spud seemed appropriate. Tub's real name was Martin. Nobody knew where his nickname came from, but Tub had always been Tub. It fit him well.

"Then it's me," said Eddie, "Spud, Kermit, and Tub. The rest of the team can camp out like we planned. We'll check it out and come back to the camp later."

"What if the coach finds out?" asked Dinky as he kicked the bat up with his foot and pointed it at the building. "He'll be mad if he finds out you camped in there."

"You a chicken?" charged Tub.

"Leave him alone, Tub," said Wags.

Everybody called Richie Wagner, "Wags", primarily because he didn't like to be called Richie or Wagner. Wags was what his name implied. He was about the same height as Spud and a slow runner. Wags had a body like a rectangular brick and it, his teammates teased, took him five minutes to run to first base. Wags was a good left fielder and a solid hitter with above average power. The year before he hit an apparent home run over the left fielder's head. It should have been easy, but the turtle slow Wags was almost thrown out at home. He wasn't fast but always got a good jump on the ball. His teammates were confident that if Wags got to a flyball he would catch it. Grounders were his specialty and he rarely made an error. He had a strong arm and could throw a runner out at home plate if he didn't field the ball too deeply. But throwing runners out didn't happen often because Wags' accuracy was, as Coach Charlie said, "a work in progress." Charlie had given Jose the task of telling Wags where to throw the ball. The reasons were twofold; he wanted Wags to learn to *hit the cutoff man*, and he wanted Jose, as the shortstop, to take control of the infield.

"Stay out of it," said Tub.

"Go play for the Cubs. You can carry Tommy Wall's bat."

"Shut up, Wags!" shouted Tub as he pushed Wags in the shoulder.

"Make me," challenged Wags as he pushed him back.

Wags stepped closer to Tub and faced him. Tub was built the same as Wags but a couple of inches taller. After a few seconds of stare down, they both backed away unwilling to fight after the other boys told them to knock it off. They had more important things to think about.

The start of baseball season was a special time. The Jamboree was a signal that school was about out, and summer was almost here. The atmosphere was relaxed as coaches, players, and parents got to know one another. All the team names were thrown into a hat. The blind draw picked two teams to play a two-inning pre-season game. After the game, a large picnic was held. To promote team unity, Charlie suggested the Oaks hold a campout the night before. Although a few parents were concerned the boys wouldn't get any sleep and be too tired to play, Charlie assured them he and a couple of fathers would chaperon and ensure they went to bed. Besides, he reminded the parents that it was a practice game meant for fun.

Tents were pitched beyond the foul line in left field next to the Community Center. Sleeping bags were laid out on the ground or on cots. The tents were placed in a circle. In the middle, the boys piled wood debris and log sections to make a large bonfire. As the fire burned to hot coals, Charlie planned to serve hot dogs and roast marshmallows toasted to make one of the kids' favorites, s'mores.

"The four of us can stay in the building until we see the ghost," said Kermit.

Kermit couldn't believe their luck. The sun and the moon would be aligned so the reflection would light up the stage.

"We have to get in and out before the coach comes back," said Spud.

"Then we can all go in," said Dinky.

"We might scare the ghost away, and if the coach comes back early, you guys have to tell him that we're out gathering firewood," said Spud.

"How do you scare a ghost?" quizzed Eddie.

"One look at Tub and that would scare her," teased Wags.

Tub pushed his other shoulder. "You want to make something of it," Tub challenged again. Wags and Tub were quickly chest to chest. Longtime friends, they knew how to push each other's buttons. The other boys were used to their tiffs and mostly ignored them.

"There's no time," said Eddie, pushing Tub and Wags apart. "After this is over you can have it out. The four of us will go in so we don't scare the ghost."

"Scaring the ghost...that sounds dumb," said Dinky.

"Didn't you ever hear that too much noise scares ghosts away?" asked Kermit.

"I never heard that. That sounds really dumb," replied Dinky, still unconvinced.

"That's a good reason only four of us should go in there," said Spud.

"What do the rest of us do?" asked Wags.

"Watch for the coach and let us know if he's coming so we can get out."

"Make sure you don't see a ghost out here. We don't know whether she'll be inside or outside," said Eddie.

"Why do you always say she? Is the ghost a girl?" asked Tub.

Spud looked at Eddie and then Kermit. "We aren't sure. We think it's a woman."

"Good," said Dinky. "Women ghosts aren't as scary as men ghosts."

Wags raised his hands high above his head and wiggled his fingers, "A ghost is a ghost."

"What's the difference? They will still scare the crap out of you," said Tubs.

"It's time; we've got to get in there. The moon is up," said Kermit.

"Does the ghost have a name?" asked Richard Cooper.

The boys nicknamed Richard, Vic, after the company, Vic Combs, a manufacturer of combs and brushes some of them used to groom their horses. Vic had unique ears. The Helix on his outer ears grew at a ninety-degree angle from his head. Vic had the best hearing on the team. His hair was cut short, except for the very front that he spiked straight up. Vic had lightning speed and was, along with Jose, one of the fastest runners on the team. On a ball hit into the gap between center and right fields, Vic could run it down and prevent the hitter from getting a double. With his strong, accurate arm, Vic once threw a kid out at first base because he didn't hustle after hitting the ball to centerfield.

"Who names a ghost?" asked Wags.

"Casper had a name, and he was a ghost," Vic reminded him.

"He's a cartoon character; nobody names a real-life one."

"Maybe we should. I don't like snakes, but if you named them, they seem more, I don't know, human," said Vic.

"Who votes we name the ghost?" asked Spud.

All the hands went into the air.

"Okay, we name her. She's a woman, so it has to be a girl's name," said Spud.

"What's a good girl name for a ghost?" Eddie asked.

"How about Judy?" offered Wags.

"Judy...that's a stupid name for a ghost," said Tubs.

Wags shoved him, "You got a better one?"

"How about Medora?" offered Kermit.

"Medora? Where did that come from?" asked Tub.

"It's a town in North Dakota. Theodore Roosevelt used to go there when he was a cowboy. I just read about it. Medora is in the Badlands."

"Medora is a good name for a ghost," said Eddie.

"Who wants to call the ghost, Medora?" asked Spud.

"Ghosts don't have names; they just scare people," said Tub.

All the hands were raised to approve the motion, except for Tub's.

"It's settled. From now on, our ghost has a name. Medora."

"Dumb," said Tub as he took a bite of jerky and started walking toward the old meeting hall. "Let's go see if Medora is out tonight. Dumb. This is really dumb."

Chapter 23

Police Chief, Joe Polanski polished his prized Wheeler cowboy boots by sliding them up and down on the back of his pants. Sometimes meeting with people in the community could be tedious, but this wasn't one of those times. Making a call on Nell Flynn was always a pleasant experience, even when the circumstances were of a criminal nature. A Portland beat cop for thirty years before retiring to become the Chief of Police in the small farm community of Canby, he had known Nell since she married Gene, *The Fly* Flynn. During *The Fly*'s years as a professional boxer, he was a fan and often volunteered to be part of Flynn's security detail. He became Flynn's friend and, on fight nights, part of his entourage. When he first met Nell, he thought she was not only beautiful but, even though a few years younger, was tough and a good balance to Flynn's blustery disposition. Polanski became police chief in the nearby town the year after Gene Flynn died. Since Gene's death, he had watched over Nell and in a sense, became, even though she didn't need it, her unofficial guardian. His longtime friend and associate, Portland Police Captain, Jack "Rip" Morrison, teased Polanski that he took the job to be close to Nell. Morrison, nicknamed Rip after he tore a thick yellow page telephone book in half with his bare hands, thought Polanski and Nell were a perfect match. Although he vehemently denied any interest, Polanski did admit it was nice to have a friend like Nell. He told Rip she helped his transition from city to small-town life. Rip, the gnarly ex-high school wrestler and Marine veteran, assured him that he was full of crap.

"You know you don't have to wait so long between visits," Nell said in jest.

"People just keep breaking the law."

"And you thought this was going to be a quiet job," she said.

"I wonder what I was thinking. Unfortunately, I wish this was a social call," replied Polanski as he put his cowboy hat on the tavern bar.

"Why did I know that before you said it? What can I get you?" she asked.

Before he could answer, Nell started to pour him a Coke. She filled the glass and slid it across the bar knowing he never drank when on duty.

Polanski thought Nell was especially pretty when her cheeks grew flushed. Since he had first met her, Nell had hardly aged a bit. She had gained a few pounds, but they were in the right places. He thought she looked like the beautiful actress, Maureen O'Hara because of her auburn hair, Irish spring eyes, and gleaming complexion.

Polanski paused, trapped. "I know. I've been busy, but I'll make it up to you."

"Not possible, but I'll let you buy me dinner."

"How about this weekend?"

Nell raised her chin and looked up as if she were checking her calendar,

"I don't know; I might have a previous engagement. I'll think about it. Now, what can I do for you?"

Polanski took the good-natured ribbing in stride. "You know we've had a string of robberies."

"I do. It's kind of scary. Any leads?"

"A few, but nothing concrete."

"John Kramer was in a couple of days ago and told me he'd been robbed. Somebody broke into his shop and stole some guns and equipment. He said a couple of those guns were antiques," answered Nell.

"He's just one of four robberies we've had in this vicinity. The main target, naturally, is money. Sometimes it's guns or tools. Other times, the thieves take valuables. They're picky."

"They? Is it a gang?"

"We don't know. Could be, but whoever it is, they know what they're doing."

"Professionals?" Nell asked.

"Sure looks like it."

Although the unincorporated areas, like Lone Elder, were the jurisdiction of the Clackamas County Police, local law enforcement agencies were often called in for support. It was understood that Lone Elder, primarily because of Nell, was an area that Polanski considered his jurisdiction. Until now, the calls were mostly for traffic accidents, teen drinking, or the occasional domestic dispute. The year before, Polanski and his deputies arrested a group of men for cattle rustling. The thieves specialized in stealing Hereford and Angus bulls. The animals were stolen and then sold to unknowing ranchers in eastern Oregon. There was also evidence that some of the animals were butchered and sold to meat markets around Portland. The men, drug addicts, were arrested in a sting operation. In a coordinated effort, ranchers used two of their best bulls as bait. Polanski set up surveillance and waited. For the greedy rustlers, the bulls were too enticing to pass up. When the rustlers made their move, Polanski was ready. An army of officers from local, county, and state law enforcement closed in and arrested the three men just as they locked the bulls into a trailer.

"Robberies happen around here, but not too often," Nell said from experience.

"I know; that's why I'm here. Have you seen anything unusual? Have there been any new people come into the tavern?"

"You mean like outsiders?"

"Yeah."

"It's been quiet. Most of the farmers are busy with their crops. It's a busy time. We're still busy Friday and Saturday nights, but like I said, it's been slow. I can't say as I've seen any strangers. We get all kinds. This time of year, we do get some migrant workers, but not many. They work long hours and tend to stay within their communities."

"It was a long shot. I think this might be a gang who hit an area, make a few strikes, and then leave."

"I haven't seen a man, or men, who might fit that description. I mostly have regulars. I did see a transient fellow. It was early morning and he was talking to a couple of kids on the baseball team. I came to work early to check on things and noticed them talking. I wasn't sure who he was. I've never seen him before."

"When was this?"

"Oh, a couple of weeks ago. It concerned me at first and I kept an eye on them, but then the man left. I think he's come into the store once or twice, but I couldn't tell if it was the same man. Like I said, we get people this time of year who follow the crops."

"Do you know who the boys were?"

"I could be mistaken, but I thought it was the Stump and Dempsey boys. There was also another boy with them. It could have been the Sharp kid. They hang around together."

"I know those boys. What were they doing out here?"

"They're part of the baseball team. It was in the morning, so they might have been camping out. Sometimes during the summer, the boys on the baseball team camp out and then play ball. Sometimes they play most of the day. I think the little stinkers crawled into the old meeting hall. They like to scare each other with ghost stories."

"Were they causing trouble?"

"Oh, no. I don't care as long as they don't get hurt or burn the place down, although that wouldn't be a bad thing. The place is about ready to fall down anyway."

"Is there a danger to them?"

"No, it's solid enough. When I bought the property, the building came with it. I'm going to tear it down. I check on it every so often to make sure everything is okay. The old building has quite a history. When Gene and I first bought this place, the locals said the meeting hall was haunted."

Polanski took a drink of Coke. "From the looks of the place, it might be. Sounds like there's a story?"

"According to the legend, a bride disappeared on her wedding day. She was never seen again, and her body was never found. She became the Lone Elder Hall ghost. Her fiancé, an ex-baseball player of some reputation, was killed shortly after in a car wreck. The story goes that he cursed the baseball field when he died because his bride's crime was never solved. They've become symbols of bad luck."

"Why do you say that?"

"The year the bride disappeared, a barn next to the meeting hall burned down. It rained all summer, destroying many crops. Lightning struck a farmer, sending him to the hospital and killing one of his cows. The string of bad luck continued for a few years and then it stopped. Nobody knows why. Then last year, Jason was killed in that terrible accident. Like the other misfortunes, his death was blamed on the ghost or the curse. Pick your poison."

Polanski bowed his head, "I know about the boy. I was there and it was tragic. The hardest thing is to lose a child. I don't know because I've never had one, but I've seen enough heartbreak to last two lifetimes. It could all be a coincidence."

Nell tilted her head. Her auburn hair hung down to her shoulders and she returned a questioning expression, "Maybe, but people, old-timers anyway, blame it on the curse. I don't believe in that sort of thing, but the ghost stories do provide a few thrills for the kids."

Polanski changed the subject back to the reason for his visit. "Back to the robberies; do you ever see Ronnie Samuels around?"

"Why do you ask?"

"His name came up. He's an ex-con. I was told he occasionally comes in here."

"I don't see him much. Comes in sometimes on Fridays to have a beer. I don't know for sure because I'm rarely here in the evenings. I remember him though. He keeps to himself. I have a feeling about him that I don't like. Is he a suspect?"

"Right now, everybody is a suspect, especially an ex-con with robbery on his resume. I do think it's odd that we are having robberies in this area and he happens to have a beer at your tavern. Once again, it could be a coincidence, but I doubt it."

"Why don't you arrest him?"

"I can't arrest somebody because they may be a suspect. I need proof that he's committed a crime. Besides, I don't want to scare him away; I want to catch him in the act or with the goods."

"How about a search warrant?"

"I have to have a good reason."

"I guess so. He's the kind of man that makes me nervous. I have to be careful living alone and all, and I have to think about Rebecca. This is mostly a family place, but there are always a few troublemakers. She can handle most men okay. It's the few crazies I always worry about. It's the downside of owning a tavern."

"Why don't you sell this place?" Polanski asked. "You certainly don't need the money. I'm surprised you even have time for it with all your other interests."

"I like the people; these are my friends. They helped me through some tough times when Gene died."

Polanski turned to see a man dressed like a logger with pants held up with red suspenders and heavy boots walk in and sit at the end of the bar.

"What makes you think Samuels is dangerous?"

Nell motioned to him as a welcome, "What'll you have?"

"Bottle of Bud," he replied.

As Nell pulled a longneck Budweiser from the ice-chest, she answered Polanski's question. "Call it intuition. Men like that, well, I always think they're up to no good, and generally, they are."

"Let me know if he comes in again," said Polanski.

"If he does, it will be on Friday," Nell replied.

"I'll remember that. I will do some checking. If you see that man around who you saw talking to the Dempsey and Stump kids, give me a call. I'd like to talk to him. I don't like vagrant men around kids. Could all be innocent but until we know for sure, I'm always cautious. I've seen too many bad things happen to kids."

"I will keep my eyes open and let some of my trusted customers know."

"I'm going to include this area on my deputies' regular patrols."

Nell shook her head, satisfied. "I'll see you this weekend."

"How about the Markum Inn for a steak?"

"Sounds delicious. I hope you catch the thieves."

"We will. I just hope we do it before somebody gets hurt."

Chapter 24

"You'll see," said Spud.

"There ain't no ghosts. The wind probably blew and you thought it was a ghost 'cause you was so scared," teased Tub as he raised his arms above his head and put his fingers in front of the moon's reflection to stretch shadows on the wall.

As usual, Tub was loud and causing trouble. With a stomach like a protruding burl on an oak tree, Tub was destined to be an offensive lineman in football. He had ears like pears sprouting from the side of his head and a flat nose so full of boogers that he never worried about going hungry. Eddie thought about telling him to go back to the camp but knew that would cause more trouble. Besides, they had to confirm the bet they made with Tub. He had to see Medora.

Kermit adjusted his glasses to see the time on the alarm clock he brought with him. "It's about time," he said.

Tub danced and swung his arms in a windmill, "What're we supposed to do? Stand on the stage and wave our arms?"

"We have to go up into the balcony," said Eddie.

Tub looked up to the ceiling, "The what?"

"You'll see," said Spud. "It happens fast, so you have to be ready."

"I'm going back to camp. I'm going to roast a hot dog," said Tub.

Eddie grabbed Tub's arm, "You can't leave now. You might scare her away."

Kermit started to climb the stairs to the balcony, "Let's go. We might miss Medora."

"How do you know she'll come?" Tub asked as he reached the top of the stairs and inhaled deeply to catch his breath.

"We don't. If she does, you'll hear music," said Spud.

"She was playing a flute," said Kermit.

"I don't believe you guys. How do you know this ghost only comes when the light comes through that window?" asked Tub.

"We don't, but that's when we saw her," answered Eddie.

Tub was adamant, "Nothing is going to happen."

Kermit pointed toward the top of the roof as the light peeked through.

"Quiet. Get down. Here she comes."

The boys ducked behind the balcony railing and waited. The light from the moon's reflection filled the window at the roof peak. As the moon rose, light illuminated the pitched ceiling and then gradually drifted down. The light rotated like a slow-moving spotlight. The boys rose from behind the wood railing and peeked over the top edge. They saw the faint shape of an image hoovering, floating just above the stage. What they saw made them hold their breath. The image was clearer this time. Medora had on what appeared to be a white dress. A black shawl was wrapped over what looked like the woman's shoulders. The boys heard a distant sound. It was high-pitched and so soft; it was barely audible. They strained to hear. The music reached an apex and then, as quickly as they heard it, the sound faded away. The light reflection faded as the stage went from shadows to darkness.

"Did you see her?" asked Kermit.

"I saw the image of a woman, but then she was gone. She just blew away," observed Spud.

"I saw a face and she was playing an instrument," said Eddie.

Tub shook his head side to side. "I didn't see anything; it was just a shadow."

"How do you know? Your eyes were closed," said Eddie.

"Were you scared?" teased Spud.

"Shut up. My eyes were open. I just got dust in them for a second."

"It was a flute," challenged Kermit. "I'm sure of it. It was a woman and she was playing a flute."

"I couldn't tell if she was playing or if it was just the wind," said Spud.

"Why would she be playing a flute?" asked Tub. "That doesn't make any sense. A ghost playing a flute."

"I don't know. Do ghosts have to have a reason for being a ghost?" asked Spud.

"Yeah," added Tub. "If a ghost doesn't scare you, how can it be a ghost?"

Eddie shrugged, "I don't know; maybe she's trying to tell us what she's doing."

Tub laughed, "What could a ghost be trying to tell us? Heck of a ghost, she didn't even yell, BOO! I'm hungry. I want a hot dog."

The boys went downstairs, keeping a wary eye on the stage. They crawled out the window and joined their teammates standing in front of their tents pitched in a circle around the campfire.

"Did you see her?" asked Wags.

"It was the wind," replied Tubs.

"Don't listen to Tub. We saw her. She was playing a flute," said Spud.

"She wasn't scary," said Kermit. "I think she's trying to tell us something."

Tub threw his hands into the air, exasperated, "Like what?"

The team crowded around to hear. "I don't know. We saw her and she's real," said Eddie.

"What happens now?" asked Ron Fox. "What if she comes back?" he asked, nervously looking around beyond the fire and into the darkness.

Fox was the team's only cowboy. Fox could ride a horse, throw a rope, and play guitar, but he couldn't track a fly ball. He swung the bat hard and occasionally hit it. When he did, it was generally an extra base hit. Kermit said Fox didn't hit for average, but he was one of the team's power hitters. Western lean with light rawhide hair and dusty green eyes, Fox was already a match for Eddie's ability to attract the opposite sex. The difference was that Eddie didn't care, while Fox made it a sport.

The boys looked at one another without having an answer. Their eyes naturally gravitated to Spud, Eddie, and then Kermit. Spud and Eddie shrugged. Kermit was the first to speak.

"I think we wait for her to make the next move."

"Next move!" yelled Tub. "What's she gonna do? Come and talk to us?" he mocked.

"Why don't we tell the coach?" Fox enquired.

"Tell the coach what?" asked Charlie.

After returning from Frank's Market in Canby to buy extra hot dogs and buns, Charlie walked up to the boys standing around the campfire.

"Ah, nothin' coach. We just saw a ghost," said Eddie.

"I hope it was a friendly one," he joked. "A ghost. There aren't any ghosts except on Halloween, unless, of course, it's a baseball ghost."

"Baseball ghost?" questioned Kermit.

Charlie saw an opportunity to toy with the boys. "Sure, baseball has gods and ghosts. Why do you think baseball hitters go into slumps, players make errors, and pitchers give up home runs?"

"That's what Mr. Nance told us too," said Spud.

"Where did you see Mr. Nance?"

"A few days ago. He told us about how baseball has curses," said Eddie.

"He's not here tonight?"

"No. We saw him by the building. He was waiting for a friend," said Kermit. "He's coming to the Jamboree tomorrow."

Feeling that something wasn't right, Charlie decided to have another conversation with Nance if he showed up for the Jamboree.

"I don't believe in that stuff," said Tub. "You make errors because you're a bad player."

"When something is hard, there's always a divine element," Charlie said looking at the blank faces. "Sometimes the baseball gods aren't on your side. That's why you can never get down on yourself for making an error or striking out. You just have to work harder and then it won't happen as often. In baseball, just like life, occasionally, everyone makes an error or they go into a slump. You have to fight through it just like big league ballplayers do."

In that moment of encouragement, Charlie realized what he said sounded reminiscent of the same message Giant pitching coach, Derek Sheets, gave to him. It was a moment of reflection and understanding that hit home.

The boys were quiet while digesting the coach's message. Most nodded in agreement, although they were not exactly sure what he meant.

"Where did you see this ghost?" Charlie asked.

"She was in the old meeting hall," answered Spud.

With a look of concern, not anger, Charlie scolded, "Boys, you were supposed to stay out of that building. I don't want you to get into trouble or hurt. We need all of you healthy for the season."

Kermit explained, "We didn't mean any harm. When the moon is just right, the reflection from the sun illuminates the stage. Then she comes out."

"This time, she was in a white dress and playing a flute," said Eddie.

"You saw that; I didn't," replied Tub.

"Your eyes were closed," said Spud.

"Playing a flute?" Charlie asked in disbelief. "Hum, this place must be haunted," he said in jest.

"She's not a scary ghost. She's nice," replied Kermit.

"It was the wind and shadows," said Tub.

"Okay. Okay, people see things differently. I think you boys have had enough for the night. Tomorrow is a big day. It's opening day and you all need to get some sleep. First, we eat and then we go to bed. I borrowed a friend's travel trailer and I'm going to park it right over there to keep an eye on things. Mr. Wagner and Mr. Cooper will be camping in their tents next to me. If that ghost comes back, you let me know. In the tents in thirty minutes," said Charlie pointing at his watch.

He wasn't really worried about the boys getting enough sleep, but he didn't want them running around all night while they were his responsibility. He had become a worried parent. With only a two-inning exhibition game and the fact that the game didn't count made it a perfect time for a team campout. The boys would be tired, but after the game and picnic, they could all go home and get some rest.

"Grab a hot dog. Breakfast at eight, then batting practice. First game is at ten," Charlie commanded as he walked back to his trailer.

Ghosts, he thought; it would make a good story to remember.

Chapter 25

"Just relax and have fun," Charlie said to a very nervous Darnell.

"I've never played in front of people. I've only played at practice," replied Darnell.

"That's what this is. It's just the Jamboree. It's a practice game. This doesn't count. And even if it did, this is not life or death; it's fun. I was a pitcher and I know how you're feeling. You are nervous; just focus that energy on throwing to Spud. He'll catch it."

"What if I walk somebody?"

"Don't worry about walking anybody. Just throw at Spud's mitt. That's the target. Don't aim it; just throw it and you'll be fine."

Darnell wiped the sweat from his forehead. His mouth was dry and when he looked down at his knee, it was shaking. This was it. He had wanted to play, but now that he stood on the mound, he wondered if it was such a good idea. He looked over at his mom and dad. They were sitting in the stands and smiling. He could tell they were proud of him, but that didn't give him any additional confidence.

"Hey Darnell, just throw at my mitt," Spud said slapping the pocket with his fist.

There's Money on the Edge

"If they hit it, we're behind you," said Eddie from first base.

It was the second inning. He knew it was just a practice game, but that didn't make it any easier. Darnell glanced over at the opposing team. They looked big in their red and white uniforms. The team was from Oregon City and had won the league last year by beating the Cubs in the championship game. He wondered how Eddie did it. He had struck out the side in the first inning. It was his turn and he faced the cleanup hitter. As he stepped into the batter's box, Darnell thought he looked big, too big for this league. Darnell looked for the sign from Spud. He put one finger down below his chest protector, signaling a fastball. Darnell appreciated that getting a sign from the catcher was part of pitching, but he really didn't need one because a fastball was the only pitch he threw. Darnell toed the rubber. Gripping the baseball without too much tension across the seams, as Charlie taught him, he went through his windup with as little effort as possible to conserve his energy. Stretching his arm back toward centerfield, he let loose with a pitch. Then he watched in horror as the ball sailed high and over the hitter's head, slamming against the backstop screen. The kid ducked. When he straightened, he looked angry and pointed the bat at Darnell.

Spud, not happy with the batter's reaction, said, "Hey kid, you better watch it. It's the first time he's pitched and he's a bit nervous. He gets wild when he gets like that."

"He throws at me again and I'm going after him," said the hitter, a kid with broad shoulders and thick arms. He wore a white sleeveless jersey with a sleeveless red T-shirt underneath. The uniform was made to make his arms look big, which they were.

"You better not," threatened Spud.

"That will be enough boys," said the umpire, a bald man with a handlebar mustache. "Play ball," he said pointing at Darnell.

"That didn't go too well," Darnell said under his breath.

With the first pitch out of the way, Darnell gripped the ball again to throw another fastball. He let it loose and this time Spud caught the baseball, but it was outside and low for a ball. The count was now two balls. Darnell thought he had to throw a strike on the next pitch. He decided to take some speed off his fastball to get it over the plate. He wound and lobbed the next pitch to the plate. He saw the hitter take a mighty swing and then watched as the ball sailed over Wags' head in left field.

"Back up home plate," yelled Charlie.

Darnell snapped back to reality and ran behind Spud. They watched as the hitter touched home plate for a homerun before Wags could get the ball back to the infield.

"Hey kid, don't throw at me again or I'll hit it harder," laughed the cleanup hitter as he walked past Darnell.

"Don't worry about it, Darnell," said Spud. "He got lucky."

Darnell grabbed the ball and walked back to the mound.

As a practice game Charlie could coach his players without worrying about trips to the mound. "Darnell," he said, "don't let up. Throw the ball. If they hit it, they hit it. As a pitcher, you always want them to beat you with your best stuff."

There's Money on the Edge

"What if they hit another one like that?"

"Don't worry about it. The only way you're going to learn to pitch, is to pitch. You're going to have a few rough starts before you get it down. You pitch to two more hitters and we'll let Fox throw a few. I want everybody to pitch today. We need the work. I don't care about the score," said Charlie as he returned to the bench.

"Okay, coach," said Darnell not fully convinced that he could throw the ball over the plate, let alone get anybody out. It was a relief to hear that he only had to pitch to two more batters.

"Hey Darnell," said Tub, "try to keep this next one in the park. That guy hit it so far Wags got pooped out running for it."

Spud had joined Darnell on the mound. "Shut up, Tub. Every pitcher gives up hits, so don't worry about it. Tub has been bombed before," said Spud.

"Yeah, I'd like to see you pitch," yelled Dinky from second base.

Tub and Dinky threw each other a 'want a fight look' and then got ready for the next pitch. Darnell took the sign from Spud. He felt a little more relaxed after giving up his first hit. The coach said not to worry about hits and focus on throwing the ball over the plate. He let loose with another fastball. He threw the ball belt high and the hitter made contact, sending a hard-hit ground ball to the shortstop. Darnell turned in time to see Jose move toward second base and field the ball. Then in one fluid motion, Jose stopped, turned, and threw a perfect strike to Eddie at first base. The umpire called, "Out!" Darnell took a deep breath and sighed with relief. His first out.

Charlie beamed. He had found a shortstop. "Great play, Jose," he said clapping his hands.

Darnell pitched to the next batter and walked him. Charlie gave him another batter and this one hit a flyball to Dinky at second. Charlie, as he said he would, brought in Ron Fox to pitch. Relieved, and a bit proud, Darnell walked to the bench. When he heard the crowd clapping, a big smile crossed his face.

"Nice job," said Charlie. "I knew you could do it. Sit down for a bit and then I'm going to put you in centerfield. With your arm, you'll make a great outfielder."

Darnell smiled again. He was a baseball player, a real baseball player. He committed to play every day to learn the game and get better.

The Oaks finished the Jamboree game with a flourish but lost to the Oregon City Reds. Charlie and the parents were encouraged by the team's performance. Tired after a long night, a picnic, and the practice game, the parents took the boys home for a much-needed rest.

"Not too bad, coach," said Rebecca.

"Funny thing is, I worried more about the parents than I did the kids," replied Charlie as he threw the equipment into his 1960 Chevrolet pickup truck.

"In what way?"

"Mostly Steve Adams and Ed Washington. They're both stern men with strong opinions. I was worried about Steve Adams meeting Ed Washington and Hector Lopez. I wonder if Steve introduced himself like he said he was going to. At this point, those men getting along is more important for the team than playing a good game."

Rebecca took a drink of cola and gave Charlie a quizzical look, "Why is that so important? The boys had a good time."

"Let's just say Steve is not used to Tub playing on a team with boys of different color skin."

"Well, he'll just have to get used to it or find another team," Rebecca said firmly. "So you don't think he likes blacks?"

"I don't know. I doubt Steve would harm or purposely impede anyone. I think it has more to do with exposure. Once he gets to know Darnell and Jose, he'll come around. Ed and Hector Lopez have to feel comfortable too. Put yourself in their shoes; they worry about their sons being on an all-white team. They know there are people out there far worse than Adams. Once we start playing games, there's no telling what some idiot fan will say."

"You think it can get that bad?"

"I'm hoping this is different than the pros. When I was in the minor leagues, you'd be amazed at what some fans yelled when we played road games. There were a couple of times when we almost walked off the field. The black and Hispanic players took it, but I don't think I could have. There are hecklers, and believe me, I've had my share, but I've never had to put up with what my teammates did. Because they pay for a ticket, some fans think they can say anything. Well, they can't."

"This is different; these are kids. Nobody's making money here."

"I wish that made a difference. There are parents who think every game is life or death. They'll do anything to throw kids off. I just don't know how Darnell or Jose will react. If it gets too bad, I'm afraid the parents will step in. At that point, I wouldn't blame them. I'd pull the kids off the field anyway."

"I think you might be overreaching a bit. Most people are tolerant and just want their kids to have a good experience. I guess you'll always have one or two bad apples who try to wreck it for the rest of us."

"It's the one or two that I'm worried about."

"I guess we'll just have to be ready."

"We?"

"I organized the picnic; I'm part of the team," smiled Rebecca.

"Want to play some catch? I have to know the ability of all my players."

"I can catch; just don't throw me any hardballs."

"We'll start with some slow toss and then see how you progress."

"I might surprise you. I haven't played much, but I know a bit about the game."

Charlie smiled. "Why do I think that before long you'll want to be the coach?"

"You have enough coaches; I want to be the general manager."

"Does that mean I have to tell you everything?"

"Everything. Now let's go. My arm is loose."

Chapter 26

Nance tossed a baseball from his left hand to his right. "I watched you pitch on Saturday. You did a good job."

"Naw, that kid hit a home run," replied Darnell.

Nance understood Darnell, like many young pitchers, was way too hard on himself. His expectation of success was to strike every batter out. Striking every batter out was as unrealistic as it was hard on arms. Darnell needed to understand there were teammates behind him for support who could make outs. Yes, they made errors, but pitchers also walked hitters. Pitchers learned there were going to be *good days, bad days, and sometimes it rained.*

"Even Bob Gibson gives up an occasional home run," Nance said talking about the great St. Louis Cardinal pitcher.

It was a hot day and Nance was given the afternoon off. It was a welcome break from the backbreaking work of farm labor. When he could, he relaxed by walking. On this day, he stopped to watch the Oaks hold a practice session. Watching the kids provided a needed distraction from his current dilemma; he still hadn't decided what to do about Ronnie Samuels.

"I've heard my dad mention him, but I don't know who he is," replied

Darnell.

"Do you get the paper?"

"Yes, we do. My mom makes me read it. She says I need to know what's going on in the world. My dad reads the sports section."

"Then he knows Bob Gibson and you should too. He's already a great pitcher and one day will be in the Hall of Fame."

"My dad told me about the Negro Leagues and Jackie Robinson. He said Robinson was in the Baseball Hall of Fame."

"It was a great honor for Jackie and baseball. He was the first African American to be inducted.

"Is Gibson a pitcher?"

"One of the best. He's tough and not afraid of any hitter. He challenges them. The better the hitter, the harder he goes after them. He owns the inside part of the plate. If you're a hitter, you'd better not crowd the plate for an advantage on an outside pitch. If you do, he'll make sure you wished you hadn't."

"What does that mean?" asked Darnell.

"Don't be afraid of any hitter. You own that strike zone and can throw the ball wherever you want it to go. Greats, like Gibson, *can paint the black;* he can hit the edges. If you hit the edges and mix in a change-up or curve ball, you will win."

"I don't know how to throw a curve or a change-up. Coach said curves were too hard on my arm and I should just concentrate on throwing the ball over the plate."

Nance sighed. He had given the kid way too much. "He's right. You have plenty of time to learn those other pitches. You just concentrate on throwing strikes."

"Yes, sir."

"One more piece of advice. Don't aim the ball. Just throw it. They call it pitching, not aiming. Once a pitcher starts to aim the ball, they lose control. That's what happened to you on Saturday when that kid hit the home run."

"Mr. Nance, why don't you coach with Charlie?"

"I'd like nothing more, but I have some other commitments. Maybe someday."

"Hey Darnell, you're up," yelled Eddie.

"Sorry, I've got to go. Thanks for the tips."

"Remember; win or lose, have fun."

Nance stood up as a police car pulled into the parking lot. He moved behind the bleachers and strolled toward the big maple in right field. He suddenly felt the need to fade away.

Polanski parked his cruiser close to the grandstand. It was warm but a light breeze had picked up. Weather reports indicated a front was moving in, possibly bringing some much-needed rain. He took a seat in the stands and watched the boys take batting practice and then work on their fielding. He noted that ground balls were easier for most boys than the flyballs. Polanski's eyes shifted to right field. Based on Nell's description, sitting with his back against a tree trunk was the man she had told him about. From a distance, it was hard to tell, but his appearance was rough.

He was older, maybe late forties or early fifties, but he couldn't tell for sure. Hard living could make people look far older than their actual age. A faded work shirt, tan pants, and a scruffy beard made him seem tangled and worn. He was smoking a cigarette and drinking from a bottle wrapped in a sack, probably a quart of beer or ale. He appeared relaxed while he watched the practice. If he was concerned about a police presence, he didn't show it. If his outward actions were by design, he was playing the part well.

"I'm Charlie Pierce."

Charlie walked out from behind the backstop. "Nell told me about you. She said she knew you in Portland before she and Gene moved to Lone Elder," said Charlie extending his hand.

"Yep, her husband was quite the fighter. I used to go to all his fights. That's where I met Nell. We've been friends ever since."

From what Rebecca told him, Charlie knew Polanski and Nell were far more than friends. Since it was none of his business, he let it pass.

"You're welcome to watch us play. I'm always open for pointers."

"Nell told me about you, and I've read a fair amount about you in the papers. I'm a big baseball fan, but I'm certain you don't need any pointers from me."

"Baseball is one of those games where even the smallest piece of advice can make a difference."

"The team looks good."

"We have a way to go, but it's early. We just played in our annual Jamboree. The boys did well. Not too bad for having a couple of kids who've never played before."

"I can envision a championship."

"I'd just be happy to finish with a winning record. The boys are coming together and having fun. That's the most important thing."

"Nell says you're doing a great job. I do have a question for you," Polanski said without looking in the direction of Nance. "Do you know who that man is in right field sitting by the tree?"

Charlie turned but Nance was gone. "There's nobody out there."

"Well, I'll be," said Polanski. "He was just there."

"I don't know him well. His name is Owen Nance. He watches us sometimes. He enjoys watching the kids play ball."

"Anything odd about him?"

"Not really. I've talked to him a few times. I met him here. It was a couple of weeks ago before the Jamboree. Can't say, as I remember how the conversation started, but he told me about Darnell and Jose."

He pointed to Darnell who was now playing shortstop. He had started another drill. Each boy was up until he hit five pitches and bunted three times before going to right field. The boys rotated around the diamond. After each successive hitter, they rotated one spot until everyone hit and played each position.

"He also told me about Jose, the kid now playing first base."

"How did he know them?"

"I think he saw Darnell after he hopped off a freight train in Barlow. He saw Jose playing catch with his dad."

"A freight train? Is he a transient?"

"I can't say, but he doesn't seem like one. He works at one of the local dairies."

"You said he helped you with the kids?"

"He sure did. We were short players. He'd seen both play and, luckily, they were the right age. Darnell goes to school with the boys. Jose just moved to the area. His dad went to work at Nell's egg processing plant."

"As you know, we've had a series of robberies. I was following up on a lead from Nell. She mentioned him. She said she saw him talking to the boys. I just wanted to make sure about him. Find out who he was. So, you're okay with him?"

"As far as I know, he's okay. He gives the boys tips. He knows the game. I considered having him help coach, but I have too many other issues to deal with. Bringing on a man the parents don't know, and who looks a little rough, well, I don't think it would be appropriate."

"Do you know any more about him?"

"He said he spent some time in California. He saw me play. He said he worked for the *Sacramento Bee* newspaper."

"Do you know what he did?"

"He was a sports reporter."

"And you didn't know him? I'd think you'd know most of the reporters that covered your team or the league."

"Not necessarily. We knew the local beat reporters because they were at every game. I played a year in Fresno. Not that far from Sacramento but also not that easy for a reporter from the *Bee* to cover the games. Reporters covering major league teams occasionally covered specific minor league players. They were generally upper-tier prospects or those about to be called up to the big club. That was routine. It happened to me before I was called up by the Giants," said Charlie with a shrug.

"I'd think you'd remember him, but I can imagine you had a lot of people around you."

"There were. Good or bad, it's kind of like a traveling family."

"I'll do some checking. Nell told me about some of the issues you're having integrating Darnell and Jose. If you need some help with that, let me know. Getting everybody to mix is sometimes very difficult. I dealt with lots of those issues when I was with the Portland Police. It's often difficult for people to change."

"Baseball is a good ambassador. I'm hoping we take a big step in the right direction."

"These are good, accepting people, who shouldn't be too much trouble."

"This is an opportunity to teach the kids how to handle things if something does happen. I don't expect any trouble from opposing fans, but you never know."

"Make sure you let me know if it does. As far as I'm concerned, there should be no tolerance for that kind of thing."

"I've got to get back. Come by anytime to watch."

"I will check on this Nance. Something tells me there's more to his story," said Polanski.

Chapter 27

Charlie's attention was suddenly distracted by Rebecca and Nell.

"What are you boys up to?" asked Nell.

"Talking baseball," Charlie said with a wink.

"What would you girls be wanting today?" asked Polanski slyly.

"Rebecca told me you had some excitement not too long ago," answered Nell.

"Right now, there's too much excitement," replied Charlie.

Rebecca reminded him, "You know, the ghost."

"Oh, that. Pretty scary," he joked. "It was last Friday night before the Jamboree. It created quite a stir among the boys."

Polanski leaned forward, "What happened?"

"The boys went into the old meeting hall and said they saw a ghost."

Polanski turned to Nell. "Is this the one you told me about?"

Nell sat back against the stands. "It is."

"When I was a kid, we used to sneak into the building but we never saw a ghost. I had my wits scared out of me a few times," said Rebecca.

"So now you have my interest. What really happened?" asked Charlie.

"I only know what I've heard. You'd have to ask one of the old-timers for the details. It happened years ago before we moved here," said Nell.

Charlie told the boys to keep playing and then turned back to Nell. "What happened?"

"It was big news because, as you know, there aren't too many murders around here; if, in fact, it was a murder. No one knows for sure because, like I told Joe, the bride disappeared. The bride, her name was Mary Ann, was about to be married. An accomplished musician, at the last minute, she decided to play her flute during the wedding. She lived five minutes away, and rather than sending someone else, she drove home to get her flute."

Charlie asked innocently. "In her bride's dress? I thought you weren't allowed to be seen in the bride's dress until after you were married?"

"That's the groom. Who knows? Maybe she wasn't dressed yet," said Rebecca.

Nell continued, "Anyway, she rushed home to get her flute. She never came back. Gone without a trace."

Rebecca was incredulous. "People let her go alone?"

"It was a couple of hours before the ceremony was supposed to start. She lived close, and in this quiet community, I don't think people gave it much thought."

"Don't people know that if something bad can happen, it will? Basic law of probability," Polanski added.

Nell rolled her eyes. "Really? This sounds more like Polanski's law of, if it can happen, it will."

"No scientific proof just my observation of things, mostly bad, happening to people. So, what happened?"

"She left to get her flute. They found her car parked in front of her parents' farmhouse, so nothing mechanical had happened. The road to her house was open farmland, but nobody saw anything. The inside of her car showed no sign of struggle. That was the last anybody saw of her."

"No trace?"

"At first, people thought she decided to skip out on the wedding, but that didn't seem likely. She loved Carl, her fiancé. They were lovers since high school but decided to wait until he returned from serving in World War Two. Carl fought in Italy and was part of Mark Clark's staff. He didn't think his chances of returning were good and wanted to hold off on getting married."

"You said Carl was never a suspect," restated Polanski.

"He couldn't have been. He was at the hall having a few drinks with his best men when it happened. He was devastated and never recovered."

"Were there ever any leads?" asked Charlie.

"I don't think so. When it happened, it was big news and even made *The Oregonian* newspaper. Nobody ever found out what happened to her. There were state and private investigators, but there were never any solid clues. No arrests were made. I still hear men at the tavern talk about it. Everybody seems to have a theory about what had happened."

His interest growing, Polanski reiterated. "No clues?"

"Not that anybody seems to remember. I heard one of the farmers who went to the wedding say that some of the deputies who worked the case are still alive. The police chief at the time is dead."

Polanski stated, "Murders are always open cases until they're solved. There's no statute of limitations on a murder."

"Why the sudden interest?" Rebecca asked.

"I was just curious," said Charlie. "Some of the kids on the team swear they saw a woman in the meeting hall. They said if the moon is just right, it reflects sunlight onto the stage. When it does, that's when they see a woman in a wedding dress. Like I said, they saw her, or something, on two different occasions."

"There have been ghost sightings in that old hall for years. Sometimes people claim to see Mary Ann and other times they see Carl. Whether they really do, well, it does make a good story," said Nell.

"Do you believe in ghosts?" Rebecca asked Charlie.

"Nope, not even baseball ones, although I'm superstitious. I jump over the foul line and my routine before a game was always the same. I've never seen a baseball ghost, but I've dreamed about a few before a big game."

Nell held up the palm of her hand, "Oh, there's one other thing I forgot."

"I can't wait to hear it," Polanski teased.

"They never found her flute. Detectives searched the farm, Mary Ann's room, her car, but they never found a trace. They concluded that she had picked it up, but that was it. There are two mysteries: the disappearance of Mary Ann and her flute. Isn't it weird that she went to get her flute and they disappeared together?"

"Interesting," said Polanski. "I think, when I have time, I'm going to look at the old case file. The case needs to be solved. What bothers me the most, is that a killer is still out there. He needs to be brought to justice for Mary Ann's sake. Maybe those boys are on to something."

"I'm sure the boys would be glad to take you to the next sighting," Charlie offered.

"I just might take them up on it," replied Polanski.

"There's nothing like a good ghost story," smiled Rebecca.

Chapter 28

Nance was unnerved by the cop. He was big and imposing. Worse, he was certain he looked his way before he started talking to Charlie. The question was, about what? Was it because there was a strange man hanging around the ballfield? Around kids? He agreed, that should never be taken lightly. Was it the robberies? He had heard about them. He could be a suspect or at least *a person of interest*. Either way, he wasn't going to wait around to find out. Nance kept careful watch. When the cop was distracted, he squeezed between two arborvitae shrubs and made his exit. Quickly, he ran to his truck and slipped away. He drove slowly, always keeping his eyes on the rearview mirror. He rounded a corner and then pulled off the highway. He turned onto a road leading to a bean field. He waited. After a few minutes with no activity, he drove back to the farm. He was fortunate the Gains' dairy was well off the main highway. Better yet, Gains didn't ask prying questions.

He should leave now. He'd been on the run long enough to know when it didn't feel right. When it didn't feel right, it was time to go. The cop was the signal. But to where, and then there was Gains. He had been good to him. Leaving before a job was done just didn't seem right no matter what the risks. Repairing the barn would be done in a day or two, then he would leave. He could also be overreacting. He was paranoid, and he knew it. He had tried to stay away from the ballfield, but watching those kids kept him from going crazy. Rarely did he go to town for fear that he might be stopped or spotted. If that cop did run a check on him, it wouldn't take too long for the Sacramento cops to figure out who he was. When they did, there would be an army of cops to take him down. He would work extra hard and leave over the weekend. He had to make his move. It was time to expose Samuels. He had waited long enough. He still didn't have any solid proof. The harmonica was evidence, but was it enough? If he didn't figure it out, all the hard work of finding him would be an effort in vain. He would just have to think of something.

As he had agreed to do, Nance helped John Gains finish repairing his barn.

"You're a good carpenter," said Gains.

"My dad was a carpenter. I learned many lifelong skills from him."

"He taught you well. Are you sure you don't want to stay on for a few more months? I have a lot to do to get this place in shape."

"You've been good to work for, but I should be moving on. It's time for me to wrap things up here and make my way back to California. I have some unfinished business there and need to take care of it."

"You're a good man and if you need any help, let me know."

"You could answer one question for me."

"Shoot."

"How well do you know the Canby Police Chief?"

"I don't know him well, but I've heard good things about him. He's no-nonsense and runs a tight ship. People who have had dealings with him say he's a fair man. He's been a cop for a long time. Nell, at the Lone Elder store, knows him well. She told me he was a beat cop in Portland in some real bad areas."

"I've heard you talk about her before. She seems like a straight shooter and reliable."

"That she is. She's a real fine woman. She owns a lot around here. She'll give you a straight answer on things."

"Thanks. I'll get my things together and be leaving first thing in the morning."

"Do you need a ride somewhere?"

"I might take you up on that. Let me see what tomorrow brings. I may need to borrow your truck for a couple of hours."

"No problem," answered Gains. As much as he liked Nance, he had an aura of mystery surrounding him. He never pressed because good help was hard to find. "By the way, if you ever need a good word, let me know."

"You never know. I just might need one," replied Nance as he returned to his trailer and started packing.

Chapter 29

"Lew," said Polanski as he rolled his desk chair close to his office door opening.

"Yes, Chief," answered Lew Fairhead, the office manager and the longest serving member of the Canby police force.

Lew had hair the color of a red burning bush, long thin fingers, and deep facial lines caused by thirty years of smoking and raising five very active sons. She thought the world of her boss. He had quirks, like the other police chiefs she had worked for, but he treated her like she was an important part of the team. She had also been around him long enough to know that when he called her name, she could expect a project.

"I have a little job for you," answered Polanski.

Polanski thought Lew was indispensable. First, she knew everybody in the small farm town and almost everything about them. As a lifelong resident, her knowledge saved time and, without revealing too many hidden secrets about its citizens, gave him the information he needed to make decisions. She listened well and she wasn't afraid to tell him if he was off the mark. Most importantly, Lew knew how to manage his many requests. Polanski realized that took special skill and often patience.

There's Money on the Edge

"Is this a local project?"

"Nope. I need you to contact the Sacramento Police Department and ask them about a man named Nance."

"Nance? Is that his first or last name?"

"Last. I'm not sure if that's his real name, but let's go with it."

"Do you know his first name?"

"Owen. He goes by Nance."

"Okay. What else can you tell me?"

"He might have been a reporter for the *Sacramento Bee* newspaper. Probably a sports reporter."

"This doesn't sound too tough. I think people will remember a sports reporter. Who's this guy? Does he live here?"

"I think he's a drifter. He works at a local dairy. I'm not sure which one. I don't want to confront him until we find out what this guy's all about. I don't want to scare him off."

"When do you need the info?"

"Yesterday."

"Of course. Okay, I'll get right on it."

As efficient as always, Lew immediately called the Sacramento Police. After she didn't hear back from them, she called back the next day. After a few apologies because her message had been displaced, she was put in contact with the homicide division. The detective in charge of the case, a John Ross, was involved in an investigation and would return her call as soon as he returned to the station. Later that day, Lew had her answer.

"He's wanted in connection with the murder of the *Sacramento Bee* editor. He's been on the run for almost two years."

"Damn, are you sure?"

"Well, according to the Sacramento Police, Owen Nance, his real name, is the prime suspect. Ross said, if it's Nance, they tracked him to San Francisco and lost his trail there. Nance was thought to have escaped the country. There were reports that Nance fled to Hong Kong. Ross did say that even though Nance was the lead suspect, the case was complex and there were many unanswered questions. Seems the editor of the *Sacramento Bee*, a man named Chester Marsh, and Nance had an argument over a story Nance had written. The story was about minor league baseball players throwing baseball games."

"Throwing baseball games? Do you mean like the Black Sox scandal?"

"What?"

"Never mind. Go on," said Polanski.

"Anyway, there is some question as to whether Marsh was involved in the scandal or was protecting those who were."

"Who was he protecting?"

"Ross doesn't know for sure. The LA mob was involved. They may have threatened Marsh or his family. Anyway, he refused to print Nance's story. They got into a fight over it. Nothing physical, but they were yelling at each other. Ross said Marsh and Nance respected each other but were often on opposite sides of an issue. There's no solid evidence against him, but still, according to Ross, all fingers point to Nance. Ross said Nance was behind the *eight ball* from the start. Seems the *Bee* convicted him before he was even arrested."

"His own paper convicted him?"

"Yep, seems like it," said Lew.

"Is there still an outstanding warrant for his arrest?"

"Yes, there is. Ross asked us to verify that the man is Nance. If he is, he requested that we arrest and hold him. Ross will come and get him and transport Nance back to Sacramento. With Marsh's killer on the loose, this is still big news in California."

"It's been a couple of days. I hope he hasn't left the country," Polanski stated. "Have Walker, Wormley, and Landon come in. I want to talk to them and create a plan. We'll have to canvas the area around Lone Elder to find out where Nance is working."

Always one step ahead, Lew said, "They're on their way to the station. They should be here at any time. Should we call the County? Lone Elder is, technically, out of our jurisdiction."

"We'll ask the county for backup when we make the arrest. I want to be careful and keep this low profile. For now, we'll handle it. We have to find Nance first. Unless somebody knows or sees something, this could take time. I'm just hoping he doesn't suspect anything."

Chapter 30

Ronnie Samuels sat in his Ford Econoline E-100 pickup truck and waited. It was Sunday and the Miller family always went to church. After church, they went to a late breakfast at the Top-O-Hill restaurant in Aurora. He calculated that this should be an easy mark. There was a watchdog, a Doberman, but they kept him locked up in a wire cage next to the house. He never robbed people with dogs unless they were neutralized with a heavy chain or locked in a pen. Ronnie was always leery of dogs. Most of them, other than Brax, didn't like him. Besides, there were too many people without dogs to rob, so why take the risk of being attacked by one.

So far, he had been smart and, although he didn't like to admit it, lucky. To successfully rob a series of houses, there was a certain amount of luck involved. People were never entirely predictable. Plans changed. People didn't stick to their routines and came home early. Hitting the Miller farm was to be his fifth and last robbery in the area. The paper had just reported six, but there was one he had nothing to do with. Sometimes that could be a good thing, especially if his counterparts were caught. Taking the route of least resistance, the police would try to pin all the robberies on them. The only difference was the other thief had robbed a residence near downtown Canby. His robberies happened in the country from Woodburn to Lone Elder. He picked the area because, besides knowing it well, people were still trusting and often left their farms unattended. There was also a convenience factor. He had an alibi. Ex-cons needed tight alibis. His was to visit a local wrecking yard for car parts or to have a beer at Lone Elder tavern. Neither of which, he reminded himself, would work today; on Sunday, both businesses were closed. He was taking a chance because it was time to move on. This would be his last hit.

He was surprised the cops hadn't questioned him. As a felon, law enforcement fingers would naturally point at him first. But there hadn't been any cops. The only potential problem was the attempted break-in at his garage. That was an odd happening that made him uncomfortable and had sped up his timetable. After the Miller hit, he would fence the last of his loot. He planned to just walk away from the garage. A distant cousin, if he wanted to, could have the property and sell it. He no longer cared. He would be long gone. He planned to disappear in California.

Ronnie watched as the Miller's pulled from their gravel driveway onto the Canby–Marquam Highway. Keeping to their routine, Henry Miller pointed his car toward Aurora and drove off. Ronnie waited until they had safely driven away, and then, to make sure there wasn't an unexpected return, he waited another five minutes. The coast was clear. The Miller farm, as many in the area were, was hidden behind a stand of trees. The only possible chance to be seen was when he drove onto the highway and then made the turn onto Miller's gravel drive. The gravel road wound through a thicket of trees. If he drove slowly, there would be no dust to alert passers-by on the highway.

Concealed behind a stack of wood bins used to transport produce to food processing plants, Ronnie carefully inched the pickup truck out and looked in both directions. The coast was clear. He edged onto the highway. Driving slowing, he kept his eyes on the rearview mirror to watch for cars. Luckily, on a quiet Sunday morning there was little traffic. He turned onto Miller's private drive. Going slow, he safely entered a tunnel of overgrown brush, thick with a variety of trees. He picked up speed and drove the half-mile that seemed like five to the farmhouse. As he anticipated, the dog barked but the farmyard and house were quiet. He backed the pickup up to the front door. Pulling on a pair of tight-fitting leather gloves, he raised his work boots and kicked open the solid wood door. There was no time to mess with the door handle, even if it wasn't locked. Time was of the essence.

Beyond the front entry was a living room with a sofa, coffee table, and easy chair. There was a piano in one corner. A red brick fireplace was centered on the back wall. He was looking for specific items. A safe for money and valuables. Guns, jewelry, precious metals, and anything else he could carry easily and fence.

He threw back an area rug only to find solid wood plank floors. He scanned the dining room. There was a cabinet full of silver goblets, crystal, and china plates. He quickly determined to come back for the silver and crystal and leave the plates. They broke too easily. He ran up the stairs to the bedrooms. He discounted the children's rooms and went to the master bedroom. He ripped off the mattress and found a pouch. It was leather and contained a few hundred dollars. Next, he searched under the bed. There was a shotgun and a box. In the box were papers; a marriage license and a bank book with deposits listed. They were of no use to him and he tossed them aside. On the dresser was a jewelry box. A quick scan told him the box was full of gold and silver. He opened it and dumped the contents into his canvas bag. He pulled the dresser from the wall to check behind it. He found nothing. He opened the nightstand and pulled the drawers open. He emptied the contents onto the floor. There was nothing of consequence until he pulled out the bottom drawer. He flipped the drawer over. Attached to the back was a canvas pouch. He ripped it off. He had hit gold. In the pouch was a stack of bills. He didn't have time to count the money but was sure it had to be at least ten thousand dollars. Satisfied, he threw the pouch into the bag and raced down the stairs. He quickly threw the silver into his pack, deciding to leave the crystal. Hoisting the bag onto his shoulder, Ronnie raced to his pickup and drove away. Safely back on the highway, he slapped his leg. His adrenaline pumping. He was careful to drive the speed limit. His plan had worked to perfection. Now, all he had to do was wrap things up and escape to California.

Chapter 31

On a routine patrol, Officer Christine Walker parked her cruiser across the street from the Lone Elder tavern. The parking lot in front of the meeting hall and next to the baseball field was a good position to watch the major intersection. From her vantage point, she could see passing cars from any direction, and they could see her. She didn't want to be hidden; this was about showing a presence. After patrolling the area, everything looked normal. Before returning to the station, she decided to take a ten-minute break and have a cup of black coffee. She glanced over at the Lone Elder baseball field. Two boys were playing catch. Nothing unusual about that, except it was a bit too early to play baseball.

The break gave her a chance to reflect. Still in the first year of her new job, she was adjusting to the culture of a small town, a challenge for a "big city" girl. It had been a big change. She had been a deputy with the Salem Police before quitting to become part of a much smaller four-person unit. She made the jump to escape big-city politics and an "old boy" network where there were few women cops. She recognized early on that there would be little chance for advancement unless she wanted to deliver coffee and perform community relations functions. The other reason was Police Chief Joe Polanski. With his vast experience, she believed she could learn far more from him than she could shuffling papers. Here, she could log real hours as a bona-fide cop without dealing with restrictions and biases due to her sex. What made her feel good was what Polanski said when he hired her. He told her she was hired because she was tough, competent, and had an even-tempered personality. Along with these qualities, she had all the traits to be not only a good cop, but one with a bright future. In his evaluation, he supposed, although there was no way of knowing until it happened, that she would be level-headed in a crisis. He said she reminded him of a female cop he worked with in Portland. The woman rose to captain. If she wanted it, all Christine needed was the experience. Polanski thought one day she might take his job when he retired.

Physically, she was middle America attractive, wore her hair in a tight bun, had a firm build, was well-proportioned to her height, and carried her strength in her shoulders. She had a quick smile without any hint of being phony. Her handshake made strong men look her directly into her eyes and weak men look away.

A plus was that she hit it off immediately with Polanski and her fellow officers. Nick Landon, "the cowboy", Clay Wormley, who she, like everybody else except Polanski, called "Mouse", and the real strength of the force, the office manager and dispatcher, Laurie "Lew" Fairhead. She had quickly become part of a family.

It had been a long night. As Saturday nights often were, it had been busy. There was an arrest for drunk driving, a raid on a teen party that garnered arrests for underage drinking, and a disorderly conduct charge. Nothing unusual, but still busier than most weekends. Then there was Owen Nance. They had found him working at a dairy close by. Later that morning, a detail of Canby and Clackamas County cops would raid the Gains' farm and arrest Nance. She was at the end of a double shift and would provide backup for Polanski, Wormley, and Landon during the raid. Until then, she was on point. Per Polanski's instructions, she was to patrol the Lone Elder area while staying clear of the Gains' farm. Because of the recent robberies, an increase in patrols would be expected by residents, but Polanski didn't want Nance to sniff they were on to him. If he did try to run, Polanski requested state and county police stakeouts at main intersections east, west, north, and south. Christine manned the major Lone Elder intersection closest to the Gains' dairy. Her position was a good distance away from the other surveillance points.

Christine took the last drink of her strong, black, caffeinated coffee. She yawned. She was tired and looked forward to calling it a night. Thoughts of a light meal, hot bath, and eight to ten hours of blissful sleep kept her going. Just as she was ready to put the cruiser in drive and return to the station, she eyed a Ford pickup truck as it drove toward the intersection. She hadn't seen the truck before, but there was nothing unusual in that there were lots of farms and lots of farmers with trucks. She did note that it was a white and blue two-tone Ford.

The driver slowed. Once again, she watched closely but saw nothing unusual; drivers often reacted by slowing when they saw a police car. Then she noted the slightest of hesitations. The driver seemed undecided about whether to turn left on South Lone Elder Road or continue toward Canby on South Highway 170. In that instant, she noted a hint of correction in his driving. She had seen the same reaction many times when a drunk driver oversteered his car in a classic attempt at avoiding detection. Now suspicious, she eyed the vehicle carefully. She assumed his thought process; if he stayed on the road, he would have to drive past her. If he turned left, he would drive away from her. She carried his thought process to the next level. If he turned left, he was avoiding the law; if he went straight, he was not afraid of it. He turned left. When he did, Christine pulled onto the road and followed him. She had no reason to stop him but wanted to know if the additional pressure might cause a reaction, a mistake. If it was Nance, she expected him to take off. Then she caught a break. The truck license plate had come loose. One of the screws had come out. The plate was tilted and looked as if it were about ready to fall off. Although there would be no ticket, she would perform a courtesy stop, inform the driver, and let him go. In the process, she could check him out. She lit up the two red lights on the cruiser's light bar. There was no need for a siren. The road was narrow with ditches on either side. The truck stopped, half on the pavement and half on a narrow strip of grass. Beyond the grass, there was a steep bank dropping into a deep ditch. There were no other cars or farm vehicles in sight. The area was strangely quiet. She approached the driver calmly, but as always, stayed alert. An officer never knew what to expect.

"Good morning, sir," Christine said.

"Why the stop? I didn't do anything wrong," answered Ronnie with a good deal of annoyance.

Christine noted the man's quick agitation and took a protective step backward. The driver was younger and didn't fit Nance's description. She noted the tattoo of a snake on the inside of one forearm. He had a tattoo on the other arm, but she couldn't tell what it was. His arms resembled a hardened drug user; they were bones covered by a sickly blend of muscle and bulging veins. The middle knuckle of each hand had a gouge and the skin was missing. His fingernails, or what was left of them, were covered in black grease. He kept his face turned away from her as if he were hiding it.

"Sir, I never said you did anything wrong. This is just a routine stop. May I see your driver's license?"

"A routine stop? I didn't know there was such a thing," Ronnie said as he reached into his wallet and handed Christine his license.

Christine was tired but her adrenalin had spiked. She didn't want to agitate the man. She studied his license and then stated evenly, "Mr. Samuels, your license plate is about ready to fall off. I thought you should tighten up the screws."

Ronnie's attitude abruptly changed, "I'm a mechanic too," he replied, cursing himself for being careless. "I'll get a screwdriver. I carry one in the glove box," he said reaching across the seat and opening the door to the glove compartment.

With her well-trained eyes, Christine noted a burlap sack stuffed down on the passenger side floorboard. She didn't want to jump to conclusions, but instinctively thought it might be a bag of stolen goods.

There's Money on the Edge

Christine handed Samuels' license back. It wasn't Nance, but this could be the thief they were looking for. Careful to control her voice, she said, "I'll go back to my car and wait until you tighten the screws. Then you're good to go."

"Thank you, officer. This won't take more than a minute," replied Ronnie.

When the cop returned to her cruiser, Ronnie reached under the seat and pulled out his Smith & Wesson .38 special. The cylinder was full of cartridges and ready. He waited until he heard the cop close her door and then tucked the gun in his pants. He grabbed the screwdriver and walked to the rear bumper. He raised it to show the cop. A woman cop, she would be easy to take. It was just her unlucky day. Unfortunately, she had seen him. He was sure she had noticed the bag of stolen goods. He knelt on one knee to straighten the license plate. One screw was missing, but he tightened the remaining screw. When he stood up, he saw that the cop was on her radio. He had to make his move.

Christine returned to the cruiser.

"Dispatch. Over," she said into her new Motorola two-way radio.

"Yes, come in. This is dispatch," said Lew taking another drink of black coffee.

"I need to run a vehicle check on a Ford pickup, license number DRT020."

"I'll run it. This shouldn't take too long."

"I may have to let him go before you hear back. I'll retain contact if this takes too long," answered Christine.

"I thought you would be on your way back to the station to join the other officers of the arresting party."

"I was on my way back until I saw this suspicious truck. I stopped the driver because his license plate was loose. There was a burlap bag on the passenger side floorboard. There's something odd here. I just don't...." Christina uttered as Samuels suddenly straightened.

In momentary disbelief, Christine watched as Samuels' reached into his pants and pulled out a handgun. His hand moved as if it were in slow motion. Leaning over the hood by the driver's side headlight, he fired from a range where he couldn't miss. Reacting on instinct, Christine threw her body out of the line of fire toward the passenger door. The windshield exploded showering her with glass. Her quick reaction saved her life, but she wasn't quick enough to dodge the bullet. She felt a searing pain and heard a dull thud as the slug tore into her shoulder. She slammed her boot against the driver's door, pushing her body onto the seat. Samuels fired again hitting the seat-back. She reeled. Her left arm was now useless. With her right hand, she fought to pull her service weapon. She found the handle of her Colt .45 semi-automatic handgun and jerked it from her holster. She flipped off the safety and forced her arm up. She caught a glimpse of Samuels moving toward her. There was death in his black, predator's eyes. Her life was now measured in milliseconds. She had to move. Then there was the sudden, deafening sound as Samuels fired into the driver's window blowing out the glass.

Luckily, the bullet hit the steering column. She raised the Colt and fired. Then fired again. Surprised, Samuels jumped backward. He fired wildly blowing out the passenger's window. Now panicked, Samuels scrambled back toward his truck.

Still on her back, Christine could no longer see him. She struggled to raise her body to a sitting position. The shooter was now near the cab of his truck. He turned, raised his gun, and fired again. Luckily, the bullet hit the firewall and logged in the dash. Christine stayed low. Taking a deep breath, she raised her gun above the dash with her one good arm, took careful aim, and squeezed the trigger. The man arched back on his heels. She had hit him. Fighting to stay upright, he forced his body forward. He swung an arm around his body and fired again in self-defense. He lunged into the truck cab. Christine fired again but missed. Now wounded, Samuels quickly started the truck and slammed it into first gear. Spinning the rear tires, Samuels showered Christine's cruiser with gravel. He sped off, fishtailing and almost losing control of the pickup. Christine fired three more times without any apparent effect. The chaos over, the scene was once again, eerily quiet.

"Christine! Christine!" shouted Lew. "Please respond."

"Officer down. I'm hit," she said fighting the pain.

"Where are you?"

"Lone Elder by the store. I'm on South Lone Elder Road. I'm hit. I'm hit in the shoulder. Send backup and an ambulance."

Lew was already on the radio calling all units with a distress call.

"Units are on the way. Sit tight."

"Don't worry, I'm not moving. The suspect is hit. He's driving south on South Lone Elder Road. He's driving a Ford pickup truck. Blue top and white body."

"Stay with me," said Lew. "I've contacted all units. They're on the way."

"I'll be here," said Christine as she tried to stop the flow of blood.

Chapter 32

"Spud, did you hear that?"

"I did. They were gun shots. They came from over there," said Spud, pointing at the Lone Elder store.

"You think somebody robbed the store?"

"It's Sunday. The store is closed on Sunday."

The boys had stayed the night at Kermit's house. After a pancake breakfast served by Mrs. Sharp, Kermit had to go to a family function with his parents. The boys decided to play catch and practice their hitting before going to the Molalla River for some fishing.

"Look, Spud. On the road, there's a police car. The windows have been shot out. Look! There's a pickup truck taking off. He's flying."

As he jumped onto his bike, Spud shouted. "Should we call the cops?"

"There's a pay-phone at the store, but we better see if everything is alright."

They rode to the police car and laid their bikes down in what seemed to be a safe distance behind it. Carefully, they crept up to the trunk, straining to see through what had been the back window.

On his tiptoes, Spud looked over the trunk. "There's somebody in there. It's the woman cop. She must be hurt; she ain't moving."

"Com'on, we have to see if she's okay," said Eddie.

They walked slowly along the side of the car to the driver's door. The door was open; the window was blown out. There were pieces of glass scattered all over the ground and on the driver's seat. Then they saw blood. It was smeared on the seat and blood covered the woman's shirt and pants. They stood staring. Stunned, the boys were not sure what to do, certain the woman was dead.

They were startled out of their trance when she slowly turned and said, "Good morning, boys."

Christine tried to remain calm and not scare the boys, but her shoulder hurt beyond anything she had ever felt.

Spud choked out a response. "Are you alright?"

"I've been better. Can you boys help me up?"

"Sure," they said in unison.

"Just give me your arm. I feel the need to stand up," Christine said.

"Are you sure you're okay?" asked Eddie.

"I think so, but I'm still bleeding."

She grabbed Eddie's arm with her good hand and slowly stood. Dizzy, she quickly fell back onto the seat.

"That didn't work too well. How about I just sit here. There's a towel in the back seat. Would you get it?"

Spud opened the back door and grabbed the towel. "There's a medical box here. Do you want it?" asked Spud.

"Yes. Open it," she said and then pointed at Eddie. "I need you to go around to the other side of the car. In the glove box, I have a box of bullets. Get them for me. You look familiar. What're your names?"

"I'm Eddie and that's Spud."

"Now, I remember you. You helped with another case," Christine said as she gritted her teeth. She focused her mind on the case. "You helped Chief Polanski find that girl. What was her name?"

"Emily. Emily Jones," answered Spud.

"Boys, if a blue and white truck comes back, I want you to run. There's a very bad man in that truck. Run into the woods and wait for the police to get here."

"You're bleeding. How do we stop it?" asked Eddie.

"I'm not sure if we can," said Christine fighting to keep from passing out.

It was early morning and Nance had completed the last of his preparations to leave. He wanted to leave at first light but had agreed to help Gains with an electrical problem in one of the barns. It was a foolish waste of time, but Gains had been good to him. By now, he was certain the police would have completed a background check on him. If they did, it wouldn't take long for them to figure out who he was and why he was on the run. The police could raid the farm at any time. He was surprised they hadn't done it already. Tired of running, if he were arrested, he would tell them about Samuels and the harmonica. It was a chance he had to take.

Gains had agreed to give him a ride to the main highway. He thought about it but had refused. After collecting his final pay, he thanked Gains for the work and his hospitality. He threw his few belongings into his canvas daypack. He made sure his Colt .38 Special was loaded. He tucked it into the pack under a sweatshirt. He swung the pack onto his back and started walking. It would take some time to reach the main 99-E highway. He would have to be careful, but he needed time to think. It was a quiet morning, but he still felt exposed. When he heard a car he hid in the brush. So far, there were no signs of the police. He thought about returning and accepting a ride from Gains but decided against it. He didn't want to trouble the man any further. He thought about hitchhiking. Problem was, there were very few cars on the road. He decided to find a secluded spot and wait until dark. He would then make his way to Barlow where he could hitch a ride with a passing motorist to Aurora.

The only possible chance to clear his name was to confront Ronnie Samuels. One way or the other, he resolved to settle things. He had to. He realized it would be dangerous and he may have to kill or be killed. If he had to kill Samuels, there would be no turning back. His would be a life on the run, hiding and always afraid of being discovered. His options were few, unless he could get Samuels to come forward and turn in the people who had hired him to make the hit on Marsh.

Suddenly, his deep thought was interrupted by the pop, pop of gunfire. It momentarily stopped and then started again. At first, Nance thought it might be a farmer scaring off pigeons or shooting some pesky varmint. He had stopped to rest in a thicket of trees concealed from the main road.

He jumped to his feet and ran to the highway. Just as he did, he saw a man crawl into a blue and white pickup truck and then sped away. The man was too far away to tell for sure, but he looked like Samuels. Grabbing his pack, he started to jog toward the scene. Out of the corner of his eye, he saw two boys hop onto their bikes and race toward the police car. The police car was shot up. From the distance, he thought he saw a woman cop, but he couldn't be sure. He was sure she had been shot. Although he hadn't seen the shooting, it had to be at close range. It didn't seem possible that somebody had survived, if they did. As fast as he could, he ran across a grass field. As he approached the car, he saw there was blood; lots of it. The officer had been hit, but she was alive. For how long, he didn't know, but she was calmly talking to the boys. She looked up at Nance.

"Where are you hit?" Nance asked.

Christine responded, "My shoulder."

"Boys, hand me that towel," he instructed as he knelt beside her.

Eddie did as he was told and then moved back next to Spud.

"What's your name officer?" asked Nance.

"Christine. Christine Walker."

"Christine, were you able to call this in?"

"The ambulance should be here in a few minutes. There are units on the way."

Nance grabbed the towel and replaced the one she had against her shoulder. He applied firm pressure to stop the bleeding."

"What happened?" asked Nance.

"It was a routine stop. The man's license plate was loose. When I approached the truck, he grew agitated. I saw a bag of what I thought were stolen goods on his floorboard. He must have sensed that I saw it. When he went to tighten the license plate, he came up shooting."

"Christine, over," her radio barked.

"Yes, Lew."

"The units are at Good's Bridge and should be there in less than five minutes. How are you holding up?"

"I have a man and two boys here to help me. Their names are Spud and Eddie. What's your name?" she asked.

"Name's Nance. Owen Nance. Do you know who did this?"

Christine didn't respond immediately. This was the man they were going to arrest. She stared at him as if she were trying to understand how he could be there.

"His driver's license said his name was Ronnie Samuels."

"I thought that was him."

"You know him?"

"I do. Been after him for a while."

"I think I'm going to pass out."

" Stay with me," said Nance. "I hear sirens. The ambulance is close. Stay with me."

"Did you see his blue and white two-tone pickup truck?"

"I saw it."

"He pulled his gun. It came from nowhere and it happened so fast, but I'm sure I hit him."

"They'll get him. You just stay calm and awake."

They were interrupted by Christine's two-way radio. "Christine, over."

Christine fought to lift the handheld mic, "Yes, Lew," she replied.

"There's an army of State and County police headed your way. They'll be there shortly. Chief Polanski is with them."

"Thanks, Lew. I'm feeling pretty weak, but I have some people here helping."

"Stay awake. Fight to stay awake," said Nance.

"Boys, there are some smelling salts in the medical kit," said Christine.

"I'll get them," said Spud.

Nance interjected, "They're little round-like capsules."

"I saw them used on my sister's boyfriend when he was playing football. He said it kept him alert," said Spud.

Spud found what Nance had described. Taking the smelling salts from the medical box he handed them to him.

Nance motioned for Eddie, "Here hold the towel against her shoulder," he said.

Nance took the capsule and broke one. He put the cotton capsule under Christine's nose. The release of alcohol and ammonia made her nose burn. She stiffened and jerked her head backward.

"That's terrible," she said shaking her head.

"Look! A police car," said Eddie.

"The ambulance is behind it," said Spud.

"Lew, the units are here. I'm okay, over."

"They'll get you to the hospital. Hang in there," encouraged Lew.

"I'll do my best. Over and out."

Chapter 33

"It's a little early for a gunfight, isn't it, officer Walker?" Polanski jested, deeply concerned about her. He did a quick check of her wound and gauged the amount of blood she had lost. The situation was serious.

He glanced at the man he thought was Nance as he started to back away from the cruiser. Spud and Eddie had backed away too. They stood by their bicycles and watched the unfolding scene. With apparent concern on his face and in his voice, Polanski bent down on both knees. Ignoring the pain, pain he gained from a long career of chasing criminals, he grabbed her hand and held it. He pulled the bloody towel away from her shoulder and peeked at the wound again. The good news is, the bleeding had stopped. The bad news was her wound looked nasty and probably meant there was considerable damage to her shoulder and the tissue around it.

"It's been a long night, and morning," quipped Christine.

"Sit tight," said Polanski. "Get the gurney," he said motioning to the two ambulance attendants. They were ready with the gurney and medical kit.

"Let's see what we've got," said the lead attendant, a short stocky man with wrestler's arms. He nudged Polanski out of the way and took his place in front of Christine.

"He caught me with a bullet in the shoulder."

While the attendant stabilized her, Polanski asked. "Christine, can you give me a description of the shooter?"

She gave Polanski the details. "The name on his driver's license was Ronnie Samuels."

"That's what Lew told me you said. Samuels is on the suspect list for the robberies. He's an ex-con. Did time for theft."

"I hit him, but he drove off. I saw a bag on the front floorboard. I guessed he was the thief we've been looking for. He had black hair combed straight back. Lots of grease. Husky, with tattoos on his forearms. He had a scar on his cheek, jagged like a knife cut. His eyes were pure evil and so deep-set I couldn't tell their color. They looked black. He was rough-looking. Tall and very thin, like a drug addict. I'm betting he's messed with the law before. He drove off that way," Christine said pointing south, the movement painful, even though she used her good arm.

"Toward Aurora?"

"Yep."

"That's in the direction of 99-E. We have an army out looking for this guy. We'll get him. That's enough. Get her to the hospital. I'll check with you later."

Christine nodded and slowly turned her legs to get out of the car.

With his siren blaring, Nick Landon pulled his cruiser to a screeching halt. He then whipped the car across the road, blocking any oncoming traffic.

"She alright?" Landon yelled as he threw the driver door open.

"She'll be okay," said Polanski.

"What happened?"

"She thinks the guy who shot her may be the thief we've been looking for. Block the road in both directions. Re-route them onto Canby-Marquam or back south on Lone Elder Road."

"We'll do chief," said Landon an Army veteran partial to cowboy boots, western-style belt buckles, and late nights. Polanski thought Landon was a good cop with a great deal of potential if he ever settled down. An infectious smile as dangerous as his good looks made Polanski wonder if he would ever make it.

"Once the county boys get here, tell them to check every farm in this vicinity for a break-in. If that guy is the thief, I'm betting he hit one of the farms close by."

"How far out?"

"I'm only guessing. Check them all within a half-mile radius."

"Focus on those off the main road first," said Christine from the gurney. "He came from that direction," she said, pointing south.

"Deputy Landon, radio Lew and see if she was able to get information on the vehicle from the state. Com'on boys, let's get her to the hospital. I want her fixed up. Now let's go."

Nance had backed away, unsure of what to do. He walked to where he saw the pickup truck take off. On the ground, he saw blood. He was in a quandary. If he stayed, it could be his end, but this may be the only opportunity to go after Samuels. If Samuels was wounded, he could die. If he died, so did any chance of clearing his name. This was his chance; maybe his only one.

As the attendants lifted Christine and the gurney into the ambulance, she motioned toward Spud and Eddie.

"Thank you, boys. You were a big help. Where is that other gentleman?"

"I'm here, officer," Nance replied as he approached.

Polanski eyed him carefully, not sure what to make of him. Then he asked in a firm voice, "Sir, are you Owen Nance?"

"Yes, sir, I am."

"Thank you, sir, for coming to my aid," said Christine.

"Not a problem. Now you take care of yourself."

Polanski faced him and said, "I have to inform you there is a warrant out for your arrest."

"I expected that might be the case."

"I'm going to have to take you into custody."

"I understand, but I know the man you're after. Ronnie Samuels is not only a thief but a murderer. Officer Walker is right; she hit him. There's blood where he stopped his truck," Nance said pointing to the ground.

"Did you see it happen?"

"I did not, but I got here right after. I've been tracking Samuels for almost two years. If you care to drive me, I'll tell you the story. I know where Samuels lives. If he's wounded, he could die, and I need to get to him before that happens. If he's not hit bad, he could take off and I can't afford to lose him again. Time is of the essence. He'll head for California and I'll never be able to clear my name," pleaded Nance.

Polanski paused, not sure if he should trust this man or not. He turned toward Spud and Eddy, "You boys tell Officer Landon what you saw today. Landon, you're in charge here. Com'on, Mr. Nance, let's go see if we can catch a thief.

Chapter 34

Ronnie pressed a shop rag against his wound. The bullet had hit him on the very edge of his side. It was painful but nothing beyond what he had experienced before. It was more like a flesh wound. He had been stabbed with a knife in prison and it was much worse. He was lucky; the bullet had gone clean through. It hurt like hell, but he didn't think there was any serious damage. He poured alcohol on the open wound. The pain was excruciating but necessary to prevent infection. He gritted his teeth and applied another dose of alcohol to his back. After wiping his wound clean, he applied disinfectant cream that he used for cuts and scraped knuckles. He put a thick layer on his side and back. He cut a white bed sheet into wide strips and applied gauze to the entry and exit holes. Wrapping the cloth around his stomach, he applied tape to hold it in place. It wasn't a professional job but would have to do until he found a doctor to stitch him up and dress the wound properly.

He had to keep moving. The shooting of a cop would receive top priority. Crimes involving cops always did. The cops would eventually tie him to the pickup truck, and probably the robberies. Smartly, he had used a customer's vehicle that was in the shop for repair. The cops would first have to trace the truck to the rightful owner. Then they would have to hunt down the owner before tracing the truck back to him. It would take time to close the loop. He should also expect roadblocks. He knew from experience he wouldn't be able to outrun the cops and their two-way radios. Traveling south on 99-E was way too risky. He would take the back roads and avoid the main highways at least until he reached Salem. The *escape ring*, as he called the immediate police search area, would initially be around Lone Elder. The search area would quickly expand. Within hours, it would range from as far south as Salem and as far north as Portland, if it didn't happen sooner. He could already feel the trap tightening. He had to leave before it closed.

He quickly counted the cash he had accumulated from the five robberies. The total was just over twenty-five thousand dollars. That was more than enough for a new start. Taking the silver and crystal would be too easily seen and cumbersome to haul. Ignoring the pain on his side, he pulled the canvas bags behind the trailer and rolled them down the steep bank. As the loot rolled noisily into the canyon, he thought how sad it was to watch all his hard work roll away. He tossed his shirt now covered with blood into the garbage and carefully put on a clean work shirt. He packed a leather suitcase with a change of clothes along with a few necessities. He decided to take two of his prized possessions, a Winchester 12-gauge shotgun and a Remington model 721 30-06 rifle. He wrapped them in a cotton blanket. He went to the garage. In one of the bays, he had parked the non-descript light blue nineteen-fifty-seven Chevrolet Bel Air Nomad station wagon. Luckily, he had just finished rebuilding the 283 cubic inch engine. The brakes and tires were new. He concealed the two rifles in the back. From his holster, he pulled his Smith & Wesson .38 special and made sure it was loaded. He placed the handgun on the passenger seat along with two boxes of shells. He folded a towel and placed it over the guns and ammo to keep a snoopy cop or passerby from seeing them. The close call with the woman cop made him realize how one small mistake could mean the end. He didn't plan on making the same mistake or being taken easily.

It was a few hours until dark. There was a risk leaving in the daylight, but he also realized he was taking a chance waiting. He had to go. He filled his toolbox with a few basic items: a ratchet wrench, ten-piece socket set, a set of box end wrenches, an assortment of screwdrivers, three adjustable crescent wrenches, and other hand tools. Tools served a duo purpose. They were needed for repairs but could also be used as a weapon if the need arose. He put the toolbox in the back of his Nomad by the rifles.

He decided to take Brax with him. The dog rested comfortably in the Nomad's back seat. He thought about leaving him behind, but he had been a good watchdog. More importantly, he had become his only friend. He closed the car door and walked back to the trailer house to make one final check and to retrieve his suitcase.

Ronnie threw the door open and froze.

"That's quite a story," said Polanski.

"I've been lucky. Lucky not to be caught and lucky that I found

Samuels."

Polanski found Nance's story believable, but still, there was no proof that Samuels had killed Marsh. "What happens if you can't get Samuels to confess?"

"I'm tired of running. You, at least, listened to what I had to say. I'll go back to Sacramento and tell my side of the story."

"You're always more guilty if you run," Polanski stated.

"Oh, I knew the risks, but I was dead either way. All the evidence pointed at me. If I hadn't received the tip on Samuels and he didn't run, I wouldn't have either. I had to track him; he was my only link. He's the only one who can identify the person who paid for the hit on Marsh."

"So, what makes you think he'll talk? Robbery and murder are two vastly different crimes. One equals prison; the other death."

"It's the chance I'll have to take. I have the harmonica; that's the only piece of evidence tying him to Marsh. I'm banking on the fact that it's still there," said Nance.

"You know that Samuels will just say you put it there."

"I'm sure he will. This is no amateur we're dealing with. This guy is a real hard case. He'd lie on his mother's grave. I'm just hoping he makes a mistake and you hear it."

"How do you suggest we do that? We're taking a risk here because we already know he's willing to shoot it out with cops. Even an arrest is highly dangerous."

"I know it's a risk, but I'm hoping you'll let me take it. The other problem is Samuel's dog. He's not the friendly sort. Samuels keeps him in the garage, but that's when he's gone. If Samuels is home, he might be out. We may have to shoot him. No matter what we do he'll alert Samuels."

"Another reason why we should call for backup and just raid the place."

"I'll make you a deal. If the dog is out, we back off. If he's in the garage, then I confront Samuels and try to draw the truth out."

"This goes against my better judgment. You might get killed. You don't even have a gun."

Nance reached behind his back and pulled out the .38. He carefully pointed the barrel down.

Polanski was instantly on guard. He wasn't sure if he trusted Nance without a gun; him having one made him uneasy.

Trying to calm Polanski's obvious fears, Nance said, "I've had it since I left California. I've never used it. Look, I've been dead for almost two years. One way or the other, I want this over."

"Just keep the gun in your pants and your hands free until we get up there," Polanski said.

Nance directed Polanski to the small park he had used previously. Polanski parked his cruiser and followed Nance into the woods. They climbed the steep hill behind Samuels' trailer house. They crested the hill and stopped behind a tree.

"The place is quiet."

"The good thing is that the dog hasn't barked. The door to the garage is open. Samuels might be in there. If he is, the dog is with him," said

Nance.

"That could be a problem," said Polanski checking his well-used Colt M1911A1 semi-automatic .45 handgun.

"We'll have to chance it. I want to get to that trailer house before he removes that harmonica. It's critical. I want you to witness that it's there."

"I'll stay close. If that dog attacks, get into the trailer house."

Just then, Samuels walked into the garage with two rifles wrapped in blankets. From Christine's description, Polanski identified the man as Samuels.

"Go," said Polanski.

Keeping his profile low, Nance crept toward the trailer house. Polanski angled off to one side. He stayed concealed behind a dilapidated storage shed and watched the garage door. Gun ready, he wrestled with whether to just take Samuels or wait until Nance had a chance to talk with him. His instincts said to arrest him. Suddenly, the garage door opened and out walked Samuels. In apparent pain, he grabbed his side. It was confirmation that Christine had shot him. Polanski made a slight move to a better position, keeping his eyes on Samuels. The man looked like he didn't suspect anything and as far as he could tell had no weapon on him. More important, he closed the garage door and the German Shepard was nowhere to be seen. He thought it odd that the dog wasn't barking. He watched as Samuels walked past. Then he opened the door to the trailer house. It was up to Nance now.

Chapter 35

"I've been after you a long time, Ronnie."

Ronnie looked and then looked again. Momentarily motionless, he said, "It was you."

Nance pointed his Colt Detective Special .38 caliber revolver at Samuels and motioned for him to sit down.

"Ronnie, I want you to be real careful. Have a seat."

"How'd you find me?"

"It doesn't make a difference. I found you. You shouldn't have shot that cop. I saw the truck when I was out here a couple of days ago."

"So you were my visitor."

"Oh, I've been here a few times. I know your habits. I caught a glimpse of your truck as you crested the hill. You're getting a bit sloppy."

"So, big deal."

"I think it is. You've put me through hell. I would like nothing more than to put a bullet in you and end this, but unlike you, I'm not a murderer. Don't make me make an exception. Take a seat and be slow about it."

Thrown off his guard, Ronnie's mind raced. He pulled a chair from under the table and sat down, doing as he was told.

"How did you find me?" he asked again.

"A bit of hard work and a lot of luck. I've been watching you for some time. Nice cover here. I didn't expect that you would come home. You shouldn't have become so famous. Having your name in the newspapers is how I found you. Without that newspaper article about you robbing old ladies and going to prison, you would have been home free.

Samuels shook his head in disbelief.

"What do we do from here? I have money, if that's what you want?"

"This is far beyond money. I don't want your money. What I do want is my life back. I want to know why you killed Marsh."

"That's my life insurance policy."

"You just shot a cop. I'm not sure you have a life insurance policy."

"It's more important now than ever. Could keep me from the chair."

"Are you sure? I hear there's a contract out on your life."

"Maybe, but it wasn't a mob hit. The people involved in the baseball thing were low-level thugs. Nothing can be proven, and besides, those players will never talk. You know if you shoot me, you're still guilty. The way I see it, you need me."

Nance ignored the comment and raised his handgun. "If you want to live, give me a name. You're not important to me. You're a killer but I don't think Marsh meant anything to you. He was just a job. A contract to collect on. What I want is who hired you and why. You tell me that and you can go on your merry way."

"You think I'm stupid? I give the name up and I'm dead. Besides, you have no proof."

"Oh, I have proof that you killed him."

"You're full of it."

"How about the harmonica in the bathroom. It's Marsh's. If you didn't kill him, how did you get it?"

"You think that's going to tie me to murder. Hell, I could have bought one."

"I think there are enough people who will remember his harmonica was missing a wood cover plate."

Ronnie shifted in his chair, uneasy. His side hurt and there was the realization that he had made a mistake. Keeping the harmonica was foolish.

"What guarantee do I have that you'll let me go?"

"None. You killed Marsh and shot a cop. Best you'll get is a head start if you give me a name. No name, no guarantee."

Samuels reached for his shirt pocket. "Careful," warned Nance.

With his thumb and index finger, Ronnie pulled a pack of cigarettes from his pocket. He put a filter-less Camel between his lips and struck a match. In deep thought, he lit the cigarette and took a long drag.

"You were stupid. Getting into a fight with Marsh made you such an easy target. The plan had nothing to do with you; you just made things convenient," said Ronnie with a slight smile.

"This had nothing to do with throwing baseball games?"

"Not a damned thing."

"Then what was this about?"

"What's anything about? Money."

There's Money on the Edge

"Money?"

"Hell, yes. Lots of money."

"Was Marsh in some kind of financial trouble?"

"No, but his brother-in-law was."

"Taylor. Taylor had him killed?" asked Nance in a stunned whisper.

Allen Taylor was Marsh's brother-in-law. It was common knowledge within the newspaper community that Taylor wanted to sell the family legacy to invest in the rapidly growing California real estate market. Marsh, a newspaperman like his father, owned controlling interest and flatly refused.

Ronnie relaxed, relieved to get the conspiracy off his chest.

"Taylor owed the mob for gambling debts. He needed money and wanted to sell but Marsh blocked it. Marsh's sister wasn't involved in the paper and wanted to sell. She needed money to support her lavish lifestyle. She was also heavily into drugs. Heroin mostly. Taylor controlled her. My opinion was that they were both real low life's."

"Odd, coming from you."

"Hey, even criminals have standards."

"Marsh loved that newspaper. For him to sell would be like cutting off his right arm. How did you know Taylor?"

"The mob, of course. They wanted their money."

"That dirty SOB. I should have known. He hated the paper and resented Marsh. Taylor was a bum; never worked a day in life. A leech that lived off others."

Momentarily distracted, Nance leaned back against the kitchen cabinet and relaxed his arm. He let the gun drop. The barrel was no longer pointed at Samuels' chest. In that instant, he lunged. Like a two-hundred-pound ram, Samuels hit Nance with the full force of his body. He drove Nance against the corner where the kitchen and hall walls met.

Gasping for breath, Nance tried to pull the gun up, but Samuels grabbed his wrist. He blocked Nance's arm, pinning it against his leg. With his left fist, Samuels connected with a vicious uppercut to the side of Nance's face. With his right hand, Samuels tried to wrestle the gun free. Nance fought, but Samuels' grip was like a vise. Samuels used his bulk to keep Nance down. They were locked in a stalemate, neither able to move in the narrow hallway. It was a death struggle.

Samuels grunted as he used maximum effort to push Nance away. Creating a gap, he hit Nance with an open hand across his face. Nance barely held on to consciousness. In a desperate attempt, Nance twisted his body to throw Samuels off. They rolled to the floor. Samuels landed on his side. As he hit, he let out a loud groan. Intense shards of needle-like pain from his wound caused Samuels' body to wrench. Nance felt the slightest ease in Samuels' grip. With all his remaining strength, he rotated his wrist and pulled the trigger. Then he pulled it again. Samuels' body shuttered. His muscles jerked. Through the smoke and smell of spent shells, Nance felt Samuels' last breath. His body wrenched and then went limp. Ronnie Samuels was dead.

Polanski threw the trailer door open with his gun drawn. There, in a twist of arms and legs, lay Nance and Samuels. Not knowing who was alive or dead, he stepped in carefully, eyeing the heap on the floor.

There's Money on the Edge

"Nance?"

"I'm alright. Get him off me. I think he's dead."

"Just the same, push your gun toward me," said Polanski. With one known and one potential criminal, he was taking no chances.

Nance did as he was told and then pushed Samuels off him.

"Did you hear?"

"I heard it all. Sorry, I couldn't get here faster. I was under the back window listening."

"He was sitting in the chair and jumped me. I had no choice. He didn't look like it, but he was as strong as a bull," said Nance still trying to catch his breath.

"Don't worry about that now. Samuels was one bad dude. Robbery was the least of his crimes," observed Polanski as he checked Samuels' pulse. "He's gone."

"I didn't want to kill him. I wanted him in court to testify. Now it's my word against that murdering brother-in-law."

"Don't forget. I heard everything."

"Taylor's wife still owes part of the *Bee*. He has resources. Without Samuels, I'm afraid he's going to get off."

"In a court of law, anything is possible, but I think you'll be okay. I need to go call this in."

"I think I'll just sit outside for a while. It's been a long time since I've been able to relax."

"Don't touch anything in here, and for sure, do not go get that harmonica. I want the crime folks to find it just where Samuels left it."

"Don't worry, I want out of this mess and away from him," said Nance pointing to Samuels.

Chapter 36

It was the Tuesday after Deputy Christine Walker had been shot by Ronnie Samuels. The area was still buzzing about the two shootings. As the story of what had happened between Samuels and Owen Nance started to filter out, people soaked up every detail. The story, as stories often do when they are told and retold again, grew to epic proportions. But life went on. The Oaks played a baseball game against a team from the nearby town of Molalla. On the mound for the Molalla Bucks was a heavyset right-handed pitcher with a quirky motion. His deliberate mechanics were slow, but he threw the ball hard, much faster than it seemed his motion would allow. Charlie described his fastball as *sneaky* fast.

He explained to the boys, "The ball will float out of the pitcher's hand. Don't watch his motion; just look for the ball. He comes over the top," Charlie said, raising his hand over his head. "Look for the ball up here. He throws strikes, so be ready to hit."

The Oaks struggled with the Molalla pitcher and, during the first four innings, were unable to score. The Oaks were behind by two runs in the bottom of the fifth. The Oaks, the home team, were up to bat. Charlie, seeing the third baseman was playing way too far behind the base, gave

Jose the sign to bunt. Jose laid down a perfect bunt. It was a hit but as often happens, Jose bunted the ball toward first base rather than down the third baseline. Charlie clapped his hands. It was a classic case of a good tactic and poor execution.

"Great job, Jose," encouraged Charlie, surprised the play still worked. Sometimes, the baseball gods were on your side.

He turned to the next batter, "Com'on, Wags. Keep your eye on it."

Charlie glanced up at the parents supporting the team from Molalla. He knew a couple of the men because they had worked on the same logging crew. Pete Long was there talking to his friends. Since his injury, Charlie had seen Pete often. Although he was a busy man, Pete was a big supporter of the Oaks and came to the practices and games when he could.

Other than the cast still covering his arm, the accident was like a distant memory. His doctors speculated he would be able to remove the cast, which had almost become a part of him, within the next three weeks. Perfect timing. The season would just be about over and he could go back to work. That was if the weather cooperated. A recent heat wave had shut down the woods due to extreme fire danger. He talked to the men from Molalla before the game. They said it would be a few weeks before logging would commence again. Charlie understood the necessity of protecting the forests but wondered what he would do if the woods were closed for an extended period.

After Wags flew out to second, Spud stepped into the batter's box and dug a small trench with his right foot. He twisted the ball of his foot and dug his spikes into the hard dirt. Satisfied, he anchored his right foot and faced the pitcher. He took a couple of practice swings. The pitcher came set and looked over his shoulder at first base to make sure Jose stayed close to the bag. Raising his left foot a few inches off the ground, the pitcher, to ensure Jose didn't get too much of a lead, sped through his wind-up. Spud's timing was off. He cocked his bat and took a short stride to gain enough momentum for the swing. He was late. Defensively, he flung the bat at the ball. Connecting, he hit a soft liner between the first and second basemen. With quick reflexes, Jose dodged the ball. If the ball had hit him before the infielder had a chance to field it, he would automatically be out. Jose raced to second base, touched the inside corner, and ran to third. He stopped at third after seeing Charlie hold up both hands. The right fielder fielded the ball and threw it to the cut-off man to hold Spud at first.

"Way to hustle. Good hit, Spud," Charlie said, pointing a finger at Spud and then patting Jose on the back.

Eddie stepped into the batter's box. He looked at Charlie for a sign. He gave him the hit away sign, which was nothing more than clapping his two hands together and pointing to the outfield. Eddie was relieved. Although he could bunt, as any good hitter did, he preferred to hit. The pitcher quickly ran the count to three balls and two strikes. Eddie stepped out of the batter's box and looked at Charlie in the third base coaches' box. With two strikes, Eddie knew he wouldn't put the bunt sign on.

Charlie clapped encouragement and said, "Two strikes, choke up."

Eddie choked up about an inch on the bat. Charlie taught them that with two strikes you choked up to make contact. Any ball in play can cause trouble; a strike out gave the team no chance. As a pitcher, Charlie liked strikeouts, but also knew how they could hurt a team. He said, "Strikeouts are errors. I'll take walks or putting the ball in play even if you make an out."

Eddie eyed the pitcher. He guessed the ball would be over the plate, but where? If it was too high, there was a good chance he would miss it. High pitches were hard to hit. A low pitch was a chance for a walk, but the team needed a hit. If the pitcher centered it up, that was a mistake he'd be sorry for. Eddie kept his hands firmly on the bat and steadied his feet. He was ready and determined. The pitch was belt-high on the outside edge. It was a pitch Eddie could neither pull nor drive back up the middle. He instantly reacted to make contact. Throwing his hips, he stepped perilously close to the edge of the plate. Slapping at the ball, he dumped it over the first baseman and into right field. He raced to first. Jose crossed home plate. Spud rounded third and scored. Reaching the ball quickly, the right fielder scooped it up, spun, and threw a perfect strike to the second baseman. The second baseman caught the ball and dropped a tag, but Eddie ran to the inside. He slid, hooking the base with the front of his right foot.

"Safe," yelled the umpire.

"Darnell, grab a bat," said Charlie. "You're batting for Fox."

Excited, at first, Darnell thought Charlie had made a mistake. He knew Kermit wasn't the best hitter, but he was even worse. His knees shook from the nerves. He walked to the batter's box. It was his first at-bat in a real baseball game. He'd batted at the Jamboree and struck

There's Money on the Edge

out. It was a practice game, but it didn't matter; he didn't like striking out. The fact that Charlie thought he could get a hit, made a difference.

"Hey kid, did you forget something?" asked the umpire.

"No sir," replied Darnell. "I don't think so."

When he realized the youth was nervous, the umpire smiled. "You can't hit without a helmet."

Darnell grabbed the top of his head. He'd forgotten his helmet. Embarrassed, he walked back to the dugout.

"Hey Darnell, you think your head is hard enough not to wear a helmet?" teased Tub.

Darnell spun around and glared at his smiling teammate. He wasn't sure if he was mad because he had been stupid or because he had to suffer, what he thought, was another racial insult from Tub. Either way, he ignored it and kept his mind on getting a hit.

"That's enough," Charlie said to Tub and the bench. It was the first time the boys heard Charlie raise his voice and they immediately stopped talking. "Even big leaguers forget things. Now let's go. We need a hit to get that run in."

Darnell strode to the plate. He took a practice swing and stepped into the box. The pitcher smiled. Now, why would he smile, thought Darnell. Was it to throw him off? Or, did he know he was a weak hitter? Determined, Darnell smiled back. The pitcher nodded, then quickly threw the ball past Darnell for a strike. Then he did it again. With two strikes on him, Darnell thought he had little chance of hitting the ball. If he bunted and fouled the ball, it was an out. It wasn't a good option, but at least he might advance Eddie from second to third. As the pitcher wound up, Darnell turned to bunt. As the ball sped toward the plate, he slid his hand up past the trademark. As he was taught, he caught the ball with the barrel of the bat. The ball trickled in front of the plate, half-way between the pitcher and catcher. Darnell was so thrilled he'd made contact he didn't immediately run. Momentarily awestruck, he watched the ball.

"Run!" yelled Charlie. "Run!"

Darnell immediately dropped the bat and took off as the pitcher and catcher ran to the ball. Out of fear or a chance to get a hit, Darnell ran like lightening down the basepath. By the time the catcher got to the ball, Darnell was closing in on first base. Knowing he had to make it, he stretched out his stride. Three, now two, now one more step, and then his right foot hit the outside of the base. Just as he was about to touch first base, he heard the pop of the ball hit the first baseman's mitt.

"You're out!" roared the umpire.

The partisan Oaks' crowd reacted with a series of catcalls, some even suggesting that the umpire should buy a pair of glasses, but the call stood.

The Oaks took to the field. Darnell pitched the last inning and did well. He walked the first batter who went to second on a sacrifice bunt. He then scored on a grounder hit to Tub at third. It was a routine play, but then the ball hit a rock and bounced over Tub's glove for a hit. The run scored.

The Oaks were unable to score in the sixth inning. The run on the bad hop proved to be the winning run as the Bucks beat the Oaks 3 – 2. Charlie was happy with the team's effort and told them the season had just begun and there was a long way to go. The boys went to Charlie's truck and cooled off with ice cream bars.

Chapter 37

There was a swarm of police cars surrounding the area near Samuels' garage. The state police sent their crime scene unit. After Samuels' body was removed, the crime unit, with an assist from local law enforcement, emptied the contents of his trailer house.

"This guy was a real hoarder," observed the head of the state police crime detail, David Craig, a studious man who wore thick, black rim glasses. Craig was seen so often in a blue shop coat, bow tie, and white shirt that it became his official uniform. The nervous type, Craig constantly shifted his head side to side as he clicked his ballpoint pen.

"What have you found so far?" asked Polanski as he surveyed what had become an elaborate scene. Off to the side was a pile of garbage deputies had removed from the trailer. Sitting on a series of tables were items investigators had tagged as evidence. Each area was sectioned off to separate items of importance from those that were not. Segmenting the evidence helped investigators determine the extent of Samuels' crimes.

After the crime scene was secured, Polanski took Nance to the police station for questioning and to take his statement. Polanski then spoke to John Ross of the Sacramento Police, informing him of what happened. They decided to allow widespread TV and newspaper coverage of Samuels' death to give Marsh's brother-in-law, Alan Taylor, a false sense of security. Under a veil of secrecy, Ross agreed to fly to Portland and escort Nance back to California. If Taylor was involved, as it appeared, they wanted to have a lockdown case before making an arrest. Polanski recorded a statement and agreed to testify to a grand jury about what he heard Samuels tell Nance.

Although relieved, Nance knew he wasn't in the clear. He wouldn't be until Taylor was arrested and convicted. Although he was eager to return to Sacramento, he realized there was nothing he could do for now. Polanski treated Nance to a hotel room for helping capture the man who shot one of his deputies. Nance enjoyed a long, hot shower, a shave, and then took a long nap.

After a day to recoup, Deputy Clay Wormley took Nance to see John Gains. Nance thought it was important to tell Gains his story and thank him for his hospitality. Although surprised, Gains told Nance he always suspected there was more to him than what he saw on the surface. Nance invited Gains, a big football fan, to California to watch the 49ers play. The next stop was the Lone Elder field where Nance wished Charlie and the Oaks well.

"I think you should give it another try," said Nance.

"I don't know. First, I'm not sure if I can even pitch. Second, I don't know if the Giants will give me another chance," replied Charlie.

"Major league teams will always give talent a chance."

"The way I left was pretty childish. What confidence would they have in me? If I were them, I'd wonder if I would do it again."

"I'm not saying it wouldn't be a problem, but there have been some big changes. The Giants fired Billy Stanton and hired Derek Sheets as the manager."

"They did? I hadn't heard that."

"Just happened. I know Sheets from the days he coached in the minor leagues. I can put in a good word for you if you want."

"Let's see how it goes. It will be at least three more months before I'm able to pitch. If I can, it will be early next year before I'd be ready."

"When I get settled, I'll be in touch. And, by the way, I think you've done a great job with the kids," said Nance.

"Thank you. And thank you for helping with the team. Recommending Jose and Darnell made a huge difference. They're about ready to become stars."

"You can bring any player forward. A player has to have the desire and ability, but it's coaching that brings out the best in them."

He hoped his accident and his involvement with the Oaks would give Charlie a different perspective on being a player. Rarely did an employee understand the perspective of a manager until he became one. There was a certain maturity that came with the transition.

Nance talked to each player and gave them some final pointers. After a short pep talk, he wished them well. As much as he wanted to watch them, it was time to go to California and put his life back together.

As one final gesture of his appreciation for helping Christine and finding Samuels, Polanski invited Nance for a steak dinner on the police department. Nell was a willing tag along.

As soon as he could, Polanski returned to the crime scene. He found David Craig immersed in piles of junk.

"We have evidence, although it has to be verified, of the robberies. We found a bag of jewelry, but he mostly stole silverware and crystal. He threw the silverware over the bank. From the looks of it, Samuels was trying to make a fast exit," said Craig.

"We got here just in time," replied Polanski.

"That's the way it looks. In the car we found a bag full of cash. About twenty-five thousand dollars. That's quite a haul. I'd say, even though this is preliminary, you found your thief."

Polanski picked up a silver plate and tossed it aside. "I'm betting you're right."

"We did find that harmonica in the bathroom cabinet. We'll log it and then dust it for fingerprints back at the lab. I know this is important. I want to get it in a controlled environment where we can do a thorough job."

"You'll probably find Samuels' fingerprints, but you may also find the fingerprints of the owner, a man named Marsh who was murdered. Both are probably old. I don't know if you'll be able to lift them. You also may or may not find Nance's fingerprints. I'm not sure if he touched the harmonica."

"Sometimes we can lift even very old fingerprints. Do you think this Samuels kept trophies?" asked Craig.

"What do you mean?"

"If he's a killer, sometimes they do. Nobody seems to know why, but they do. It's kind of a perverted record, like a notch in a gunfighter's gun for every person he's killed in a shootout."

"I've seen crazier things. What did you find?"

"We not only found the harmonica, but we also found some other musical instruments. From what we're seeing, Samuels doesn't seem like the kind of man who can play an instrument, although you never know."

"In the first four robberies, I don't recall musical instruments being listed on the items list. I'll have Lew, my office manager, do some checking. What else?"

"County animal control was brought in to remove the German Shepard Samuels had locked in his Nomad. The dog had to be restrained, but it was in good physical shape. One of the Marion County deputies remembered the animal as a service dog for the Woodburn Police. The dog had been retired. Samuels probably bought or stole him. The deputy knows the handler and will contact him."

"Service dogs are well trained and will only become aggressive when commanded to do so or to protect their territory," said Polanski.

"I suspect this one was just doing his job. He was trained to be a watchdog and that's what he did. It shouldn't be too much trouble to rehabilitate him. The deputies thought he would be alright. How's your officer?"

"Christine is doing very well. She's had a couple of surgeries, but she came through them well. The doctors say she'll need extensive therapy on her shoulder, but they expect her to make a full recovery."

"Will she stay with the force? It's never good when we lose an officer."

"I've been wounded before and know a few cops who've been shot. Everyone responds differently. It's never easy to come back. You must be sure. If you aren't, a moment of hesitation can get you, or someone else, killed. If you can move beyond it, then come back; if not, well, there are other ways to make a living."

"I hope she makes a full recovery. From what I've heard, she's one brave cop. We need people like her."

"We sure do. I'll let you get back to work. I'll be around if you need anything."

"Do you know what else Samuels might have been involved in?"

"Other than the burglaries and being part of a murder investigation in California, no, I don't. Why do you ask?"

"I don't know. This guy has been a criminal for some time. Maybe his whole life. Guys like that are always involved in far more than it seems. I think we'll take our time here. I have a gut feeling we might find something else."

"Wouldn't surprise me one bit. I'll be in touch," said Polanski.

Chapter 38

The next two weeks flew by. It was already the season midpoint and Charlie was satisfied that the Oaks were coming together as a team. The Oaks' record stood at three wins and three losses. After the tough loss against the Molalla Bucks, they lost a tight one to Oregon City. Then they lost to the Cubs in a lopsided game 7 to 2. They played well in every game, but inexperience, errors, and not getting hits with runners in scoring position were the reasons for the losses. Then, as sometimes happens, the Oaks started to gel. Eddie pitched a shutout against Whiskey Hill. Then Darnell, starting his second game, gave up a few hits, but a slick-fielding play by Jose on a sharply hit ground ball with the bases loaded prevented Mulino from scoring. The Oaks won on a double by Spud and a home run by Eddie. The Oaks pushed their record to five hundred with a win over Hubbard. The Oaks were set to start the second half of the season in a league where each team played the other teams twice.

Charlie was proud of the boys. Spud, Eddie, Tub, and Wags were the core players. But Jose, Darnell, and Dinky were becoming solid contributors. Kermit, Vic, Fox, Thumbs, and Doc each made significant contributions to the team.

Substitute catcher and left fielder, Stuart "Thumbs" Dean was seriously injured the previous winter in a calf roping accident. The boys thought Thumbs was an appropriate nickname after he lost his right thumb when he tried to dally a rope around his saddle horn in a team roping event. His thumb, pinched between the rope and the saddle horn, was ripped off when the calf bolted unexpectantly. Excluding his missing thumb, Thumbs was ready to play. Short of stature and tough as nails, Charlie played Thumbs as a substitute left fielder because he was still learning to grip the ball with four fingers and what remained of his thumb. Unable to swing the bat hard, Thumbs specialized in contact hitting. During his first game back, the Oaks were down one run to Mulino. Thumbs came to the plate with two outs and hit a "Texas Leaguer" between the shortstop and centerfielder. Thumb's bloop single scored the winning and go-ahead runs for the Oaks' win.

Larry "Doc" Rayburn was the youngest boy on the team. The son of a veterinarian, Larry got the nickname, Doc, because he told Thumbs his horse had colic after he noted the animal was restless, sweating profusely, and pawing at the ground. When Larry's dad confirmed the diagnosis, he became Doc. Freckle-faced and wiry, Doc filled in for Dinky at second. Against Whiskey Hill, Doc walked, stole second, and scored the winning run on a single by Darnell.

Charlie didn't want to get overconfident, but he felt sure the Oaks could be competitive with any team. Charlie had seen it before; when a team gets hot, they can be tough to beat.

Jose was quick and had the natural quickness to get to any grounder or fly ball. He could make plays at shortstop that most infielders on other teams could not. Against Mulino in a critical situation, Jose fielded a ball deep in the hole between third base and shortstop, and then threw the runner out. He had an accurate arm and it was getting stronger. Jose was also a good teammate. He never said anything negative about the other players and had a good attitude whether the team was winning or losing. Jose Lopez loved being part of the team as much as he loved to play the game.

Darnell had a way to go when it came to hitting, but as a pitcher, he was quickly becoming one of the better ones in the league. Eddie was still the number one pitcher on the team, but Darnell was almost as good and still improving. The Oaks were much stronger as a team with two excellent pitchers. Charlie marveled at how calm Darnell was, even when he gave up a few hits or runs. Darnell was tough and determined. If Darnell or Eddie had a bad game, Charlie could go to Vic Cooper, their left-handed centerfielder. Vic didn't throw too hard, but he was a left-hander and had natural movement on the ball. Better yet, Vic threw the ball over the plate. Another option was Tub Adams. Tub was wild. Most of the batters were afraid of getting hit and they often swung at balls way out of the strike zone.

Spud described Tub as a pitcher. He said, "Tub wasn't fast, but deadly."

Charlie worked with Tub on his accuracy, but quickly realized that Tub liked being wild. Tub relished scaring hitters. To his delight, one batter peed his wool pants while another, after Tub sailed the ball over his head, ran back to the dugout. Tub didn't scare everyone. Called in to relieve Darnell against the Oregon City Rangers, Tub faced their cleanup hitter, a kid named Louie who had a head the size of a basketball, a stomach big enough to devour two large pizzas, and three long whiskers protruding from his chin. Tub wasn't concerned about Louie's size but was intimidated by the three straggly whiskers, each about three inches long. The whiskers were beyond his imagination. Unnerved, Tub threw the ball down the center of the plate. Louie hit the ball so far over Vic's head in center field that by the time he retrieved the ball, the extremely slow Louie had circled the bases for a home run. Tub was stunned. As Charlie yelled for him to backup home plate, all Tub could do was watch Louie round the bases. Charlie called in Vic to relieve Tub.

There was still a long way to go, but Charlie, against his better judgment, started to think about making it to the playoffs. He was about to learn a big lesson.

Chapter 39

"How is Officer Walker?" asked Nell.

"She'll be fine. It'll take a few months for her shoulder to mend, but the doctors say she'll make a full recovery," answered Polanski.

"That's wonderful news. And that man Nance?"

"He's back in California. Detective John Ross said a grand jury has convened and they are about ready to issue indictments. He said the district attorney and the police have built a good case against the brother-in-law."

"So, the brother-in-law did it?"

Polanski leaned against his cruiser and took a drink of water. "It looks that way. Although, they'll have to convict him, it might take some time, but Nance is off the hook."

"Did the sister and brother-in-law sell the newspaper?"

"Ross said no. He wasn't sure what happened, but Marsh's wife retained control and took over. She blocked the sale."

"They killed her brother for nothing?"

"There was more to it than that. Besides owing the mob money, Taylor was jealous of Marsh. They hated each other."

"So much for a loving family."

"The two serpent heads, greed and jealousy, have struck again."

"Poor Nance. It sounds like the man went through hell," said Nell.

"He sure did, and almost got killed too. It turned out good. Have you seen the boys today?"

"There were a few boys in here earlier buying sodas. Big game this week."

"They're playing the Cubs. It's all over town. The Oaks have won three straight games. Charlie has them playing good baseball. Why do you want to see them?"

"Oh, I never had a chance to thank the Dempsey and Stump boys for helping Christine. Nance told me they were on the scene before he was. It takes some brave boys to do what they did. I wanted to thank them."

"They might still be at the field. The boys were helping Charlie get the field ready for the big game. Oh, I'm moving ahead with tearing the old community center building down. I'm moving ahead with my plan to build a warehouse and office. It's time that building came down."

"What about the ghost?"

"I guess Mary Ann will have to find a new place to play."

"When does this happen?"

"I'll wait until the baseball season is over and then have it done. If I did it now, there would be too much of a mess."

"What happens to the baseball field?"

"I haven't decided yet. If there are enough boys to field a team, I will keep it."

"The boys are having fun. Why wouldn't they play together again?"

"Charlie said it depends on how many boys want to play. We may not have enough kids. He thinks between the Oaks, Cubs, and Whiskey Hill, they might have the nucleus of a team to beat anybody in the state."

"It's a good group of kids. It won't be long before they're in high school. If they stick with it, and if I'm still around, I'll be watching them."

"Where are you going?"

"No place directly, but I've been a cop for a long time. It might be time to let the younger people run things. I wouldn't mind doing some traveling. I think Arizona sounds awful good during Oregon's long wet winter months. Sunshine just makes the joints work better."

"I just might take you up on that offer."

Polanski smiled, knowing he didn't offer anything. "What about the store?"

"It's time to sell it. Running the store, tavern, and egg processing plant is way too much."

"I don't think the folks around here will be happy with that. You're a thread that holds this community together."

"But material gets old, and like you say, it might be time for the young folks to run things. Rebecca has decided to go to law school at Stanford. She might come back, but not to run the store. If she wants to, I'll step aside and let her run things. If not, after a few more years I'll sell everything."

"I could always use a traveling partner."

"You didn't think I was going to let you have all the fun, did you?"

"Where should we go first?"

Chapter 40

"It was the curse," speculated Kermit.

"How do you know that?" asked Tub.

"First, the policewoman was shot. Then we lost to Molalla on a fluke play," said Kermit.

"The ball just happened to hit a rock," he said, picking up a rock about the size of a filbert.

"How could a rock that size send the ball over your mitt and into left field? It doesn't make sense. It's too small," said Eddie.

"Like I said, we got the whammy. It's Carl telling us to solve the mystery of Medora," said Kermit.

"Oh, boy. Here we go again. We won other games and there was no curse. I've never heard Carl whistle so he ain't even watching," Tub countered.

"Just because he hasn't whistled, doesn't mean Carl ain't there. When you don't expect it and everything is going well, a jinx jumps up and bites you. That's the way a curse works. Happened to the Boston Red Sox after they traded Babe Ruth to the Yankees. They haven't won a championship since. How about the Chicago Cubs? They haven't won a

World Series since they insulted the pet goat of a tavern owner and he put a curse on them. Like Mr. Nance told us, 'there are curses in baseball,'" replied Kermit.

"We don't need Carl against us," said Eddie as he raked the dirt around third base.

"I spit on my bat before every game," added Spud. "I ain't superstitious, but I also ain't takin' any chances of a slump."

"I haven't changed my baseball socks all year. I'm afraid if I do, I'll jinx the team," said Wags as he pulled a weed and tossed it into the outfield. "My mom almost washed them. She said they stunk and wouldn't let me bring them into the house. She made me hang them on a clothesline outside. I'm not washing them until we win the championship."

"My mom won't let me bring my dirty uniform into the house. She makes me take it off in the washroom," said Darnell.

"My dad said he never washed his baseball pants all through high school," said Eddie.

Darnell nodded his head up and down, "After I heard what Mr. Nance said, I started jumping over the foul line. I saw a major leaguer do it. I don't know if I'm superstitious but I ain't takin' any chances, especially when I'm pitching. Charlie said when he pitched, he never changed his routine."

Tub threw his hands up. "You're all nuts."

"I saw you spit on your glove," said Kermit.

"Every infielder spits on his glove," said Dinky.

"I spit in my catcher's mitt and grease it to keep the leather soft.

Makes the ball easier to catch. Leather gets dry and the ball slips out," said Spud as he picked up his mitt and threw a ball into the sweet spot.

"I pee on my mitt. Brings me luck," said Tub.

"I thought I smelled something. It was you who smelled like piss," Spud said.

"Who pees on a mitt? I thought you said you weren't superstitious?" asked Kermit.

"I thought his underwear was dirty," said Darnell.

"Shut up, Darnell. You always stink," said the defensive Tub.

Darnell dropped his rake and jumped in front of Tub to confront him. He looked him in the eyes and said, "What's that supposed to mean?"

"You heard what I said."

"You saying I stink?"

"Yeah, you stink."

"You think I'm dirty because I'm black."

"You said I stunk because I wear dirty underwear. You called me dirty first."

"Just because you smelled like piss. How was I supposed to know you peed on your mitt? I didn't call you dirty. You called me dirty. Now take it back."

"You think you can take me? Go ahead and try," Tub replied, throwing his chest against Darnell's.

Darnell took a step forward and pushed back. Darnell suspected that Tub was resentful because he was on the team. His anger had bubbled to the surface. Teammates teased, but Tub had gone too far. He had disrespected him.

"I don't like you talkin' about black people. You want to fight, we'll fight, but I ain't listenin' to you talk bad about me. I ain't dirty. I think you stink; not your mitt."

Tub stepped back and then charged Darnell. Darnell sidestepped and grabbed Tub around the neck. Rotating his hips, he threw Tub to the ground. Tub rolled and got on top of Darnell. Darnell rolled back on top of Tub. Some of the boys watched, not knowing what to do while others thought Darnell and Tub should get what was bugging them out of their systems.

"I knew this was going to happen," said Eddie.

"What should we do?" Dinky asked.

"Let them get it out. It'll clear things up," said Spud.

"Tub's got it coming," said Wags. "He's been mouthing off for too long. He took the Cubs side in the big brawl."

Tub wrapped his arms around Darnell's waist and squeezed. Darnell held Tub's head in an armlock and pounded his head with his fist.

Darnell squeezed tighter, "You had enough?"

"I'm just gettin' started," said Tub.

"What's going on here," demanded Charlie. "That'll be enough boys," he said.

"He started it," said Darnell. "He said I stunk."

"I did not. You said I smelled like piss."

"You said I was dirty 'cause I'm black. That's what you meant."

"Okay, enough. Now get up. What's the matter with you two? You're teammates. We've got a big game coming up and you're fighting."

"He doesn't like me 'cause I'm black. I don't care about that, but he ain't gonna disrespect me. I've let him get away with it long enough. He wants to fight, it's okay with me."

Tub was quiet, never expecting to be challenged.

"What's going on here," demanded Barbara Washington.

"Nothing, mom," said Darnell.

"Young man, you know fighting is not allowed in this family. Now you get your mitt and get into the car. Your father will be home tonight. You'll have to explain yourself to him."

Charlie wisely kept quiet, realizing how upset Barbara was.

"He said I was dirty and stunk," said Darnell pointing at Tub.

"You fight over that? You know what your father will say. Now, young man, you get into the car. Charlie, I'm sorry, but this is unacceptable. You're the coach; you can't let this happen."

Charlie didn't argue the point. It was his team and he was responsible. "I'm sorry Mrs. Washington. I didn't see this coming. Boys will be boys, but this should have never happened."

"I think you'll have to talk to my husband. I'm not sure how he'll take this, but he has a strict rule about fighting."

"Let me sort this out and I'll come and talk to him," said Charlie.

Charlie had witnessed enough fights between teammates to know sometimes brothers fought. What he couldn't allow were the racial undertones. There was no place for it on his team. If Tub was the instigator, keeping him on the team could be difficult. Kicking him off the team could backfire and cause him to be resentful of Darnell. The other question was Steve Adams; where would he fall on the matter? Had he said something to Tub about Jose and Darnell being on the team? If he had, then having an instigator around may make repairing the damage difficult. Suddenly, there was a threat to the team, and it wasn't on the field. That the fight happened right before the biggest game of the year made him wonder if the curse was real. Curse or not, he was potentially going to lose two key players. If he did, he would pull the team together and go on, but realistically, the chances of beating the Rangers or the Cubs or winning the championship had just flown into the potato field in left.

Chapter 41

Charlie was still a bit stunned as he picked up the remaining equipment. Not because Darnell and Tub got into a fight—that sometimes happened between little and big leaguers—but because he might lose both players.

Polanski parked next to Charlie's pickup truck.

"Well, coach, how's the team doing?"

"Good afternoon Chief Polanski. Right now, not so good."

Polanski noted that the boys were sitting on the bench with their heads down.

"What happened?"

"Couple of the boys got into a fight. Things were said, and, well, you know how that goes."

"Boys will be boys. I hope it's nothing too serious."

"I'm afraid it might be. The fight was between Darnell Washington and Tub Adams."

Polanski tilted his head as if he knew what might have happened. "Did one of the boys say something?" Polanski didn't like to assume anything, but his experience was that if there was an issue between the races, a slur often started it.

"I'm afraid so. They exchanged insults. Darnell took offense to what Tub said. It's been coming for some time. Even young boys know when they're not shown respect. Darnell and I talked about how to handle spectators from other teams. I told him that some fools might make a derogatory comment. There's always that one person willing to say something just to throw off your game. If it happened, I told him to ignore it. But from experience, I know that is far easier said than done."

Polanski picked up a bat and put it into the equipment bag, "Ignoring it, depending on what is said, can be very hard for anybody at any age."

"I talked to the boys. These are good boys and they get along well, but you never know. I just hoped it would never happen. I talked to the team about respecting other players and thought that was enough. I guess it wasn't. Now I worry about how Ed Washington will take it," said Charlie.

"Don't be too hard on yourself. Sometimes it's better to get these things out in the open," counseled Polanski.

"Maybe, but we may have lost Darnell. His parents may not let him play. They do not allow fighting. I know when they say something, they mean it. I'm not sure about Tub and his parents either. Tub will have to change. I'll go see Steve. I can't have this on the team. I don't care if we win another game; the boys have to learn from this."

"Do you want me to talk to them?"

"Thanks, but I don't think that's necessary. Let's just see what happens."

"How are the rest of the boys taking it?"

"They know how Tub is and they like Darnell. If I was going to guess, I'm guessing they're on Darnell's side. That's good because it shows they know the difference between right and wrong. It might also mean they know Tub can be mouthy."

"How about the game this Saturday?"

"The boys are looking forward to it. I just hope this is all settled by that time."

"I did come here for a reason. I came to talk to the Stump and Dempsey boys. They did a very brave thing when they helped Officer Walker."

Charlie pointed in the direction of the baseball field. "They were brave boys. Go ahead. It might be a good distraction."

Polanski nodded as if to say everything would work out. As he walked toward the field, he heard the boys talking.

"My dad said they're going to tear down the meeting hall," said Kermit.

"What happens to Medora?" asked Spud.

"She won't have the stage to play on. Maybe she goes away," said Eddie.

Throwing a baseball into his mitt, Kermit added, "Ghosts don't go away; they just kinda hang around until they get what they want. Then we might have a problem."

"What?" asked Eddie.

"Hi boys," greeted Polanski.

"Hi Chief Polanski," said Eddie. He knew Polanski better than the other boys because his parents' hardware store was just down the street from the police station. His dad and Chief Polanski worked with other

There's Money on the Edge

business owners to prevent shoplifting and other crimes. Following Eddie's lead, the other boys said hello or raised a hand in greeting.

"Are you boys ready for the big game on Saturday?"

Without saying much, they all nodded in agreement.

"What's this I hear about a ghost?" Polanski asked in jest.

"We saw her," said Eddie.

"She was on the stage," added Kermit.

"Tub thinks it was the wind, but we saw her. We named her Medora," said Kermit.

"Well, I'm sure Medora would have liked that."

"Chief Polanski, what happens if they tear down the building?" asked Spud.

"Yeah, what happens to Medora? She loses her home," said Wags with a concerned look.

"I'm sure she'll be alright," soothed Polanski.

"She won't have a place to play," said Spud.

"Place to play?" asked Polanski to clarify.

Kermit pointed toward the meeting hall, "You know, there won't be a stage for her to play the flute."

"Play the flute?" quizzed Polanski.

"When the moon is up. The reflection from the sun shines on the meeting hall stage. Medora sits on the stage and plays the flute until the reflection is gone," Eddie explained.

"Interesting," said Polanski.

"She's pretty good. Tub thought it was the wind, but it sounded like a flute to me," said Spud.

"Well, I guess it makes sense," Polanski theorized. "The bride's name was Mary Ann. She was going to get her flute when she disappeared."

Polanski gave the boys a summary of what happened on Mary Ann's wedding day without going into too many details. The boys listened intently. Odell told them a bride had disappeared but didn't tell them about her flute. They also didn't know her real name was Mary Ann.

"I guess we should call Medora, Mary Ann. That's her real name," said Eddie.

"Maybe that's why she's playing the flute," said Kermit absently. "Maybe she lost it and wants it back."

"That doesn't make any sense," said Spud. "If she lost her flute, how could she be playing it?"

"I've never seen her flute; it just sounds like one," said Eddie.

"Come to think of it, I've never seen it either," added Spud.

Kermit jumped up. "She could be trying to tell us something."

"Like what?" asked Spud.

Out of nervous tension or to pass the time, Wags tossed the baseball into the air and caught it with his mitt. "Ghosts scare you. Since when do they try to communicate with living people?"

"Casper does," said Spud.

"That's a cartoon. In real life, ghosts just scare you. It's their job," said Vic.

Polanski listened, slightly amused. It was always surprising how intelligent boys and girls could be at a young age. Ghosts. Well, he thought, the boys would have a story to go with memories of the baseball season. They would almost certainly remember the ghost as much as they would about playing baseball. Later, when he looked back on it, he couldn't remember what one of the boys said or which part of the conversation it was, but suddenly, what they said registered. The boys may have just solved a "cold case" and helped make sense of a mystery that had eluded authorities for twenty years. It was a longshot, but he knew that sometimes that's what it took to catch a killer. After thanking Spud and Eddie again and saying goodbye to the boys, he rushed to his cruiser and called Lew.

Chapter 42

Charlie was nervous. After the incident between Darnell and Tub he hadn't talked to either Steve Adams or Ed Washington. His first stop was the Washingtons. He had called ahead to ensure Ed would be home. Barbara didn't sound happy, an indication of what he might face when he arrived. On reflection, he wished he had been more forceful with the two boys, and for that matter, the whole team. He felt responsible and, in many respects, he was. Tub was Tub. He'd grown up with boys like him. They said things to get attention, and often what they said caused problems, or as happened with Darnell, fights. Boys learned early that saying the wrong things had consequences. Tub was also like his friend, Tommy Walls, a bit of a bully. Was this racial, Tub being a bully, or a good bit of both? Charlie wasn't sure, but he was sure of one thing; in relation to the Oaks, it stopped now. Baseball was now secondary. Now all he hoped to do was the right thing for Darnell and Tub. Baseball, like other sports, served the important social function of putting boys and girls together, not pushing them apart.

As he drove up to the Washington house, he noted a car that looked familiar but one he couldn't immediately place. He parked behind the black Chevrolet sedan and took a deep breath.

He shook his head and said silently, "And I thought coaching would be easy."

He slowly pushed the door of his Chevrolet pickup truck open and walked to the front porch. There was talking inside and he hoped he wasn't interrupting anything. He knocked on the door. At first there was no answer, then Barbara opened the door with an unexpected smile on her face.

"Hello, Charlie. Come in," she said.

"I hope I'm not interrupting anything," Charlie said, questioning why he had come.

Barbara could tell Charlie was on edge and she replied evenly, "Oh no, you're just in time."

Just in time? For what? He wondered. He stepped through the threshold. To his surprise, sitting in the living room on the couch were Steve and Tub Adams. Across the room were Darnell and Ed.

"Welcome," Ed said, extending his hand.

Charlie shook it but didn't respond. He was still at a loss for words. He relaxed but was a bit confused.

Somewhat dumbfounded, before he could respond, Ed said, "Mr. Adams and Tub have come for a visit."

"I can see that," said Charlie. "I hope everything is resolved."

"We don't know if it's resolved, but Tub and I thought it was time to sit down with Mr. Washington and Darnell to apologize. What Tub said was offensive. We do not say those things in our family."

Ed held up his hand. "And we apologized to Steve and Tub for what Darnell said. We have a rule against fighting. Darnell broke that rule and will have to be punished."

Charlie didn't necessarily agree with the non-fighting rule because there were times when there was no alternative, but he did understand the message Ed was trying to send. When Ed said punishment, Charlie hesitated, sure that he would have to make the argument that both boys should continue to play on the team.

Charlie took the highroad, "Sometimes teammates have disagreements. They unknowingly say things that hurt or are offensive. Although fighting is never the solution, it's good to get things out in the open. Then we can learn from our mistakes."

"Darnell made no mistakes here," said Steve Adams. "I agree with you that sometimes people say the wrong things or make comments they don't mean. I've done it and have regretted it. Tub needs to be careful about what he says. I'm hopeful he'll think twice before making another offensive comment, especially to someone that's a teammate and he considers a friend."

"Why don't you boys go outside and play catch for a few minutes and let the adults talk," suggested Ed.

Relieved, Darnell and Tub quickly stood up and rushed out the front door.

"I hope the boys will be able to play the remainder of the season," Charlie said, more as a question than as a statement.

"Darnell was wrong, but I think taking him off the team will do more harm than good. No, his punishment will be a good talking to and additional chores."

"That's really good news. He's come such a long way in a short amount of time. He's become a key part of the team and has become a very good ballplayer," Charlie said with enthusiasm.

"I've never seen my son happier. To take baseball away would almost devastate him. I was wrong not to let him play earlier and I don't want to make the same mistake."

Charlie's respect for Ed Washington as a parent and as a man continued to grow. Relieved, he turned his attention to Steve Adams.

"I know. I should do the same thing for Tub, but it's a bit more complicated. This isn't the first time Tub has gotten into trouble because of what he's said to another kid. He was almost expelled at the end of the school year for fighting. He has to learn that his behavior is unacceptable. It's my opinion that you have to discipline early. If you don't, you'll pay for it when the child gets older. Tub has to be punished for this."

Charlie held his breath. He expected the worst.

Steve Adams leaned back on the sofa. "I too believe that taking Tub off the team would be counterproductive. As a kid, I'm afraid he might blame Darnell for what is his responsibility. I also feel responsible for his actions. I don't think we are a racist family, but after what has happened this summer, I'm going to rethink how I approach things. I certainly could have been more tolerant of Darnell and Jose joining the team. I will make it a point to try understanding what people of race face. I apologize and intend to do better. So, what to do for punishment?"

"Whatever you decide. I think the boys have learned from having each other as teammates. What the team has been through this summer has brought them closer together. They've had experiences that will last a lifetime," said Charlie.

"Ah, the beauty of sports," said Ed.

"If it's okay with you, Ed, I think I'll let Tub play."

"I don't really see this as my decision, but seeing the boys interact today, well, I think they crossed a barrier that some people are never able to do. You," Ed said to Steve, "coming to my house today shows that you are a man who does the right thing. It takes guts to apologize, and more guts to change."

Steve extended his hand, "Ed, I hope this doesn't sound artificial, but it's my desire that we can become friends."

Ed extended his hand and Steve shook it.

Steve turned to Charlie. "I think Tub has to miss the next game. He can be part of the team, but he can't play. Keeping him away from the game in some respects is easier on him. Being with the team and not playing sends a stronger message. Missing a game and doing additional chores for what he said are his punishments."

Charlie nodded in agreement. Winning the next game without Tub would be difficult, but what Steve Adams was trying to do was far more important. As he left the Washington house, Charlie considered the outcome. A disaster had been averted. In some respects, it couldn't have gone any better. Now all he had to do was bring the team together and figure out how to win the games against the Cubs and Rangers.

Chapter 43

Polanski called David Craig of the crime lab to meet him at Samuels' trailer house. Luckily, Craig was at the scene, having returned to gather additional evidence. The army of police, county, and state vehicles were long gone. The area was still roped off. The only indication that a few days before the place was a beehive of activity was the large pile of trash sitting next to the trailer house. Most of the evidence Craig and his team recovered had been carted away. Polanski could tell that the evidence collection had been very thorough. He made his way to the trailer house where Craig was busy at work.

Craig was focused on inspecting a hunting knife with a rusty the blade. "Chief Polanski," he motioned with a raised hand.

"Interesting piece of evidence," said Polanski looking at the knife.

"We found it at the bottom of a toolbox. At first, we didn't think much of it, but then one of the technicians noted a trace of blood where the blade connects to the handle."

"Human or animal blood?" asked Polanski.

"We won't know for sure until we do some further analysis. Samuels was a hunter and it's a good bet he used the knife for skinning."

"That makes sense."

"What doesn't is where we found the knife. Why would he bury the knife at the bottom of a toolbox? Probably nothing to it, but it does seem odd. I would think a hunter would keep his skinning knife with his hunting gear or some other place where there was easy access. This was buried, like he was hiding it. Like I said, there may be nothing to it, but it's worth a closer look."

"Especially since the murder in Sacramento involved a knife. If it's the knife Samuels used, it will be the damning piece of missing evidence."

"We've been in contact with the authorities in Sacramento. They never found the weapon, and like you say, it's the final piece of evidence that will close the loop on one Ronnie Samuels. We should know in a few days."

"Keep me posted. Now for the reason why I came back out here. I remember you mentioned there were other musical instruments. Besides the harmonica, what did you find?"

"An old guitar and a flute. The guitar didn't have strings and the flute was rusted and pitted. Both look to be very old. Why do you ask?"

"It's an old case. Years ago, a bride disappeared on her wedding day. Right before she was to be married, she went home to get her flute. She had decided to play at her wedding. The bride's body was never found. Her flute was never found either."

"Do you think Samuels was involved?"

"I have a theory. When Samuels was young, he worked for his uncle. I'm betting he was here at the same time the bride disappeared. Then he got involved in the theft ring and spent time in the Oregon pen. After he got out, he went to California and then came back after he murdered Marsh. His uncle had died, so Samuels took over the garage. If this is the knife that he used to kill Marsh, he could have brought it with him. Like the harmonica and flute, it could be a kind of weird trophy."

"Boy, you got me. Why would he keep them unless he wasn't at all worried about being a suspect? It's hard to believe he kept both items."

Polanski continued to theorize, "He may have intended to dispose of them but got sloppy or just forgot them. I don't know and it doesn't matter now. If we can link the flute to the bride, then we may have solved a cold case."

Craig tossed his clipboard onto the table and took his glasses off. While cleaning them, he said, "The flute is in the trailer laying on the table next to the guitar. We didn't think they were important and left them here. They are both tagged."

"Okay if I take the flute?" asked Polanski.

"Fine by me. Just sign the evidence sheet. The investigation may go on for a while and we need to make sure we keep track of things."

"I'll bring it back to you. I want to show the flute to the woman's sister."

"Good luck."

"Sometimes that's what it takes."

Polanski guessed Misty Arnold to be in her mid-forties. She was plump, but not fat, had silky shoulder-length black hair, and cheeks that he imagined could flush red if she were angered. Her eyes darted from Polanski to one of her four children ranging in age from, he guessed, ten to fifteen. The younger boy and girl politely kept quiet while the older children shook his hand. They went back to their homework while eating apple slices and pieces of cheese.

Misty motioned for Polanski to follow her into the living room. There were pillows arranged on the back of the sofa and matching chair. They were fluffed and placed strategically in the corners. One pillow was propped up in the center of the couch. He guessed the living room was Misty's show piece. He suspected the living room was off-limits to the children to keep it clean and organized for guests. It was also a conundrum for him. He never felt comfortable sitting on a couch that screamed, *don't sit on me!*

"Mr. Polanski, please have a seat," Misty offered with an open hand.

"Call me Joe," Polanski responded, thinking mister was a bit too formal and made him sound old.

"Okay, Joe. Now, what can I do for you?"

"I'm here to talk about your sister."

"I kind of figured this was about Mary Ann. I didn't think this was about my kids. They aren't perfect, but they don't cause too much trouble. My husband doesn't cause too much trouble either, but he's away on a business trip."

"We might have some new evidence that may shed light on what happened to Mary Ann."

"You know, after all these years, I still think of her and that terrible day. A day that should have been one of the happiest of her life, wasn't. It was a terrible tragedy."

"She was your older sister?"

"Yes, by three years. I was her maid-of-honor. To this day, I don't know why she decided at the last minute to go home and get her flute. I guess it was just fate."

"I have a theory of what may have happened."

"A theory?"

"At this point, yes."

"There have been so many. My parents went to their graves tormented about what may have happened. As much as possible, I, along with my brother, try to put theories out of our minds. They're just too hard to think about."

"I know, and I apologize. I wouldn't trouble you unless I thought this one had some merit."

"Then I'm all ears," Misty said straightening her back.

"I think you heard that one of my deputies was shot while making a routine traffic stop."

"Yes, I did. I hope she's going to be alright."

"Yes. Doctors say she'll make a full recovery. It turns out the routine traffic stop may be the huge break we needed. After Christine, Officer Walker, was shot, we tracked a suspect to Aurora. After confronting him, he was killed."

"I have no sympathy for criminals who shoot at cops or anybody else," Misty said, her tone determined and uncompromising.

"Unfortunately, they're out there. The suspect had a long record of criminal activity. Primary among his crimes was theft. For that, he spent time in prison."

"I read about him in the Canby Herald and the Oregonian. I don't like to see anybody get hurt or killed, but it's good he's off the streets."

"Samuels was a hardened criminal. He was involved in several robberies around Lone Elder. He had just committed one when Officer Walker stopped him."

"The paper was inconclusive about that. So he was the thief?"

"After he was killed, detectives from the state crime lab did a thorough investigation of his trailer house. They found a few interesting items linking him to the robberies. During the investigation, we found an old flute."

"Really?" asked Misty with heightened interest.

"That's where my theory comes in."

"Was it him?"

"I think so. What I think happened was that your sister interrupted a robbery. I think Samuels had cased your parents' farm and planned to rob it while the family was at the wedding. This was not about Mary Ann until she showed up for her flute. It was just a tragic case of bad timing. My guess is Samuels killed her because she could identify him."

Misty held her breath, "Are you kidding? This was all about a robbery? But nothing was taken."

"Mary Ann must have surprised Samuels before he had a chance to take anything. He may have panicked. I don't know."

"Unbelievable."

"What's more surprising is that Samuels kept the flute," Polanski said as he reached into his briefcase and pulled out the flute he had wrapped in a plastic bag.

He took the flute out of the bag, carefully holding it on the ends. He was careful not to smear any fingerprints. The chance of lifting an old fingerprint on the round surface was small but he still proceeded with caution. He leaned forward to enable Misty to inspect the flute.

Misty took a deep breath and held it, "That's hers. That's Mary Ann's."

"Are you sure? Don't you want to take a closer look?"

"I don't have to. I know that's hers. It's a side-blown flute like you see in symphony orchestras. My dad always dreamed of us, especially Mary Ann, playing in one. She was very good. Her music teacher at school said she was as good as any player she'd ever heard."

"There are millions of flutes. What distinguishing marks tell you it's your sister's?"

"You see that small dent by the embouchure hole?"

Polanski shrugged with a confused look on his face. "The what?"

"There on top. It's the hole where the flutist blows air through the tube. There's a small dent."

On closer inspection, Polanski found the embouchure hole and dent. "I see it."

"You'll also find the manufacturer's name near the head joint. The manufacturer is Haynes. We had an uncle who lived in Boston and he worked for the William S. Haynes Flute Company. He gave the flute to my sister."

Polanski shook his head. Everything Misty described about the physical characteristics of the flute was true. Now he was certain that he held in his hands Mary Ann's long-lost flute.

"For the official record, I'll need a statement of what you just told me."

"I'll do whatever is necessary. You really think this Samuels is my sister's killer?"

"I do. It makes too much sense. He was a thief and he killed Mary Ann so she couldn't identify him."

"If you found the flute at his residence, do you think that might be where my sister is buried?"

"That I don't know, but since you've identified the flute, there might be a possibility that he could have buried her there. I'll guarantee you one thing; we'll dig the place up to find out."

Chapter 44

The Oaks needed a spark. After the Cubs scored two runs in the first inning and two more in the fourth, the boys had suffered two hard gut punches. Charlie heard somebody behind him say the four-run lead was too tall a task to overcome. But he knew the Oaks. They would never quit. In the bottom of the fourth, Jose's hard-hit ground ball off Tommy Walls scooted past the shortstop and rolled under the centerfielder's glove for a double. It was a blow to Walls who had boasted he would strike out every Oaks' hitter. With Jose on second, Spud hit a soft liner into right field. Jose scored. Getting two hits and a run was the spark Charlie was hoping for. It was a small victory, but the Oaks were still down three runs. Then Eddie stepped up to the plate and on a two-strike and one ball count, hit a towering home run that landed deep among the potatoes in right-centerfield.

Tommy Walls ripped off his hat and threw it on the ground. "You're lucky," he said.

Eddie walked to the bench, slapping the hands of each teammate who had lined up to congratulate him.

An angry Walls said, "If this cow pasture of a field had a fence that would have only been a double."

"Hey, Walls," said Tub who had to sit out the game. "If there was a fence, that ball would have sailed over it by a mile."

"It doesn't matter. We've still got you by a run," jabbed Walls. "You ain't getting any more."

Walls struck out Vic to end the fourth. The score: Cubs 4—Oaks 3.

Charlie had a decision to make. Eddie had pitched the first three innings and had given up two runs on successive errors. Wags substituting for Tub, threw the ball over Darnell's outstretched arm on a slow roller up the third base line. The runner ended up on third base and scored when the next batter hit a flyball to Kermit in right field. Kermit misjudged the popup, allowing the ball to drop in for a hit. The runner went to second when Kermit threw the baseball to home rather than to the cutoff man at second. On the throw, the Cub's runner advanced. It was a mistake Kermit rarely made. Charlie had drilled into the outfielders' heads the necessity of throwing in front of the runners to keep them from advancing into scoring position. Hit the cutoff man, he preached. It was a basic rule of defensive baseball that many major leaguers fail to comply with. Some of it was lack of basic baseball instinct and some of it was nothing more than ego. As Charlie had learned, powerful arms were good if they were supported by sound fundamentals.

The second run was on an infield hit. It was a tough play to Dinky's right. With two outs, the runner was going on the pitch and had rounded third base before Dinky got to the ball. He stopped the ball but had no chance of throwing the runner out at home.

There's Money on the Edge

Charlie made a pitching change and brought in Darnell. Unlike many coaches, Charlie kept track of pitch counts. He allowed Eddie, Darnell, and his relievers to only throw a certain number of pitches per week. He did it because when he was young some of his youth coaches often made him pitch every game. Luckily, he hadn't developed any arm trouble from the experience, but knew of many other pitchers whose careers were cut short because of arm injuries caused by overuse. Not only was he protecting their arms, but he was saving Eddie and Darnell because he wanted them strong for the rest of the season. Naturally, he hoped the Oaks would make it to the championship game, which was still a long shot. First, they had to beat the Cubs.

It was the sixth and final inning. The heart of the Cubs' lineup was coming to the plate. Charlie was going to bring in Ron Fox, the lefty, but decided to let Darnell pitch to the clean-up hitter, Tommy Walls. Charlie knew Darnell wanted to face Walls after he hit a home run off him in the first game they played at the start of the season. The Cubs had won the game handily.

Darnell looked in at Spud for the sign. Spud gave him the standard one finger signal to throw a fastball. Darnell shook him off. Spud, a bit confused, called timeout and ran to the mound.

"What's the matter?" asked Spud. "Didn't you see the sign?"

"I saw it, Spud. The last time I pitched to Walls, he hit my fastball for a home run."

"I know that, but that's the only pitch you have. Don't throw it down the middle. Hit the edges like Charlie said. Your fastball is a lot faster than it was. You hit the corners and Walls will never be able to hit it."

"Yeah, but I've been working on a change-up. I'm gonna fool him."

Spud was skeptical, "When were you going to tell me about this pitch? You've never thrown a change-up. A big game is a heck of a time to try it."

"I've been working on it at home."

"Practice would have been a good time to try it."

"Just once. I know he's gonna expect my fastball. We've got to confuse him."

"Walls ain't smart enough to confuse."

"Okay, boys, let's go," said the umpire, a man with a red face and bald head he covered with what looked like a black beanie cap without the propeller.

"Let me throw it one time. It's gonna drop, so be ready."

"Does coach know about this pitch?"

"Nope. Like I said, I've been working on it at home. I saved it for Walls."

Spud looked at Darnell and then took his catcher's mitt and tapped him on the chest. "Let's get him. I'm gonna put down one finger in case Walls sneaks a peak. Throw it on the first pitch. Then we throw a fastball. I'll give you two fingers for the change-up after that, if it works."

Darnell waited until Spud was set. He took the sign. As Spud thought he might, Walls tried to steal the sign.

"Why you lookin' at me?" asked Spud.

"I ain't. I can look where I want."

"Boys, play ball," said the ump.

Darnell held the baseball in the space between his index finger and thumb. He tucked it in tight and gripped the ball around the center. As he had practiced, his motion had to look to the batter like he was throwing a fastball. He couldn't rush the pitch. If he did, the ball would land too far in front of home plate. If the ball did that, Walls would have enough time to react and not swing. No, he had to relax and extend his arm. He wanted the ball to break down right before home plate and drop into the dirt. If it worked Walls would think it was a fastball and be way out in front of the pitch. Darnell wound, and in a fluid-motion, released the ball. Walls caulked the bat to take a mighty cut. It looked like a fastball right down the gut. Confident, Walls stepped toward the mound with his front foot. Then he knew. He was way too early. He watched as the ball spun and seemed to float. Fooled badly and off-balance, he lunged. In a futile attempt, he threw the barrel of the bat at the ball as it bounced in front of home plate and into Spud's mitt.

"Strike one," bellowed the umpire.

"What a pitch," yelled Eddie from first. "Great pitch, Darnell."

Darnell held his smile back. It had worked, but there was still work to be done. Walls was a dangerous hitter, but the self-assured Walls no longer appeared so confident. Spud called for a fastball. Darnell missed the plate, but Walls took a wild swing and missed. He was way too late. The ball was in Spud's mitt before he completed his swing. Darnell was in Walls' head. He didn't know what pitch was coming next. Darnell had two strikes on him and watched as Walls dug in.

"He wants me to throw a fastball," Darnell whispered to himself.

Darnell waited for the sign. Spud gave him two fingers. He and Spud were on the same page. Darnell wound up and let loose with a change-up that was even better than the first one. Walls froze; his knees buckled. All he could do was watch as the ball broke over the plate.

"Strike three," yelled the umpire.

"That wasn't a strike," moaned Walls.

"Right over the plate, son. Too good to take."

"Hey, Walls. Like I said he would, Darnell struck you out. You owe me a buck," said Spud as he threw the ball back to Darnell.

"Good luck collecting on that bet," said Tommy as he turned and threw his helmet against the fence.

"Keep the money, Walls. It was worth it to see you strike out," said Spud as he put his catcher's mask back on.

"Coach. Get control of that player or he's out of the game," said the Umpire to Walls' father.

"That was a bad call, ump," said Mike Walls.

"Great pitch," retorted the umpire. "Play ball."

Charlie looked on in disbelief. "Time out," he said as he walked to the mound and motioned for Spud to join them. "What was that?"

"My change-up," said Darnell.

"I could see that. Since when do you have a change-up?"

"He does now. It's a beauty. It really spins," said Spud slapping his mitt.

Charlie smiled. "Well, it's a good pitch and, I guess, you can throw it.

Who taught you that pitch?"

"I learned it from that man who watches us sometimes."

"You mean Mr. Nance?"

"Yeah, Mr. Nance."

"Well, I'll be damned. No curve balls, but you can throw the change to keep them off-balance, but not too much. Stick with the fastball and work on hitting the edges. I'll be damned," Charlie said again as he scratched his head and walked back to the bench.

After that, Darnell struck out the final two Cubs hitters. The Oaks were up with the season on the line at the bottom of the last inning. It was the bottom of the order. Vic, Darnell, and Kermit. Vic walked on a three and two count. Darnell, now a proficient bunter, moved Vic to second on a perfect bunt to first. On a close play, he was thrown out. Kermit stepped to the plate.

"You can do it, Kermit," Charlie encouraged from third base.

Kermit looked at Walls. He knew from following professional baseball that pitchers got tired toward the later innings. The only problem was, Walls looked as strong as he had in the first inning. He could wait for a walk, but Walls had good control and threw strikes. Looking for a walk would surely mean that he would strike out. He also noted that the umpire recognized when the hitters just looked for a walk. If he thought they did, he expanded the strike zone. Kermit calculated that his best bet was to bunt. Bunting wasn't a part of batting that he did well, but neither was hitting. The first pitch was a fastball down the middle.

"Strike one," yelled the umpire in a loud voice that startled Kermit.

The next two pitches were in the dirt as Walls got a bit wild. The second pitch got past the catcher and Vic advanced to third.

"*Ducks on the pond*, Kermit. *Ducks on the pond*," said Charlie, clapping his hands.

Determined, Kermit twirled the bat. Walls smiled and held the ball out for Kermit to see. The implied challenge was, see if you can hit this. It was now or never. Walls wound and delivered the pitch. Kermit squared to bunt and then jumped back into the hitter's stance. He took a powerful swing. When Kermit squared to bunt, the first baseman, a tall skinny kid, with a goose-like neck and a toothy smile, took a step toward the plate. He was no longer set, his movement awkward. He tried to stop and stumbled backward. It was enough. Kermit made contact and hit a grounder. The ball hopped, then scooted, then danced as it dribbled between Goose's legs. Vic scored and Kermit, running as fast as a scared rabbit, stood safely on first base.

"The baseball gods are on our side today!" yelled Kermit.

Jose came to the plate. Walls was demoralized and walked Jose on four pitches. Wags followed with an infield hit to deep short, which the shortstop couldn't make a play on. Spud came to the plate with the bases loaded and one out. Walls quickly got ahead in the count; no balls and two strikes. Spud stepped out of the batter's box and considered what Walls would be throwing. Walls was one of the few pitchers who threw a curveball. Most did not because it was too hard on a young arm. Ahead in the count, Spud knew it was coming. It would be a good pitch to hit if it didn't break. If he hung it, Spud would be ready. Walls' motion was slower. He had tipped his hand. Spud knew what was coming. Rather than break, the ball floated. Spud held back and waited. He made a smooth swing and slapped the ball over the shortstop's head. It rolled into the gap between the left and center fielders. Spud stopped at second, but three runs had scored. Game over. Final score: Oaks 6 and Cubs 4.

Spud was mobbed by his teammates. The Oaks had beaten the mighty Cubs and had won their biggest game of the year.

"Line up," commanded Charlie. After each game in a show of sportsmanship, the teams walked parallel with each other and slapped hands as they walked by.

"We're still tied for first and you guys have to play the Rangers. They're going to kill you and then we'll play them for the championship," said Tommy Walls.

"We'll see about that," said Eddie.

"After we beat the Rangers, we'll see you in the championship game," added Spud.

"We're on a roll," said Darnell.

"No way. You guys just got lucky," said Walls.

"We'll see about that," said Wags.

"We're still in it," cheered Charlie. "We're still in it. I knew you guys could do it. It's time for an Oaks' huddle."

Gathering the team in a circle, Charlie, as he did after every game, recognized key contributors, win or lose. The parents listened as he made positive comments about each player. After the short ceremony, he brought out the team's favorite, ice cream bars. No matter what happened the remainder of the season, they had achieved a major accomplishment. They had beaten the Cubs.

Chapter 45

"I've decided to attend Stanford Law School," said Rebecca.

"Good for you. You'll make a great attorney."

Rebecca paused, not sure if she really liked Charlie's response. She thought he had answered too quickly, but as she had expected. She sighed, feeling an unexpected letdown. Disappointed, she had wanted Charlie to tell her no.

"What will you do?" she asked.

"I'm not sure. Summer will be over soon. I'll go back to the woods and work for a few months. Then I'll make my decision."

"Decision?" Rebecca asked holding her breath.

"On baseball. Being around the kids got my juices going."

"I thought you were done. You said you were never going back."

"I never thought I wanted to until I coached these kids. I made the decision too quickly. I was wrong. Watching these kids struggle as they learn the game made me realize how hard you have to work. There are ups and downs; you just have to accept them. That's true of kids and major leaguers. The learning process never stops. I thought when I had my struggles I had peaked, and my career was over, but it was just a deep trough."

"I thought you said the game was no longer fun?"

"I did, but the kids showed me how much fun it could be. Coaching them showed me that. Sure, it's a business, but it's still a game and one that I miss a great deal."

"Do you think they'll give you another chance?"

"I don't know. I walked away like a baby. I might have to crawl back like one. They might not give me another chance. If they don't, I'll work in the woods for a while until I decide what to do."

Rebecca held her breath and asked. "What about us?"

"I don't want to stand in your way. You have a great career in front of you."

"What if I decided not to go?"

"I wouldn't let you. Look, my life is a bit undecided right now. Even if I make it back, there is no guarantee that I'll make it. If I don't, then what? I don't have much to offer."

"You could help me run the egg business. My mom has decided to sell the store and tavern. She's going to keep her properties and the egg processing plant, but she wants to have more time to travel and enjoy life. She might even move to California part-time while I'm in law school."

"I don't know much about chickens or eggs. What I do know a little bit about is baseball. I know less about eggs than I do logging, and that ain't much."

"You can always learn."

"Probably, but I don't want to live off you and your mother. Besides, you have a good crew at the plant; they don't need me telling them what to do."

"You have to have a boss. Mom is backing away, and I'll be too busy."

"I'll give it some thought, but right now, my priority is to stick with the boys and get healthy."

"How does your arm feel now that you have the cast off?"

"Weak. It's healed, but it will take a few months for my strength to return. I think working in the woods is a better place to do that than an egg processing plant. Maybe someday, but if there is a chance to pitch again, I need a conditioning routine and some hard work."

Rebecca could feel her face flush. She felt a thick lump grow in her throat. Fearing that she might start to cry, she turned and walked back to her car.

"Good luck today."

"The boys are ready. It should be a good game. Are you coming back to watch?"

"Maybe. I have some things I promised to do for mom before I leave. I'd better start on them. The next couple of weeks will fly by."

"Will I see you later?"

"I'll be around," Rebecca replied, knowing she wouldn't.

Chapter 46

"They found her flute," said Eddie.

"Her flute?" asked Spud.

"The flute Mary Ann went to get on her wedding day," interjected Kermit.

"How do they know it was Mary Ann's flute?" asked Spud.

Kermit wiped his glasses clean. He tracked his bobber as it drifted slowly in the calm Molalla River backwater. "It was in the paper. The guy who shot the policewoman had it at his trailer. He's the guy they think murdered Mary Ann. Her sister identified the flute he had in his trailer as hers," said Kermit.

Spud took a bite of peanut butter and jam sandwich. "Do you think Mary Ann's ghost will go away?"

"I don't think so," answered Kermit.

"Why not? The case is solved," said Eddie. "They found her killer."

Spud was one step ahead of Kermit, "She doesn't have the flute."

Kermit laid back against a section of log the sun and water had bleached to a light shade of brown. "Mary Ann wants her flute."

"You guys don't know that. The case is solved. Why would she come back? To get her flute? I don't think so."

Eddie reeled in his line and readied another cast. "What about her boyfriend, Carl? How about him?"

"I think if she goes away, he goes away," Kermit theorized.

Eddie reacted as the tip of his fishing pole snapped down. Jumping up, he grabbed the cork grip and jerked it upward. His attempt at hooking the fish came up empty.

"Bit too strong, Stump. Bye, bye fish. You jerked the hook right out of his mouth," ribbed Spud.

Eddie shrugged, then answered Kermit, "Oh sure, ghosts stick together. I don't want to go on another wild goose chase. Carl will go away."

"Well, people started seeing Mary Ann the same time they started to say the baseball field was cursed. Mary Ann and Carl were going to be married and they died at about the same time. Carl will leave when Mary Ann leaves," speculated Kermit.

"If the baseball field is cursed, why have we been winning? If there was a curse, then something would have happened. We would have lost," rebutted Eddie.

"Don't forget the first game of the year. We lost to Molalla on a bad hop. That could have been Carl," said Kermit.

"Charlie said it was the *baseball gods*," replied Spud.

"What if we just calmed Carl down a bit?"

"What?" asked Eddie. "How do you calm down a ghost?"

"We tried to help Mary Ann," said Spud. "That's it. Carl saw we were trying to help Mary Ann and he calmed down."

Eddie wasn't convinced, "So, all the bad stuff that's happened is because Carl was mad. You think he was angry because nobody was helping Mary Ann? That's crazy."

"What if it's true?" quizzed Kermit.

"If it's true, what are we supposed to do? How do we make Carl happy?" asked Spud.

"There's only one way to find out. We've got to return Mary Ann's flute. That's what she's waiting for. She's waiting for her flute," said Kermit.

"How do we do that? We don't have the flute," said Eddie.

"We have to do this before the big game with Oregon City. I think Carl will only be so patient. The moon is about right. The game is going to be at Lone Elder on Saturday. We have to give her flute back before Saturday," said Kermit.

"The first problem is," said Eddie. "We have to get the flute."

"Chief Polanski has it. It's evidence," Kermit said.

"We have to get it," said Spud.

"We can't steal it. If Polanski has the flute, it's at the station under lock and key."

"We'll have to tell Polanski what we're doing," said Kermit.

Spud threw a piece of his bread crust into the water and watched as a fish came to the surface and snatched it with his mouth.

"Great, you won't bite the hook, but you'll eat my bread. What makes you think Polanski is going to let us take the flute? He'll think we're nuts, like we probably are."

"He's good friends with Mrs. Flynn. We can ask her, or we can ask Charlie. He's a baseball player, and like Mr. Nance said, 'all baseball players are superstitious.' He won't want to help."

"Mrs. Flynn knows about Mary Ann and Carl. She'll believe us. She'll help," thought Eddie.

"Charlie might not let us do it before the big game," said Kermit.

"Then we can't tell him. If we get the flute, what do we do then? How do we return the flute to Mary Ann?" asked Spud.

"Why don't we just set her flute on a chair in the center of the stage? She can swoop down and pick it up," Eddie joked.

Kermit jumped up, excited. "That's exactly what we should do. How else would we do it? She's not going to take the thing, but she'll see we tried to help. That will make Carl happy and he won't put a curse on our game. We need him on our side, not Oregon City's."

Eddie started to reel in his fishing line. "We only have a couple of days. We'd better go talk to Mrs. Flynn."

"We'd better hurry," added Spud. "I don't want Carl to be mad at us. We've been playing good baseball. I don't want him messing things up."

"I think we should tell the whole team. If they don't come, they'll never believe us," Eddie said.

"The whole team?" asked Kermit.

"Yep, I agree with Eddie. This is a team thing. Like Charlie says, 'We win as a team, and we lose as a team. One person doesn't win or lose a game."

"To the team," said Spud.

"To the team," said Eddie and Kermit in unison.

Chapter 47

"The last game of the season, for this field anyway, is this Saturday. If the boys make it to the district tournament, it's at Kelly Field in Oregon City. You can start demolition on Monday."

"We'll bring in the equipment this week," said Jim Webb.

Jim Webb was a stout man with a rough, reddish face and a tattoo of the Statue of Liberty on his right forearm. His company had numerous projects, all of which he managed. He was known for always being on the move and for chewing on a cigar he never lit.

"Jim, you better hold off until after the game. It should be a big crowd and we'll need the whole parking lot for cars."

"Those boys are playing some great baseball. I'll be at the game. You can't miss this one. The game is the talk of the town," he laughed.

"It's been a long time since this area has been so involved in a team. After they beat Canby, Charlie said they just got hot. They're an exciting team to watch."

"Mom," yelled Rebecca from the store counter. "There are some young men here to see you."

"Excuse me, Jim. I'll see you on Monday."

"We'll get started bright and early. If something comes up, I'll be at the game."

Nell shook Jim's hand and walked into the store from her office in the adjoining house. "Hi boys," she said to acknowledge Spud, Eddie, and Kermit. "What can I do for you?"

"When are you going to tear down the meeting hall?" asked Eddie.

"I just talked to the contractor. He's bringing in the equipment on Monday. He'll start the teardown next week."

"Good," said Kermit. "We were afraid you were going to do it before Saturday."

"Okay, boys. What's going on? Is this about Mary Ann?"

The boys were a bit taken back when she mentioned Mary Ann. How did she know it was about her?

"Uh, yeah," said Spud. "We've got to give her flute back before the game on Saturday," he blurted out.

"What?" asked Rebecca.

"This couldn't be about Carl, could it?" Nell asked.

"Yes," said Spud.

"We've got to give Mary Ann's flute back. If we do, Carl won't put a curse on us," said Eddie.

Nell glanced over at Rebecca and winked. "Maybe you boys should tell me what's going on."

Eddie told Nell and Rebecca about their theory. They listened intently, occasionally smiling at their youthful imaginations.

"You boys think that if we don't return Mary Ann's flute, Carl may get angry and take it out on the team. You've been playing some great baseball; what makes you think he wouldn't curse the team from Oregon City?" asked Nell.

"Because we're from Lone Elder. He'll take it out on us."

"Does Charlie know about this?" asked Rebecca.

"We haven't told him because he may not want us to do this before the big game," said Spud.

"Oh, I think Charlie will go along. He's pretty superstitious when it comes to baseball," replied Rebecca.

The boys nodded in agreement. "We told the other kids on the team. If we can get the flute, the whole team will be there tomorrow night to see if Mary Ann will show up and take it," said Eddie.

"If I'm not mistaken, the reason you're telling me this, other than to find out when I'm going to have the building demolished, is to talk to Chief Polanski to get the flute back, right?"

Spud looked down a bit sheepishly, "Well, yeah."

"I would, except I don't think he has it. The man who murdered Mary Ann is dead and the case is closed. Chief Polanski gave the flute back to Mary Ann's sister. You might have to talk to her."

A collective sigh could be heard from the three boys. They hadn't expected that Polanski would have given Mary Ann's flute away.

"Mom, what can it hurt? I think we should help the boys. You sure don't want them cursed," said Rebecca with an encouraging tilt of her head.

"I'll tell you what. I think I might be able to help. At what time do we have to be at the meeting hall?"

"The moon will be right tomorrow night. The reflection will light up the stage just after dark," said Kermit.

"No guarantees. I'll talk to Chief Polanski and Mary Ann's sister. Is it okay if Misty comes?"

"I don't think Mary Ann or Carl will care how many people are there as long as she gets her flute back," said Kermit.

"I'll see what I can do. Now you boys run along. I'll see you tomorrow night. Play hard on Saturday. Win or lose, you've had a great season. Oh, and grab a candy bar on the way out. It's the least I can do for team spirit."

Rebecca chuckled, "I don't want to miss this, and I bet Charlie won't either."

"I thought you quit seeing each other?"

"Mother, we're just friends. We had a talk and worked things out. Besides, I wasn't really seeing him, you know, in that way."

"Sure, Rebecca. Sure," replied Nell with a smirk.

Rebecca returned an annoyed gaze, "What if Misty doesn't want to give up the flute?"

"She'll get it right back. If she's worried about it, she can be there to make sure she gets it back. If Mary Ann takes it, listen to me, I sound like the boys, then she will want to see it."

"You really don't believe we're going to see Mary Ann, do you?"

"It's one of those times when it's kind of fun to be a kid again. I'm pretty sure we won't see Mary Ann, but it sure could be fun. Ghosts?

Those boys sure have vivid imaginations. I guess I'd better call Joe and have him come with me to see Misty. This will be the final meeting at the hall. Maybe this will also give Misty a bit of closure. If nothing else, it will be interesting."

"I'm going out to see Misty today," said Polanski as he read a report about the evidence found in Samuels' trailer house.

"Why?" asked Nell.

"I just got a call this morning. They found Mary Ann's body."

"My heavens. Where at?"

"Samuels dug a grave under the workbench in his repair shop. David Craig of the crime lab said he noticed a depression under the workbench. It was a dip where oil collected. The floor is dirt and uneven. Still, he thought it was odd. They moved the bench and dug down. They found the body a few feet below. She still had on her wedding dress."

"So I guess that's it. The crime is solved and now there's a body."

"I guess so, but now I wonder if Samuels' uncle was involved. Maybe the bench wasn't there, but that doesn't seem likely. If the work bench was there, Samuels would have needed help to move it. It took four officers to lift the darn thing."

"Do they know how she died?"

"Not much to go on there. I guess it doesn't matter at this point."

"Misty and the family will at least have closure."

"Not a happy ending, but yes, after all these years, they will have closure."

"The also found a hunting knife. There were traces of blood, human blood, found on the knife. It's the same blood type as the Sacramento newspaper editor, Chester Marsh. They analyzed the knife wounds and they are certain they were made by the same type of knife. Hard evidence that Samuels killed Marsh."

"If he wasn't in the clear, Owen Nance is now. For what he went through, it has to be very good news. Speaking of news, I have a request and it happens to include Misty."

Nell related what the boys had said and the need for Mary Ann's flute.

"I'm not sure, Nell. I have to give her the news about Mary Ann. I'm not sure how she'll react to your request."

"I know; it's a bit farfetched and the timing is awful."

"I guess it just depends on whether or not Misty believes in the tales about her ghost."

"Will you ask?"

"I'll pick you up in fifteen minutes. I think I may need some help on this one," said Polanski as he hung up.

Chapter 48

Kermit worried there were too many clouds. What had been an overcast Oregon day had turned partly cloudy.

"I don't know if this is going to work. If the clouds get too thick, there won't be any reflection," sighed Kermit.

"It's a bright night; it won't take much light," said Spud.

"If there isn't enough light, I don't think Mary Ann will be able to see the flute," replied Kermit.

"Don't you think ghosts can see in the dark?" teased Tub. Since his suspension for the Cubs game, Tub had become a real team player on the field. Off the field, he was just Tub.

"I hope she can. If not, Carl might make the ball bounce over your mitt," said Darnell.

"What if Mrs. Flynn doesn't bring the flute?" asked Vic.

"Then we're toast. Carl will be mad at us and he could curse the game on Saturday," said Kermit.

"You can't think like that; you'll jinx us," said Spud.

"Carl doesn't matter; we'll win anyway," said Eddie.

"No curse is going to beat the Oaks," boasted Thumbs.

"Yeah, we can't let a ghost scare us into losing. We've got the baseball gods on our side," said Wags.

"I ain't afraid of no ghosts," said Dinky. "Except I would like Carl on our side too."

"Gods or ghosts aren't going to win or lose the game; we just have to play better than them. We do, we win. We don't, we lose. We just have to give it everything we got," said Spud.

"Yeah. Well, I'd just as soon keep Carl happy," added Kermit.

"I don't want him mad either," Spud agreed.

"Boys, over here," motioned Charlie.

"Com'on, it's the coach," said Wags.

The team ran from the stands behind home plate to the entrance of the meeting hall. There to meet them was Chief Polanski, Nell, Rebecca, Charlie, and Mary Ann's sister, Misty. In Misty's hand was the flute.

"Boys, I'd like you to meet Misty, Mary Ann's sister."

The boys raised their hands or nodded. They said a collective, "Hi."

"You think Mary Ann is waiting for her flute?" Misty asked.

Nobody answered at first and then looked at Kermit. "We think so. We think that's what she's looking for. This is our last chance to give it to her before the game on Saturday and before the building is torn down."

"You boys don't need to worry about a curse. You're a good baseball team and you've earned the right to play for the championship. Just remember that if Mary Ann doesn't show up," said Charlie.

He thought it was okay for the boys to have fun but didn't want them to not be confident in their playing ability.

The boys nodded in agreement.

"What do you want me to do with the flute?" asked Misty.

"We're going to put it on a chair at center stage and wait for the sunlight to reflect off the moon. The light will shine through that window at the top of the peak and illuminate the stage. That's when Mary Ann appears," said Eddie.

"You've done this before? You've seen her?" asked Misty.

"Twice," said Spud.

"I never saw her," said Tub.

"I saw her," said Eddie.

"Me too," said Kermit.

"Well, I guess there's one way to find out," said Nell as she unlocked the front door to the meeting hall.

"It's about time," said Kermit.

"I'll put a chair at center stage for the flute," said Spud.

"We need to be quiet and get everybody into the balcony," said Eddie.

"Let's go see Mary Ann," said Nell, grabbing Polanski's arm.

Off duty, Polanski wore a pair of jeans, his cowboy boots, and a white shirt. "I've never seen a ghost," he chuckled.

"Charlie, are you afraid?" Rebecca asked.

"Boo," he whispered, "if you get scared, I'll protect you."

"I'm not sure I would trust that protection," Rebecca said nudging him in the ribs.

"We have to be quiet," said Eddie as the group climbed the stairs to the balcony.

"Get down," said Kermit. "Stay below the railing."

Eager with anticipation, a hush fell over the group. Polanski and Charlie turned off their tube flashlights. The balcony and main floor were pitch black, except for the moonlight that filtered through the large maple tree next to the field. Just then, they looked up as the moon's reflection illuminated the ceiling and slowly rotated toward the stage. Not a sound could be heard. It was like the group was put into a collective trance. Then suddenly, it was dark as the moon passed behind a cloud. The boys held their breath as the cloud passed and a beam of light hit the stage again. Center stage was suddenly bright. The light was brighter than the boys had seen before. A spotlight beamed on the chair and Mary Ann's flute. A swirling breeze blew the front door open and swept a gust toward the stage, creating a slow-moving whirlwind. The whirlwind stopped at center stage. The almost imperceptible sound of rustling leaves could be heard in the background. A woman appeared. She rose from a light blue haze. She hovered next to the chair. She was dressed in her wedding gown, and her once black veil was now white. The veil was wrapped loosely around her face and draped over her shoulder. An almost imperceptible smile could be seen through the veil. Long waves of golden hair flowed softly down onto her chest. She reached down with her long delicate fingers and lifted the flute. She held the flute up toward the balcony. Her veil dropped and Mary Ann smiled as if to say, thank you. Suddenly, there was another whirlwind. Carl drifted onto the stage close to Mary Ann. He knelt and kissed her left hand. Then he lovingly slid a ring onto her finger. Mary Ann swept her hand over Carl's head.

Then she lifted the flute to her mouth and softly started to play. After hearing the sound, she stopped, smiled again, and, with Carl, bowed to the balcony. Then as suddenly as they appeared, they were swept away into the night.

The balcony was totally silent. Nobody spoke, afraid that saying anything could wreck a divine moment. What they had witnessed was beyond beautiful. Submerged in their own thoughts, for a few seconds, they remained motionless. What they had seen was beyond belief, but now everything made sense. They had witnessed closure. For this one small piece of the universe, all was now once again in harmony. Mary Ann had her flute and Carl was with Mary Ann. They were now part of eternity.

Misty was first to speak. She couldn't hold back the tears. "She was so beautiful. She was just how I remembered her on her wedding day. They loved each other so much. It wasn't right that they weren't together. Now I know they'll be together for ever. Boys, thank you for making this possible. I'll never forget this night."

"I wouldn't have believed it if I hadn't seen it," choked Polanski, a man who rarely showed emotion and who thought he had seen it all.

"And I thought these boys were seeing things. Boys, I'm sure glad you figured this out. If I wouldn't have seen it, I never would have believed it," said Nell.

Rebecca gripped Charlie's hand extra tight and then grabbed his arm as if she never wanted to let go.

"Hey, Tub, did you see her?" asked Spub.

Tub couldn't answer but nodded his head up and down.

"Well, we don't have to worry about Carl. If we lose to Oregon City, it's because we didn't play well. Now we have no excuse," said Eddie.

"I think it's time for everybody to go home," said Polanski.

"One more thing," said Misty, "I want to see if Mary Ann really took the flute."

In mass, the group descended the stairs and rushed to the stage. In the dark room, Polanski and Charlie shined their flashlights to the chair at center stage. The chair was empty. Mary Ann had taken her flute.

Chapter 49

The parking lot was full. Cars were parked on both sides of the main roads. Deputies Landon, Wormley, and two county officers controlled the traffic. The stands were full. People stood behind a rope running parallel to the left and right foul lines. The rope extended from the backstop to the potato field in left and to the row of arborvitaes in right. Four high school cheerleaders manned a booth that served hot dogs, popcorn, candy bars, and four different types of sodas. Nell committed half the proceeds for new cheerleading outfits. An announcer's table was set up behind home plate to provide color commentary. It would be the first time many of the boys had ever heard their names announced when they were introduced and came to bat. The league provided four official-looking umpires dressed in dark blue. John Gains used his Ford tractor to groom the infield with a fine screen. Parents raked the infield and removed as many rocks as they could find. Two men from the Canby Public Works Department dressed in official-looking coveralls chalked the foul lines, making sure they were straight. They put a dusting of chalk on the bases, cleaned home plate, and chalked the batter's box. The outfield grass was mowed to a length of one and one-half inches. Gains pulled a heavy roller filled with water around the outfield to flatten gofer mounds or raised spots. For the first time, a homerun fence circled the outfield. A hit over the fence would land in the potato field, a true home run. A hard-hit ball would be stopped by the fence. Rather than rolling into the potato field for a home run, the hitter would be held to a double or triple depending on how fast he rounded the bases. Lone Elder field had never looked so good. The only thing that needed to happen was the game.

"You guys were lucky," said Tommy Walls as he walked behind the Oaks' bench.

"Quit whining," said Tub. "You shouldn't have choked and lost to Molalla. I heard you struck out three times."

In a twist of fate, the Cubs had lost to Molalla and ended their season with four losses. The Cubs did do the Oaks a favor by beating Oregon City. The Oaks and Rangers stood tied at nine wins and three losses. The winner of this game would move on to the district tournament.

"Want to make something of it?" hissed Walls.

"Sure," interjected Darnell. "Anytime."

"Yeah, bring your boys," said Spud. "We'll see how tough you guys are."

Charlie heard the chatter and let it go for a few moments. He liked that the Oaks were sticking up for each other but wanted them focused on the game.

"Okay, that's enough. Com'on boys, we've got a game to play. No distractions."

"We got this coach," said Eddie.

Charlie held up his hand to give Eddie a high-five. He had experienced anxiety as a player, but this was different. He was nervous. He had hardly slept. At five o'clock in the morning, he was out of bed and pacing. He reminded himself these were just kids, and young ones at that, but it didn't seem to help. He was confident but anxious for them. It was much tougher to watch them play than it was to play. If this was what it was like being a parent, then he doubted if he was ready for that big step. The stress would kill him.

He agonized over the lineup. During the last two games, Eddie had pitched a lot of innings. Today, he would give the ball to Darnell. He had come a long way and was ready. It also gave the Oaks a better defensive infield. Spud catching, Eddie at first, Dinky at second, Jose at shortstop, and Tub at third. Wags would play left, Vic in centerfield, and Ron Fox in right. Kermit, Thumbs, and Doc would play no later than the fourth inning. Every kid would play at least two innings and have one at-bat. It was a team effort that got the Oaks to the championship game and they would all be part of it, win or lose.

Both teams showed their nerves. The first two innings went quickly. Darnell and the opposing pitcher, a big right-hander named Cole Sims, were on their games. In the third inning, Jose made a sparkling defensive play at short. He went deep into the hole and backhanded a ground ball and then, in one fluid motion, rifled a throw to first to get the runner out by a step. The score after three innings was 0-0.

The Rangers broke through first. Darnell walked the leadoff hitter. He moved to second on a sacrifice bunt and then stole third on a close play. The runner scored on a ball hit to Dinky's left. Dinky had no chance at making a play at home but threw the runner out at first. Darnell struck out the next batter. Darnell was pitching his best game, but so was the opposing pitcher. The crowd was growing tense and not a single person had left.

The score remained unchanged and stood at 1-0 until the fifth inning. In the fifth, the Rangers scored when the clean-up hitter ripped a double and then scored on a bloop single to right. The Oaks got their bats going when Vic hit a *frozen rope* for a single into left field and Jose doubled to drive him in. Wags struck out to end the threat. After five innings, the score stood at 2-1 Rangers.

In the sixth, Eddie came in to relieve Darnell. After walking the first batter, Eddie settled down and struck out the side. It was the bottom of the sixth and final inning. The Rangers made a pitching change. They brought in a reliever; a big lefty who stood six inches taller than the other kids.

"That guy looks like Frankenstein," said Tub.

In a voice with a slight quiver, Wags observed, "He has whiskers."

"Ya, don't hit his whiskers," said Spud. "Just watch the ball and forget about the pitcher. We can hit anybody."

"That's the attitude," Charlie encouraged. "Let's go boys. One run to tie, and two to win. We've come back before and we can do it again."

When Spud stepped into the batter's box, he looked toward the pitcher. There was no question, he was the biggest pitcher he'd seen all year. He wondered why he wasn't on the Rangers when they played them before.

Given they had lost to the Rangers by five runs in their first meeting, it was probably a good thing. Nor did they see the kid in their second meeting when the Oaks scored six runs in the fourth inning and held on to beat the Rangers to give them a split for the season.

The first pitch sailed over Spud's head for a ball. That was intended to scare me, he thought. The second pitch was off the plate, wide. The third pitch was down the middle for a strike. Spud stepped out and picked up some dirt. With his eye on the pitcher, he rubbed the dirt between his hands and then spit on them. He grabbed the bat firmly, but not in a death grip. He waited. He expected the next pitch to be thrown down the middle of the plate. He was ready. The pitcher wound and let loose. The ball came fast and was thrown down the middle as Spud had anticipated. He swung hard and made solid contact. The ball hit the bat in the sweet spot and soared over the third baseman's head. It rolled all the way to the left field fence. By the time the left fielder got to the ball and returned it to the infield, Spud stood on second base with a double.

"That a boy Spud!" yelled Charlie. "Great hit. Now we're going Oaks. Let's go!"

As the crowd and his teammates erupted, Spud looked at the Rangers. They looked downhearted. Their expectation was that their pitcher would strike out the side. Now he saw concern, and downright fear, in their faces. The Oaks players and fans could sense a momentum shift. But this was baseball. Momentum lasted only until the next strikeout, the next great play, or the next big hit. In baseball, you couldn't let up; you had to earn it.

Eddie stepped into the batter's box. Spud had shown the way and if he could get a hit, so could he. He and Spud were great friends, but that didn't mean they didn't compete. In some respects, their competitiveness strengthened their friendship. He respected Spud because he was tough, competitive, and never quit. He liked him because he was fun to be around and loved an adventure. But this was more than a competition between him and Spud; this was for the team. He loved the Oaks. He had to get a hit; he had to score Spud from second.

The first three pitches were around the plate. The count was two balls and one strike. On the fourth pitch, Eddie was frozen when the pitcher, like Darnell had done to Tommy Walls, threw him a change-up. Eddie was way out in front and missed the ball for a strike. With the count even at 2-2, Eddie debated about what the pitcher would throw next. He thought he could expect another change-up, but if he looked for it and the pitcher threw a fastball, he would have no chance to hit it. The ball would be past him and in the catcher's mitt before he swung the bat. No, he had to expect a fastball. He set his feet and took a deep breath. He positioned his hands and focused both eyes on the spot where the pitcher would release the ball. When the pitcher threw it, Eddie quickly picked up the ball. He had guessed right. The ball was coming fast and down the middle. Eddie made a short stride and timed the pitch perfectly. He took a hard level swing with a slight uppercut. It was a perfect connection, a tremendous impact. The ball exploded off the bat. Later after the game, Charlie, Ed Washington, Steve Adams, and others marveled at how far Eddie hit the ball. The Rangers' left and center fielders didn't make a move as the ball rocketed over their heads. The ball cleared the home run fence. A group of young boys ran to find the ball, but it had landed so deep into the potato field it took some time for the boys to find it. Final score: Oaks 3 – Rangers 2. The Lone Elder Oaks were the league champions!

Bedlam erupted. Oaks players charged the field. Spud trotted around third, jumping up and down. He jumped on home plate. Eddie took one quick look at the ball and knew it was gone. Excited, he sprinted to first, skipped to second, sailed to third, and threw his hat into the air as he floated to home. His teammates stood in a semi-circle around the plate. He made sure he scored by stomping on home plate. The umpire watched to ensure he touched the plate. With the score official, the team jumped up and down; the wild celebration had begun.

Charlie waited a few seconds for the team to calm down, then held up his hand and said, "Okay champs, let's line up."

Charlie beamed; the Oaks had completed a great transformation. In a short amount of time, they had progressed from last place to league champions. The team had gelled, and at the right time. He recalled the series of events that made the Oaks a team. The recommendation, almost divine intervention, by Nance to bring Jose and Darnell onto the team. Both boys had made a huge difference. The bonding of the team after the scrap with the Cubs. The clash between Darnell and Tub. And, the most unusual of all, solving the mystery of Mary Ann and Carl. It had been a wild, yet wonderful season. He rubbed his arm. Was it fate that he had quit the Giants and then hurt his arm? He didn't know, but fate certainly couldn't be discounted. As the team celebrated, he looked for and found

Rebecca. She had a big smile on her face. She walked over to him.

"Way to go coach," she said, giving him a big hug.

"We're the champs," he said into her ear.

"You would have been a champ to me, win or lose."

Charlie squeezed Rebecca tight. "I guess I found more than a baseball team when I came to Lone Elder."

Nell beamed as she watched Rebecca and Charlie hug. "It's on to the district playoffs, but I think I may have found a son-in-law," she said to Polanski.

Looking on, he said, "I think you might be right."

"How do you think we'll do?" Steve Adams asked Ed Washington.

"Depends on how we play. I guess, it really doesn't matter. These boys coming together and winning the league is achievement enough. If we do well in district, that's just, as they say, *the icing on the cake.*"

"It's on to the district tournament," said Rebecca.

"Then it's time to get my life together. I thought I'd give pitching another try. I heard from Nance. He talked to the new manager of the Giants, my old pitching coach, Derek Sheets. He's willing to give me another shot. If my arm heals and I can pitch again, I'm going to spring training next year. It's a long shot, but I'm willing to take it."

"What about the Oaks?"

"Steve Adams and Ed Washington have agreed to coach the team next year. They both travel and reached an arrangement to share the responsibility. They're good men and will be good with the boys."

"The boys will miss you."

"I'll miss them too. This has been one of the best experiences of my life."

"I hope I was part of that."

"You were the best part," Charlie said as he gave Rebecca a big kiss.

Epilogue

Charlie stood on the pitcher's mound. He picked up some dirt and rubbed the baseball. He glanced over at the stands behind the Giants' dugout. He saw Rebecca. She wore a wide-brimmed hat to shield the sun. Her auburn hair flowed from the hat to her shoulders. She had on a Giants jersey with his name and number on the back. A student at Stanford Law School, she never missed a home game when he pitched. As newlyweds, they had become the darlings of the San Francisco press. Next to her sat Nell. After selling the Lone Elder store, she spent most of her time running the egg business. Once a month, she came to visit Rebecca. A big baseball fan, she always came to watch him pitch. Joe Polanski sat beside her. Although he talked about retiring as police chief, he couldn't pull the trigger. Now that Officer Christine Walker had fully recovered and was back on the force, Polanski and Nell were spending more time together. Nell had finally talked him into taking a vacation and they were planning a trip to sunny Arizona.

In the stands next to them were the Oaks players. Their season had just started, and they were already 3-0. The team was playing well. They were riding high after just beating the Cubs. They were the team to beat.

As a special treat, Charlie bought them airplane tickets to San Francisco to watch him pitch. This was the Oaks' first Giants game. The boys wore Giant hats and met all the players. They were in awe as Willie Mays, Willie McCovey, Juan Marichal, Orlando Cepeda, Gaylord Perry, and other Giants signed autographs. Making it extra special, their ex-coach was on the mound. Owen Nance, once again a sports reporter for the *Sacramento Bee*, wrote an award-winning story about Charlie and the Oaks. The *San Francisco Chronicle*, and other papers up and down the west coast, ran it. Hollywood loved the story and there was talk about a movie. The Lone Elder Oaks were stars.

Charlie shook his arm. His arm had comeback stronger than it was. More important than his arm, his attitude had turned around a hundred and eighty degrees. Was it because he had experienced real work as a logger? There was nothing like hard work for a man to consider his options. Or was it because of coaching the Oaks? There was no question the experience gave him a different perspective on life and baseball. Then there was Rebecca. She had become the biggest part of his life. She was his rock. She kept things in perspective when the ups and downs of playing professional baseball conspired to overwhelm him. Nell and the people of Lone Elder were there for support too. Pete Long and the other members of the logging crew sent him notes of encouragement, but also jabbed him when he hung a curveball. They were his constant supporters.

The last few months had been a whirlwind, but he had changed, and changed for the good. It was still early in the season, but his record stood at five wins and one loss. He was leading the league in strikeouts and his control was the best of his career. Yes, he knew he would hit tough spots, and he might even go into a pitching slump, but this time, he had the confidence to fight his way through them. Baseball was a game of punches. Coaching the Oaks had taught him that you had to be able to take them, and then, make the adjustments. Funny, he thought, how kids could teach adults lessons. Faced with adversity, kids are resilient. The Oaks never gave up. They didn't quit until it was over. If they lost, the loss didn't linger if they had done their best. If you left everything on the field, it would go down in the loss column, but never be a charge against guts, character, or spirit. The Oaks made him remember what was important. That didn't mean it would be easy, but now he was able to deal with the distractions, just like he taught Darnell and Jose.

Charlie didn't know how long his career would last, but now he had family and friends to fall back on. He could handle whatever came. He took one final look at the stands. The Oaks stood up, and in unison, like the team they were, tipped their hats to him. Charlie stepped off the rubber and tipped his hat back to acknowledge them. The crowd, understanding what had just happened, roared. Charlie stepped back onto the rubber. It was time to go to work.

The umpire yelled, "Play ball!"

The End

There's Money on the Edge

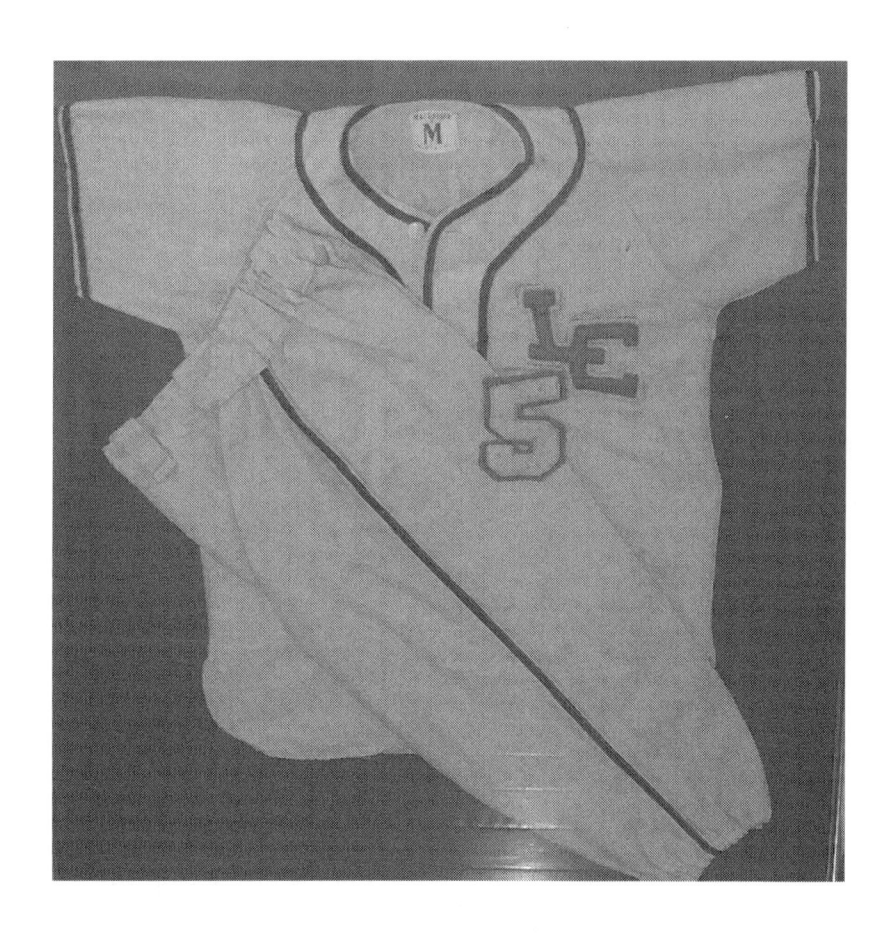

Thank You

I hope you enjoyed reading *There's Money on the Edge,* **the fourth in** *The Adventures of Spud Dempsey and Eddie Stump* **series.**

Other books in the series include:

The White Oath
The Scarlet Luce
King Norman

You may also enjoy reading one of my other publications:

Managing the FUZ
Jerome's Edge

All my publications are available as E-books or in paperback.

Acknowledgements

Technical Editing: Glow_Writer

Book Cover: Pro_Designers123

Formatting: dadal123

Special Thanks: Vicki Adamson, Betsy Jankowski, Barbara Reifschneider, and Sandra Mortensen for their input and catching so many of my errors, omissions, and downright stupid stuff. Because of their input the work is much better.

The errors are solely my responsibility.

The Adventures of Spud Dempsey and Eddie Stump Books

The White Oath—The year is 1943 and White Rose resistance leaders are arrested for distributing pamphlets documenting Nazi atrocities. Before their execution, they steal artwork and jewels worth millions from the Nazis who have cruelly confiscated them from political prisoners and Jews. Entrusted with the vital sixth pamphlet and the location of the valuables, Katharina Hermann escapes but is cornered at a small Porto, Portugal café by the brutal SS Officer, Karl Brunner...It's twenty years later. When they hear a faint cry for help, Spud and Eddie investigate and are thrust into a swirling mystery that ends on the Argentinian freighter, Evita Star...Hunted for a crime he didn't commit, Malcolm Lee, a young Asian and African-American runaway, places his fate in the hands of strangers until he is forced to make a fateful decision, does he go to the police or run?

The Scarlet Luce—The old crow, Peck, circles the pasture carefully watching. Suddenly, sensing danger he dives...The magnificent filly, Scarlet Luce, suffers a devastating injury. Her future looks bleak until she is rescued by the enigmatic Tom Crane...JD Sims' dream of become a jockey has come to a heartbreaking end after she is critically injured in a tragic car accident. Depressed, all seems lost until a chance encounter gives her renewed hope...After saving Luce, the old war horse, Temecula, and the Shetland pony, Flop, from a disastrous fire, Spud and Eddie, with the help of Police Chief Joe Polanski, face the challenge of a conspiracy and the mystery of Tom Crane.

King Norman—Severely wounded, the puppy escapes his cruel masters. Driven by instinct, he faces death-defying perils as he wanders aimlessly into the unknown... To "protect" her from having epileptic seizures, Emily Jones is locked in her room. Alone and depressed, all seems hopeless until... Devastated by the tragic death of his son, Oregon lumber baron, Henry "Hap" Jones becomes a recluse until a mysterious telephone call threatens what he holds dearest... After a chance encounter, Spud and Eddie fight evil as they attempt a heroic rescue... After receiving a desperate call for help, Police Chief, Joe Polanski, defies conventional wisdom and takes a huge risk to save a life.

Other Publications

Managing the FUZ—It's late and Myra Gates, a young, talented, and fast-tracking executive, has been drinking with her new boss, Trig Davis. When Davis invites her to his room and then attacks her, she fights back but her career and reputation are in jeopardy...Ed Cooper's life is in shambles. He struggles with a new management team, gets demoted, and then his hated rival becomes his new boss...After a company cutback costs him his job, Joe Rinaldi hits bottom and puts a gun to his head...Outspoken Barbara Russell challenges management and then suffers the consequences...When Lucas Moore fails he puts his career at risk but then he's given one more chance to be a star. *Managing the FUZ* is available Kindle, Nook, and in paperback via CreateSpace.

Jerome's Edge—After the devastating loss of her brother, Lilly Jerome is on the verge of losing her family's company. The scheming of her greedy Uncle Earl and the betrayal of a close friend have her reeling until a mysterious woman surfaces from her father's past...After surviving a brutal assault on her small Colombian village, Rosa Vargas flees to the dangerous Bogota slums. Evil men lurk, but she is determined to expose the people who murdered her father. She has nowhere to turn until the fearless newspaper reporter, Maria Hernandez, and the hardened ex-operative, Turp Arnold, help her uncover what may be an international conspiracy. *Jerome's Edge* is an E-book and is also available in paperback.

Contact Info

boonmort@gmail.com

boonemortensen.com

Made in the USA
Monee, IL
24 May 2020